MEN in UNIFORM

Courteous, courageous and commanding—
these heroes lay it all on the line for the
people they love in more than fifty stories about
loyalty, bravery and romance.
Don't miss a single one!

MEN
in
UNIFORM

JULE
McBRIDE

AKA: MARRIAGE

HARLEQUIN®

TORONTO • NEW YORK • LONDON
AMSTERDAM • PARIS • SYDNEY • HAMBURG
STOCKHOLM • ATHENS • TOKYO • MILAN • MADRID
PRAGUE • WARSAW • BUDAPEST • AUCKLAND

If you purchased this book without a cover you should be aware that this book is stolen property. It was reported as "unsold and destroyed" to the publisher, and neither the author nor the publisher has received any payment for this "stripped book."

Recycling programs
for this product may
not exist in your area.

ISBN-13: 978-0-373-36296-7

AKA: MARRIAGE

Copyright © 1998 by Julianne Randolph Moore

All rights reserved. Except for use in any review, the reproduction or utilization of this work in whole or in part in any form by any electronic, mechanical or other means, now known or hereafter invented, including xerography, photocopying and recording, or in any information storage or retrieval system, is forbidden without the written permission of the publisher, Harlequin Enterprises Limited, 225 Duncan Mill Road, Don Mills, Ontario M3B 3K9, Canada.

This is a work of fiction. Names, characters, places and incidents are either the product of the author's imagination or are used fictitiously, and any resemblance to actual persons, living or dead, business establishments, events or locales is entirely coincidental.

This edition published by arrangement with Harlequin Books S.A.

For questions and comments about the quality of this book please contact us at Customer_eCare@Harlequin.ca.

® and TM are trademarks of Harlequin Books S.A., used under license. Trademarks indicated with ® are registered in the United States Patent and Trademark Office, the Canadian Trade Marks Office and in other countries.

www.eHarlequin.com

Printed in U.S.A.

JULE McBRIDE

When native West Virginian Jule McBride was a pre-schooler, she kept her books inside her grandmother's carved oak cabinet, to which only she had the key. Every day at reading time she'd unlock the cabinet— and the magical worlds contained in the books inside. Only later did she realize the characters she'd come to love weren't real, and that's when she knew she'd one day be a writer herself.

Jule graduated from West Virginia State College with honors, then from the University of Pittsburgh, where she also taught English. She's worked in libraries and as a book editor in New York City, but in 1993 her own dream to write finally came true with the publication of *Wild Card Wedding*. It received an *RT Book Reviews* Reviewers' Choice Award for Best First Series Romance, and ever since, the author has continued to pen heartwarming love stories that have repeatedly won awards and made appearances on romance bestseller lists.

Today, Jule writes full-time, and often finds the inspiration for her stories while on the road, traveling between Pennsylvania, where she makes her home, and her family's farm in West Virginia.

For Maribeth Jameson—
there's always someone watching over you.

CHAPTER ONE

SHE'S SURE GOT some body. And those legs...

Seen through high-powered binoculars, Delilah Fontenont, a.k.a. Lillian Smith, had a stocking-clad pair to die for. They were like everything else about her—her neck, her arms, her enticing feet. Long and slender, with tapering swanlike curves, they looked as soft as feathers, as long as miles, and as smooth as whipped cream. Yeah, Shane Holiday could almost hear those legs when she walked, whispering together like lovers. Whispering softly, only for Shane.

That's right. Talk to me, baby.

He wiggled his black Stetson farther down, flattening his sleek blue-black hair but keeping his favorite hat safe from the tidewater breeze. Then he wedged a muscular thigh against the starboard rail of the FBI boat anchored in the Hudson. Inching the binoculars upward, while keeping them trained on Lillian's penthouse window, Shane felt a slow burn in his gut, and he vaguely wondered if it was from the subject's creamy legs, his vengeful anger, or the heat wave baking the city. He felt around blindly with a lean tanned hand for his coffee cup.

"Damn—" He winced as he sipped. "Cappuccino with no sugar?"

"Oh, Shane, don't tell me you're still missing the

doughnut shop and that creek water they call coffee in East Texas." Agent Finley Huff, otherwise known as Fin, turned his broad back to the breeze, moving with surprising ease given that he was fifty years old and fifty pounds overweight. His navy-and-red tie caught the wind, flapping over the shoulder of a white button-down shirt, and his wavy red hair blew wildly.

Shane shrugged. "How you Yankees survive stake-outs wearing suits instead of jeans, and on nothing more than steamed milk and juice-sweetened muffins is a mystery to me."

"Kind of like the mystery of how you Southern boys manage to drink coffee at all in this criminal heat?"

"All I know is real men need some sweets in the a.m."

Fin chuckled. "Lillian's legs might qualify. Besides, all the sugar in the world couldn't make you sweet, Shane."

Shane merely nodded, keeping his unwavering gaze fixed on Lillian. "The pictures of her on file sure never do the woman any justice," he murmured.

"Her legs belong on a Madison Avenue runway." Fin jokingly swished his hips to demonstrate.

"Or in irons," Shane returned dryly. "Her curves flow like the mighty Mississippi, but any man who's swept up in the current's going to drown."

"Too bad. It sure is a waste of a good woman." Fin sighed. "How's it feel to be this close to getting your justice?"

Shane took in the plush Southern-style decor of Lillian's apartment—a far cry from his empty log cabin back in Texas—then he lowered the binoculars just long enough to send Fin a slight smile. "Fine. At least if you can believe I'm about to propose marriage to the woman."

"I'm beginning to think that no crime's so bad she deserves you for a husband." Fin sobered. "Look, Shane, you're awfully close to this case. Are you sure you can handle it? Sure you want to go undercover? I mean, with her what man wouldn't? But…"

Shane shot Fin a glance of censure. "I bet her picture's on your office bulletin board, prominently pinned among the other most-wanteds."

Fin rolled his eyes. "Right. If I pinned up a fugitive with legs like hers, Mary Ann would have my hide." Mary Ann was Fin's wife. "And anyway, since we're trapping Lillian this way, the case isn't really official yet. I can bring in a few agents to back you up without getting into trouble. Otherwise, you're on your own."

Shane barely heard. *Wives*…he thought distractedly. The idea of marriage—even contemplating a false one for the sake of making an arrest—thoroughly unsettled Shane. He just wasn't the marrying kind. Only for Lillian Smith and the FBI would he make an exception. As he continued sizing her up, he took another sip of coffee, licking in annoyance at the frothy steamed-milk mustache. Shane definitely liked his coffee weaker, blacker and with a lot more sugar. A soft grunt of disgust over the fancy coffee died on his lips. She was definitely gorgeous.

As if reading his mind, Fin fanned himself. "She's so hot, this heat wave pales by comparison."

She could make a man blister. And she was definitely a Lillian. Not a Lily or a Lil, both names of which made Shane think of naive girls who had hearts as wide open as lily pads, skin as pale, and nothing to hide.

Lillian Smith gave Shane pause. A lot of pause. Just looking at her made him feel he was smoking a sweet hand-rolled cigar after eating a rich cream dessert. She made him ache, then melted him, and in addition to the hard evidence he sought, Shane sometimes just wanted more personal proof that her moist soft skin smelled of fragrant oils in thick summer heat. Or that her voice was husky with the intrigue of a past she didn't even know they shared.

To say she'd gotten to him was an understatement. It was unprofessional, too. But she reminded him of the Southern bayous where she'd spent her youth and where he'd spent part of his. Now Shane's heart pulled, and still eyeing her, he tried to tell himself it was only because he wanted to arrest her and get the hell out of New York City. He missed shelling crawfish on the front porch while humming to birds and cicadas, and the soothing classical music he loved.

He was a hard man, an ex-detective, but somehow, Lillian Smith managed to make him feel as homesick as a snot-nosed kid. Shane damned her for it, too, since his quest to find her had landed him up North for two lousy years. He'd kill to be back in his log cabin in East Texas, which was on a puddle-sized pond thick with frogs. Or else down in Louisiana, on Bayou Teche with his Aunt Dixie Lynn, where the long hot nights were quiet and fireflies blinked from the briar bushes and sugar cane.

In New York City, Shane couldn't even hear himself think. Except about her.

Over the years, he'd mulled over her more than he should have. She was tall, statuesque and classy. Twenty-five, which meant she was too young for him. But then, she possessed a high-born manner of money and privilege that made her seem ageless. Generations of Louisiana blue blood had given her a haughty lift of the chin, erect carriage, and a controlled composure that always reminded Shane he was no more than the son of a dirt-poor Texas farmer. Every time she walked across the penthouse—floating on those dreamy legs—Shane felt restless.

No, he and Lillian hadn't said so much as howdy-do—at least, not yet—but she was already under his skin, making him itch to pull her down. Which was why he was going to propose marriage today. Not that he'd get anywhere near an altar, since he'd arrest her first.

His gaze swept from the knot of her blond French twist to the feathery bangs on the high forehead of her oval face. Blond strands spiked into black eyebrows, enhancing dark eyes that held innocence Shane knew better than to trust. Her natural hair color, like her eyes, was dark. Stripped of blond dye, it would be the color of twilight fracturing through a cut-crystal jar of molasses. Suddenly feeling strangely unbalanced, Shane braced his thigh harder against the boat's rail, biting back a sigh of frustration at his own lack of control.

He half wished she'd close the curtains over her terrace doors. But like all Liberty Terrace's wealthy tenants, she seemed to think facing the Hudson River afforded her privacy. Most tenants didn't even lock their doors, but instead relied on internal security. As if they were in the boondocks, instead of Manhattan. Every curtain in the high-rise was wide open.

So was Lillian's white silk blouse.

Not even Shane's thigh against the rail could steady him as she tucked the loose tails into a short, half-zipped navy skirt. Her slip had lace cups she amply filled, a strand of pearls fell into her deep cleavage, and even though Shane had seen women wearing less, that hardly eased his tension. He was a lawman, but man became the operative part of the term whenever Lillian was around. Shane wasn't proud of it.

"Amazing," Fin murmured. "Can you believe we get paid for watching her dress for work?"

"Like they say, it's a tough job, but somebody's got to do it." Wincing at the trace of huskiness in his voice and feeling determined to deny it, Shane stared abruptly from Lillian to lower Manhattan's skyline. The morning haze was burning off the river, and on the island hard sunlight was glinting off steel and glass; high-rise buildings shot like silver rockets into the cerulean sky, and nearer, in the water, tour boats—*Miss Liberty* and the *Circle Line*—chugged toward Ellis Island and the Statue of Liberty.

Shane lifted the binoculars again. "Besides, *you're* getting paid, Fin," he said, picking up the conversation. "I'm the one with the personal vendetta, so I'm a volunteer. After this, I go to a real job."

"That's what I like about you, Shane," Fin returned with a another soft chuckle. "You're so selfless."

"That's me. Candystriper for the FBI."

"A candystriper? Does that mean you'll be tending to Lillian's ills?"

She was buttoning her blouse; Shane's voice turned dry. "She looks healthy enough to me."

"You can say that again."

Shane could concentrate better without Fin's running commentary. Especially now, when Fin started tapping his foot and humming "Let's Call the Whole Thing Off." At least it wasn't the wedding march. Again.

"Fin, if I didn't know you were happily married and packing a lethal weapon, I'd worry about you. Some mornings, I think you'd rather be in a chorus line on Broadway."

Fin mock-growled, "Want to see me do the can-can?"

Shane shrugged. "Go ahead. Dance if makes you feel more manly."

Instead, Fin started humming. This time it *was* the wedding march, and Shane decided it was no use trying to tamp down his aggravation. On stakeouts, he was just too accustomed to being a lone wolf. A natural-born tracker and watcher, he'd been the only detective in Texas who ran solo. In spite of his good looks—an ex-cop's lean hard body and weathered face, razor-straight raven hair and blue-silver eyes—he had an talent for passing unnoticed.

Which was why he could sneak up on people like Lillian.

No, she'd never guess he'd pursued her for seven years. Or that he already knew everything about her, down to the general layout of her home and of the office where she worked for Wall Street financier Jefferson Lawrence.

Fin sighed. "I wish you'd found a chink in her armor."

Silk though it is... Her life was like her stockings— smooth and seamless. She was punctual, responsible. A hard worker and night-school graduate. Most Friday nights, she baby-sat, free of charge, simply because she liked kids. But there was more to Lillian than met the eye.

"Shane, if I were you, I'm afraid I'd wind up *under* the covers, not just undercover."

A wry smile flickered over Shane's lips. "A man can never go too far in the interest of law and order."

"Right. Sleeping with her would be a public service."

"An all-American duty."

"Well, soldier, if you get the urge to raise your flag—or was that your terrible swift sword?—" Fin paused, humming a few bars of "The Battle Hymn of the Republic." "Just don't forget we've got you under surveillance."

"Fin—" Shane sighed, putting the joking aside. "Give me a little more credit. I'm a professional."

Not that Shane didn't occasionally walk the razor's edge. Still, he figured it was too late in the game for any woman to tame him, much less claim his aching heart. Maybe he'd even lost his heart forever, way back on a little East Texas farm years ago. Now, no half-dressed sultry blond siren whose every move probably spelled trouble was going to help him find it again.

Fin quit humming the wedding march. "Ready to tie the knot?"

Shane grunted softly. "Don't you mean the noose around her neck?"

Fin chuckled appreciatively at the word play. "Some neck," he commented.

And it was—a sweet-looking column of peaches and cream that any man would long to taste. Shane sighed again. In the end, it was just dumb luck he'd found her. Two years ago, he'd gotten a lead she was in New York. Turning in his detective's badge in East Texas, he'd moved to Manhattan, becoming chief of security at the Big Apple Babies adoption agency, a job his brother, Doc, helped him secure. Shane didn't mind the work. It was lower-risk than what he'd had on the force, with regular hours. On his own time, he'd kept tracking Lillian.

But the trail turned cold.

Until now. Recently, just as if she was a regular citizen, Delilah Fontenont, a.k.a. Lillian Smith, had walked right into Shane's arms. Literally. He'd bumped into her when she'd come to Big Apple Babies, hoping to adopt an available newborn boy. The shock of that first fleeting touch had stunned Shane; the rich scent of her, so hard to name, hadn't left him since. While Ethel Crumble, her caseworker, hadn't found out about Lillian's past, Ethel had decided to deny the adoption application this afternoon, even though Lillian had already met the baby. After lengthy consideration, Ethel felt Lillian needed a husband in order to adopt.

Combining their professional skills, Fin and Shane had scoured Lillian's psychological profile. She was superficially reserved, but a risk-taker at heart, and she'd wanted a child for a long time, probably badly enough to consider marrying a stranger to get one. Regarding men, she responded to old-fashioned chivalry and Southern charm. It wasn't exactly Shane's style, but he was prepared to wing it. By tonight, he hoped to be living in Lillian's apartment, researching every aspect of her life. Undercover, there was nothing he'd leave untouched.

Nothing.

Maybe not even Lillian. He pushed aside the unwanted thought, reminding himself he was here merely

to solve a crime that had haunted him for seven years—
the death of his Aunt Dixie Lynn's husband, Silas. The
man had been like a father to Shane, and he'd been
killed on the night of Lillian's ill-fated marriage to a
mobster named Sam Ramsey.

No one really knew what happened that night—
except Lillian. She was the key that could unlock the
past. But Shane knew enough: both his Uncle Silas and
Lillian's husband had died the night of her wedding,
and Lillian had fled the scene with three million dollars belonging to the Mob. She'd been living under an
assumed name ever since.

And Shane had finally found her. Not about to spook
her into running again, he meant to find out everything
he could before she was officially brought in for questioning. She'd eventually be arrested, if only for falsify-
ing her identification papers.

"Glad it's almost over?" Fin asked again softly.

"Yeah."

A thousand times, Shane had imagined Lillian outside Big Apple Babies today. She'd be heartbroken, with
the tears she so rarely shed filling her dark deceptively
innocent eyes. He'd appear from nowhere, a gallant
knight sweeping a cowboy hat from his head. She'd
say, "If I had a husband, I could adopt my baby…"

He'd raise an eyebrow. "A husband?"

She'd nod, looking lost and in need of rescue.

And then Shane would make Delilah Fontenont,
a.k.a. Lillian Smith, the one offer her psychological
profile said she could never refuse: marriage.

CHAPTER TWO

"KIND AS YOUR offer is, I have to refuse. Earlier today, I know I expressed interest and invited you over so we could talk privately," Lillian began, hiding her nervousness as she fixed a drink tray at a side bar in the living room of the penthouse. "But then I came to my senses."

"I promise—" Shane swept off his black cowboy hat, holding it over his heart as he seated himself on a red cotton-upholstered sofa. "I'd never force a woman to the altar, especially not if she'd lost her senses."

"My, my, aren't you the gentleman?" she chided with a smile. "But personally, I think *any* woman who marries probably has a few screws loose."

"You may have a point there."

Shane's deep Southern drawl slid inside Lillian with the ease of butter, stirring old memories and making her wistful for home. Maybe it was that, or because she hadn't gotten the baby today, but tears stung her eyes. Not that she'd cry in front of Shane as she had earlier. In fact, she rarely cried—at least, not anymore. The past seven years had taught her to be tougher than that. That's what she told herself.

"Feeling better than this afternoon?"

"Much better," she lied.

But her eyes were still red-rimmed, and her head

ached. She didn't even want to think about her meeting with Shane today at the Big Apple Babies adoption agency. She'd been so distraught that she remembered little—only the kind security guard's warm strong hand under her elbow, and how he'd offered her his handkerchief. Most men didn't even carry them anymore—especially not men up North—and the old-fashioned gesture had reminded her of her daddy. For years, Charles Fontenont had mopped her impulsive girlish tears with handkerchiefs monogrammed with his name.

The Fontenont family name she'd so naively sold down the river.

Don't think about it, Lillian. Or about how magically Shane Holiday had appeared, seeming so gentle and sweet. Or about the baby. God, she'd wanted that child. Which made Shane's offer of marriage sorely tempting. What did Ethel Crumble have against single women, anyway?

"You'd be a wonderful parent, Lillian, but you need a husband," Ethel had explained.

Another husband? Not in this lifetime, thanks.

"So, you're marriage-shy?" Shane prompted now.

"Shy?" Lillian managed a wry laugh, returning her attention to the drink tray. "More like totally averse. I mean, if shy's being a wallflower in the corner, then I left the room a long time ago. The *building*," she amended emphatically.

"Oh, no. Am I in the company of a man-hater? Should I draw my weapon, ma'am?"

Shane's mild flirtation lifted Lillian's spirits. It was as if he'd read a codebook on how to ease the skittishness she'd felt around men since her disastrous marriage. "I

do hope you're not really carrying a gun. I hate guns."
And with good reason.

He patted his dark sports coat. "Sorry, comes with the job."

"Well, please," she drawled, "don't shoot little ol' me."

His answering chuckle was deep and rich. "Not even if you posed a real threat," he promised, casually setting his hat beside him on the sofa.

Her eyes drifted over his stone-washed jeans, dark linen sports coat and black-cherry cowboy boots, which gleamed from a recent polish. She shrugged, her hands rising gracefully from a sugar bowl and fluttering in mock helplessness. "Who knows? Maybe I do deserve some sort of punishment." *Oh, Lillian, what are you saying?* It was as if guilty confessions from her past were seeping around her words, trying to get out.

"Punishment for?"

"Being so wicked on Wall Street."

He smiled. "You're really a corporate raider then?"

"Close enough. I work for one. I'm the personal assistant to Jefferson Lawrence." When Shane's eyes flickered with recognition at the name of her well-known employer, her expression softened. "Actually," she admitted, "Jefferson's more of an angelfish than a shark. He spends hours reviewing charities that need contributors."

"And being his assistant fills your days? You're not interested in marriage? I mean *real* marriage?"

Been there, done that. And I have no intention of talking about it. Lillian stopped dropping tongfuls of ice into tall glasses long enough to shoot Shane another quick smile. She noticed something fleeting in his eyes, maybe male appreciation, and feeling suddenly unsteady on her navy high heels, she involuntarily lifted a hand, smoothing her French twist. "Believe me, I'm committedly single."

"At least we've got that in common."

That and the Southern upbringing. Every time Shane Holiday spoke, his achingly familiar voice flooded her with memories of the headstrong passions that had fired her careless young blood. She remembered running barefoot along the bayou near the old tumbledown plantation of her girlhood with her tangled hair blowing in the wind. Oh, the Fontenonts had been wealthy once, and she'd learned good manners and some necessary sophistication, but otherwise, her parents had let her run as wild as a gypsy, catching crawfish and hiking in the woods.

It had been her undoing. She'd grown up strong and bold—and had loved too freely. She'd trusted her husband, Sam Ramsey, without question, until she realized how mercilessly she'd been used. Now Lillian silently cursed Shane Holiday for stirring the memories of a betrayal—and husband—better left buried. Smoothing her navy skirt, she regained her iron-willed control. For seven years, ever since the events that had rocked her life and cost her everything she loved, she'd reined in her natural passions. She'd tried to forget her old self, dark-haired Delilah Fontenont, wild child of the gentrified Louisiana backwoods, and to become nothing more than Lillian Smith—blond, poised, well-manicured Wall Street professional.

Her life, since she'd changed her name, might lack excitement, but at least she was safe. Not that she couldn't ably defend herself against physical danger, but she meant to make sure no man ever again messed with her heart.

Which was why she wished she hadn't invited Shane here. Usually, she had better sense than to entertain law officers, and now she was enjoying Shane's company too much. Besides, considering a risky marriage to a near stranger was something the younger, more impulsive Delilah would have done. She'd definitely smartened up since the night she'd changed her name to Lillian. Now, no matter how much she wanted that baby boy, she had to accept Ethel's denial of the adoption application. Keeping her voice light, she arranged cookies on the tray. "So, you're not the marrying kind, either, Shane?"

He shrugged. "I confess, I'm married to the law."

Another reminder that an ex-cop was in her home made her heart skip a beat. "I thought being married to the law was for world-weary detectives. Can't security guards punch out and go home at five?"

He laughed easily. "Whatever I do, I like to go the extra mile. Besides, I am an ex-detective."

Not just a cop. An ex-detective. Wonderful. She pushed down her fears. "A world-weary one?"

"Nothing so glamorous. I'm fuzzier than a kitten."

Lillian almost believed him. He definitely looked as if he'd feel more comfortable carrying handkerchiefs than handguns. He was glancing around now, looking comfortable in the heat, his gaze only mildly curious, his nondescript body relaxed inside the wrinkled bulk of a linen jacket that wasn't altogether flattering. He took in the open airy room.

"Great apartment."

"Thanks. It belongs to my boss. It's a real estate investment. When he sells, I'm out on the street."

"Nice of him to let you live in it."

She shrugged. "As I said, Jefferson's big on charity."

"And you accept?"

Was Shane implying she might accept something more personal from Jefferson than the use of this apartment? The suggestion was almost funny. After losing the woman he loved years ago, Jefferson had become a decidedly fussy middle-aged bachelor. But no, Shane's dark eyebrows were merely raised in polite inquiry. "Wouldn't *you* accept?" she asked, turning the tables.

"Sure. It'd be a great place to live. I like the paint job, would have picked the colors myself."

"Thanks, I chose them." The living room walls were green. Elsewhere, they were lilac, mustard and salmon, set off by chalk-white doors and moldings. Ceiling fans lent a Louisiana flavor, as did all the wrought iron outside—the rail along the Hudson river promenade, the old-fashioned lamps and park benches, and the formal landscaping of Rector Park, which was visible through a window behind Shane. She was a five-minute walk from her Wall Street office—and yet a world away from noise and crime, tucked in a safe enclave of Battery Park City, near waterfront restaurants, pristine parks, and the Manhattan Yacht Club.

When Shane glanced down the long hallway she'd hung with countless gilded mirrors, she followed his gaze, glancing at the furniture she kept for Jefferson—a stately grandfather clock and a marble-topped table next to the front door. Her heart suddenly fluttered. Surely

Shane's interest was only academic, but he was glancing curiously toward the shut door of her bedroom.

Ignoring a rush of self-consciousness, she carried over the drinks tray, her high heels clicking until the hardwood floor gave way to carpeting. As she arranged napkins and glasses, her eyes drifted over Shane's jet hair. He wore it slicked straight back from his high forehead; it brushed his collar in back, and a bluntly cut strand fell over an eyebrow. His white shirt, she suddenly noticed, smelled faintly of lemon and starch.

"Sugar?" she inquired.

"Three heaping spoons."

"Unfortunately I have cubes. And these are tongs."

He looked momentarily thrown. "Five then."

"Four," she compromised dropping in the cubes. "Five is too unhealthy. I mean, you could drop dead or something. And I don't even know CPR."

He chuckled. "See. You're talking like a wife already."

"If I was a wife, I'd ply you with sugar and inquire about your life insurance policies."

"Cynical," he murmured. "Not a good quality in a spouse."

She rolled her eyes drolly. "I told you. As much as I appreciate the offer, I'm not getting married."

"Then quit lecturing on my blood sugar levels."

She was still smiling and stirring his iced tea when she got a powerful urge to look at him again. He'd seemed so harmless. But just now, as she'd looked away, she'd taken a disturbing impression. His body was hard. His face, weathered and chiseled. Below dark slashes of eyebrows, his light eyes were the bluish silver of cold dry ice. Razor-sharp, too—as if he'd watched her for

years and didn't like what he saw. It was nonsense, of
course. When she double-checked, those eyes didn't
hold so much as a glimmer of interest.

Settling into a matching red armchair opposite him,
she casually sipped her tea. "I do thank you for coming,"
she continued. "As I said, I was really upset this afternoon." She smiled at her own folly. "I was so distraught
that marrying a near stranger seemed reasonable…"

"Well, let's toast to the shortest engagement in history." Shane lifted his glass. "I'll always think of you
as the woman who got away."

"Who got away?" She leaned and clinked her glass
to his. "Why, Mr. Holiday, you make me sound like a
criminal." Wincing, she told herself to quit compulsively
homing in on the topic of criminality, as if she was in
need of a confessor.

Shane's smile wrinkled the corners of his eyes. "A
woman who works for an angelfish? Somehow, I doubt
you pose much threat to society, Lillian."

She relaxed a little more, gracefully leaning back,
crossing her long legs. "So, pray tell. Did you really
mean what you said outside the adoption agency today?
You were willing to marry me, just to help me get the
baby?"

"Yeah."

"Why?"

"Out of the goodness of my heart."

She absorbed that. It was hard to believe, but he did
seem nice. And he wasn't really a total stranger. She'd
bumped into him—literally—on her first trip to Big
Apple Babies. While waiting for an interview, she'd
also overheard Ethel talking about both Shane and his
brother, Doc. Clearly the caseworker thought highly of

the two men. She'd been telling a coworker that Shane had helped put his brother through medical school, and that the men were close, visiting during the work day, taking their lunch breaks together. "Your brother's the pediatrician at the Big Apple Babies agency, right?"

Shane nodded. "I'm real proud of him."

"You're a nice big brother."

Shane merely shrugged. But he was nice. The way he'd approached her today was proof he cared. Appearing from nowhere, he'd seated her in a private corner of the agency's lobby and soothed her.

"You know—" Her lilting tone made clear she wasn't really considering his proposal. "Because you're employed at Big Apple Babies, there would be a conflict of interest if you tried to help me adopt from them."

"People affiliated with Big Apple Babies have already adopted from the agency, so there's a precedent. Besides, we could always try elsewhere."

But the baby I already love—my baby—is at Big Apple Babies. She'd decorated a nursery for him, and was already calling him Brandon. She wagged a finger. "You do make it sound reasonable."

"It is reasonable."

She laughed, really laughed, for the first time that day. "I'm not doing this!"

He held up a tanned hand. "Believe me, I'm not pressuring you."

But Shane's offer could change everything. He could help her bring Brandon home. And she needed the baby, someone to whom she could give all the love she'd locked up inside herself. *And a man. Eventually, Lillian, you've got to forget what Sam did to you and love a man again,* said a voice inside her. *Forget about it,* came a swift denial. *I won't love a man again as long as I live.*

"I just felt so bad for you today, Lillian…"

She shot Shane a fleeting smile. "Thanks." As she ran her fingers up and down on her glass, the cool moist condensation gathered on her fingers, suddenly making her shiver in spite of the room's heat. "Is it too hot?" she suddenly asked. "I could have turned on the air-conditioning."

"I love the heat."

"Even in this heat wave? It's a scorcher."

"The hotter the better."

Suddenly, he seemed to be talking about another kind of heat. The soaring city temperatures, the baking side-walks and sun glancing off steel skyscrapers paled to whatever flowed between them. She tensed, aware of a whole other silent conversation that was taking place between their bodies—her fingers sliding up and down on the drink glass, her legs crossing and recrossing. His opening slightly as his arm stretched, draping on the sofa back. For a second, she couldn't breathe. Beneath her silk blouse, her slip felt tacky against her skin. She fought the urge to fidget, and assured herself the flash of attraction was only in her imagination. Shane had never even removed his loose, lumpy jacket.

"I never use air-conditioning," he was saying casually. "I'm used to hot weather. Like I said, I grew up in East Texas. Louisiana, too."

"I'm from Mississippi," she lied, taking a sip of iced tea that soothed her unaccountably parched throat, chilling her system. Mississippi was close enough to Louisiana that Shane wouldn't question the accent she'd worked so hard—and failed—to lose.

"Miss the South?" he inquired.

She nodded. *With all my heart.* "You?"

"Oh, yeah. My parents died when I was eight, so I spent winters in Texas, then summers with my Aunt Dixie Lynn in Louisiana, near Bayou Teche."

"I lost my parents, too," Lillian murmured, registering that she and Shane had that in common, as well, and still thinking of her family home—of the lattice trellises where her father tended roses in view of the white-columned porch. At least she'd grown up farther south than Shane, on the old Fontenont plantation on Bayou Laforche, a world away from Bayou Teche. Newspapers carried the story of what happened after her wedding, but it was old news now. Besides, if no detectives—ex- or otherwise—had shown up by now, none were coming.

"So, you were a detective in Texas, not Louisiana?" she asked with more casualness than she felt.

He nodded. "Until I gave it up altogether."

"Why'd you quit?"

He shrugged. "Getting too world-weary. Besides, I really can punch out at five now. And my little brother settled here. Other than two aunts, he's the closest family I've got."

Because Lillian craved a family, she was touched by the closeness Shane shared with what remained of his. Especially when emotion flickered in his eyes. "I guess I can admit the real reason I approached you is because I'm an orphan myself."

"Ah," she said simply. So, it wasn't only from the goodness of his heart; still, empathy was a noble motive.

"I'm not in favor of doing anything unethical," he

assured, "I'm an ex-cop and I work for the agency. But I've seen the baby you want to adopt. It'll be a shame if he doesn't get a home."

She leaned forward, telling herself she was drawn to him by her interest in the baby, not the pull of Shane's voice. "Isn't he the sweetest thing you ever saw? I wanted to name him Brandon. I always liked the name." She gestured helplessly toward the hallway. "The nursery's all fixed up."

"Brandon," Shane murmured in approval. After another pause, he continued, "I—I'm sorry, but after you left today, I looked at Ethel's file. I was having second thoughts, too. I mean…I'd proposed marriage to a woman I didn't even know."

Faintly embarrassed color tinged her cheeks. "I acted so impulsively," she admitted, "inviting you over like this. I mean, not that you're not nice, it's just…"

"I understand perfectly," he interjected. "From Ethel's files, I know you lead a quiet life. Belong to Trinity Church. Work hard. Baby-sit." He sighed. "I…I'm just sorry you can't have kids of your own."

His eyes touched hers now, imparting sympathy. Something inside Lillian wavered. She quickly said, "I really have no intention of marrying you."

He smiled. "So you keep saying."

"I mean it," she warned.

But she'd never marry for love again. What if Shane Holiday's offer could really give her Brandon? He was so helpless. An accidental pregnancy for a young girl with no possible means of supporting him. Even the girl, just a teenager, had wanted her to have Brandon.

And then Ethel said no.

Lillian had been stunned. But could she marry Shane,

to bring home the infant she already felt was hers? It was risky. She did have good identification cards, including a Social Security number in the name of Lillian Smith. And if Ethel hadn't found out about her past by now, she probably wouldn't. Besides, now Ethel would be more interested in Shane's attitudes toward fatherhood, and since Ethel already knew Shane, Lillian figured he'd pass muster.

Not that Lillian trusted ex-detectives or security guards any more than the average man, which was to say not at all. "And the marriage would be strictly a favor?"

Shane's deep hearty belly laugh warmed Lillian's soul nearly as much as the baby who was so much on her mind. "Sweetheart," he drawled, "I'm not the marrying kind. This would have to be business, pure and simple."

Sweetheart. It wasn't in the Wall Street vocabulary, and it had been a long time since a man called her that. She didn't mind it. "If it's business, what do you get out of the deal?"

"Besides the knowledge I've done some real good in the world?" He looked faintly embarrassed. "Well, I could really use somewhere to stay right now. My landlord just sold the building where I live and since my lease was up, I'm going to be out on the street in a few days. I'm desperately looking for a new place. My stuff's already packed, movers are lined up. The works."

"But you can't find an apartment?"

He shook his head.

She could certainly sympathize. His was just one more story in the ongoing saga of Manhattan real estate, where overcrowding brought skyrocketing rents. Complete strangers were frequently doubling up as roommates. She glanced around. She'd been far luckier than most since Jefferson let her live here as long as she kept up the maintanence payments. If she continued doing so during Shane's stay, Shane would definitely be getting a deal. "So, you're thinking you'd move in immediately, then?" she said. "And we'd sort of be roommates while we get to know each other's habits, life-styles, backgrounds…"

He frowned, resting his hat on his knee and study-ing the brim as if thinking. "I spoke impulsively. But it would work, if I moved in and we presented ourselves as newlyweds. We could pretend we met down South, that you visited some relatives near Bayou Teche in the summer…"

Lillian picked up the thread. "We could say we met again outside Big Apple Babies, where you were work-ing and I was trying to adopt, and then we immedi-ately hooked up, rekindling a previous romance. If Ethel thinks we were involved before, it won't look like a quickie marriage." Her heart skipped a beat, making her wonder if she'd really become as tough and cynical as she professed. "It could be very romantic."

"Yeah, lots of flowers and dinners—" Shane nodded curtly, as if to emphasize this was only business. "I'd live here awhile, for the sake of authenticity. Right before the wedding, we'd set up another appointment to review your adoption application. Maybe my connections at Big Apple Babies would even help."

"You'd really do all this for me…a near stranger?"

His gazed fixed on hers, steady and unwavering. "Yes," he said simply. "I don't want a family of my own, and I'm not interested in marriage. But I do like to see orphaned kids get placed." He flashed a quick smile. "Besides, as I said, I really could use a place to stay right now. It'll give me more time to look, and I won't have to jump on the first apartment I can get my hands on."

She really would be doing the man a favor, she supposed. She swallowed hard. Brandon was so adorable. As small as could be, with a whisper of black hair as straight and fine as Shane's. And Brandon was an active baby. No doubt, he'd be a high-spirited hellion, just as Lillian had been.

Shane's voice was coaxing. "He's cute."

She smiled wistfully. "So, you like kids?"

"To tell you the truth, I've never been around them much. Just at work. And I'm not in the nursery often." He frowned. "Honestly, they make me nervous."

She felt more disappointment than she should have. Was she really hoping he'd say he liked children? "Well, if you moved in," she reminded, "you'd meet some kids, since I baby-sit."

Baby-sitting seemed to pose more of a challenge to him than marrying a stranger. "I guess I could handle it."

She surveyed him carefully. They were no longer talking theory. They'd crossed the line, and now they were talking marriage. "Don't you think people would notice if we got divorced right after I got the baby?"

"I'd stick around for the agency's follow-up visits. Besides, how many marriages last nowadays, anyway?"

"True." Seven years ago, Lillian's had sure blown up. Along with a boathouse and a pier. One minute, she'd been a blushing bride wandering through the plantation house, looking for her new husband. The next, she'd confronted Sam Ramsey's betrayal—and she was on the run, driving away in panic with men chasing her. She remembered staring back as an explosion rocked the earth, sending red sparks spraying into the dark night sky. Even now, what all she'd seen wasn't clear. She only remembered shadows. Gunfire. And other things she'd willfully pushed from her mind and banished to the realm of dreams. Or nightmares. "Trust is hard to come by these days," she finally murmured in understatement, thinking of her deceased husband.

Shane's voice turned deeper, strangely unreadable. "You really aren't interested in love, are you, Lillian?"

Striving to lighten the mood, she shook off the dark shadows of the past and sent him a mock ominous glance. "No, Shane," she announced drolly. "That part of me is dead."

The sudden curve of his mouth gave her a start. Even though the smile communicated bemused irony, the firmness of his lips said he was a man to be reckoned with. "Well," he said with a soft chuckle. "I hope you buried that special part of you in a shallow grave." His intriguing smile tugged harder. "In case you decide to dig it up again."

Her need of men, like her past, was buried for good. She shook her head. "No chance of that, Shane."

"You never know," he warned.

"Believe me," she assured. "I know. And anyway, you said you didn't want to get married, either. Why not?"

"I just don't."

There was definitely more to this man than met the eye. Ignoring the warning bells, Lillian found herself sizing him up again, the way she might have when her name was still Delilah and she drove too fast, talked too loud, and hadn't thought twice about challenging men who were far better-looking than this one. Shane was definitely teasing out the part of her she'd suppressed. She leaned forward, nodding sagely. "Ah, the proverbial lone wolf."

Her long perusal hadn't fazed him in the least. "I've been called worse."

"Hmm." What was it about this mild, nonthreatening man that was drawing her? Was it a matter of pride? The fact that, in spite of their casual flirtation, he obviously wasn't interested in her as a woman? She frowned. He wasn't even interested in women in general. Which, she tried to assure herself, suited her just fine.

"Ever been married before?" he asked now.

The question, which wasn't exactly casual, made her heart miss another beat. "No," she quickly lied.

"Me neither," he said, telling the truth.

When he set aside his tea glass, she felt faintly relieved. "Well…I guess I'd better be going." Before she could move, he reached over, swiftly closing his remarkably strong fingers over hers, applying soothing pressure.

"Look, Lillian—" His solemn drawl stirred more than memories now, while each nuance of his touch further reawakened the woman in her. "I'm sorry things didn't work out."

She barely heard him. She was too busy trying not to notice how much she liked the feel of his tanned hand. It was dry in the heat. Lean and long-fingered. Like him, it was a blend of smooth and rough—his palm silky, his fingertips slightly coarse. Just the touch of it made her suddenly wish she hadn't changed so much in the past few years. Because Delilah Fontenont would have jumped at this man's crazy offer of marriage. But then, a lot had happened to make Delilah change her name to Lillian.

When he released her hand, she felt strangely bereft. Even more so when he stood to go.

"Wait, Shane."

She floated gracefully upward on the long stems of her legs, the word seeming to come from somewhere else, maybe from the deeper, more adventuresome nature she fought so hard to hide. "Wait," she repeated. "Let's do it."

In the following heartbeat, she told herself the decision had nothing to do with the pull of his voice, or how compelled she felt to discover what lay beneath the surface of the man.

"Okay," he said simply.

"Okay," she repeated, feeling stunned.

Shane leaned and lifted his tea glass. "Here's to it."

Could it be this simple? Would marrying Shane Holiday really allow her to adopt Brandon? *My son.* Joy bubbled inside her as she imagined Brandon in the crib she'd readied in the nursery. Lifting her glass, she clinked it against Shane's. "So, will you marry me, Shane?"

"Lillian—" He inclined his head in a nod. "I accept."

Her voice hitched with excitement. "So, you can move in soon?"

He looked relieved, no doubt over having found a temporary apartment. "Why not tonight?"

CHAPTER THREE

"So, IF IT'S A fake marriage," Fin mused aloud, "can I still get wild and crazy at your bachelor party?"

"That's you, Fin," Shane returned dryly. "Always asking the hard, academic questions."

Fin chuckled. "You ready?"

"Yeah." Shane held open the elevator door. While Fin and two other agents wearing coveralls with pocket logos that read Manhattan Movers unloaded Shane's meager belongings into Lillian's plush upstairs hallway, Shane's shaggy three-legged gray-and-white dog, Lone Star, began sniffing the carpet.

Ignoring Fin, who was now trying to goad Shane by humming the wedding march, Shane focused on the job. *Don't slip up and call her Delilah. You're undercover now. A security guard at Big Apple Babies, nothing more. You're a nice guy, helping Lillian get a kid out of the goodness of your heart, and she won't suspect differently until you find out everything you can. Eventually, she's going to be arrested, if only on fraud charges. Don't forget it.*

Unfortunately, when Lillian swung open the apartment door, Shane's mind went blank and his body responded to her with a tight hard knot of heat that smoldered inside him as surely as his angry frustration over the fact that he couldn't control it.

For the second time today, they were face-to-face. And no less than this afternoon, when he'd trained his considerable energies on convincing her that he was harmless, Shane was struck by her poise and beauty. She was so close, just across the threshold, and her scent, that rich thought-stopping musky aroma, made his chest tighten.

Moving in with her was definitely the toughest assignment he'd set himself yet. He'd always liked challenges. But this... Dammit, this was impossible. As his gaze traced the tall legs that ended on navy high heels, he found himself fixating, wondering about the creamy hollows at her ankles. He pretended not to notice how she was sizing him up. It had been risky, and he still wanted to appear unthreatening, but Shane had quit slouching and changed into threadbare jeans and a T-shirt, such as he usually wore when he was off duty. Maybe it was male pride. But if he was moving in with Lillian, she might as well get used to the way he looked without an oversize sports coat.

"That really was awfully fast." Her eyes still trailing over him, she reached up and nervously smoothed her French twist.

He raised an eyebrow. "I thought we agreed that I'd move in tonight? Did we get our wires crossed?"

"Well, no, but..."

"I had a stroke of luck," he interjected, lowering his voice as if not to jeopardize their charade in front of the movers, the agents who were trudging past her, carrying boxes. "Turns out, the movers could come immediately." He mustered a smile. "When I told them we were getting married, they put an extra rush on it."

She looked anxious, but she nodded as if this was a good omen. "Things are working out so easily."

Things are working out because an angry ex-detective and the FBI have been tailing you for seven years. "Only trouble was, I had to bring my dog. I forgot to mention that before." Shane held his breath. To a man, all the agents had absolutely refused to take Lone Star, and if Lillian wouldn't, Shane would have to put the dog in a kennel. He couldn't stand the thought of the dog being caged.

"Dog?" Lillian slowly turned, zeroing in on Lone Star, who'd already sneaked past her. Looking positively appalled, Lillian fiddled anxiously with her pearl neck-lace. Her reaction wasn't exactly promising and made Shane feel strangely defensive on Lone Star's behalf.

"What kind of dog *is* that?" Lillian lowered her stricken voice another notch in deference to the movers, as if she, too, feared they'd sense that she and Shane were barely acquainted.

"What kind of dog?" Shane wasn't really sure. "A three-legged medium-sized mutt?" he ventured, not sure if that was the sort of answer Lillian was after.

She considered. "What happened to his back leg?"

"Her. And I don't know. She was a stray. She was minus the leg when I found her."

Lillian's gaze returned to Shane's. "Does she have a name?"

"Lone Star."

"Very feminine," remarked Lillian dryly.

Shane shrugged. "Dogs don't care about names."

She merely nodded. "Ms. Lone Star and the lone wolf, huh?"

"Just Lone Star," Shane corrected. "No Ms."

"I thought you said dogs don't care about names." Lillian's eyes suddenly sparkled, reminding Shane of how moonlight looked sometimes on the dark water of his pond back in Texas. "Anyway," she said, "I take it *you're* still the lone wolf?"

For some reason, Shane allowed an answering flicker of humor to touch his eyes. "Always."

Lillian stared at the dog again.

It didn't look promising, and Shane could only hope his well-laid plans weren't about to unravel. Not that he'd really thought this cool, classy young woman was going to let a dog into her apartment, especially not when the dog looked as unkempt as Lone Star. But Lillian surprised Shane by chuckling softly.

"I hope you don't mind me asking," she drawled, "but has Ms. Lone Star ever had a bath?"

Shane decided not to push his luck by correcting the name again. And he started to say yes, of course he bathed Lone Star—then he frowned. "Well...I guess I gave her a good scrub the last time my Aunt Dixie Lynn came to visit."

"And that was?"

Shane winced. "A while back."

Before Lillian could respond, Lone Star, who seemed not at all inconvenienced by her missing leg, frisked merrily toward the kitchen, sniffing everything in her path. Fin grunted loudly, readjusting a heavy box on his shoulder and mustering a tough-sounding Brooklynese so unlike his usual accent that Shane smiled. "What's in these boxes, mister? Lead?" Fin scowled from the other end of the hallway, playing the part of the irate mover. "And where did you want this stuff, anyway?"

"The bedroom," Shane said.

Shane's gut tightened when he finally stepped across the threshold. He couldn't believe he was really inside. There was no going back now. He edged down the hallway, but then had to stop to give the agents maneuvering space. Lillian bounced against his back, and he felt her softness against him, the instinctive touch of a hand she used to steady herself against his waist. Glancing at her over his shoulder, he could swear her cool composure faltered again, as if the shock of contact wasn't lost on her, either. But it was hard to tell.

She was staring at him warily. "So...you've completely moved out of your place? And you brought all your belongings?"

Hadn't he explained that? What had she been expecting? He frowned, glancing around. There were only a few boxes. "Yeah. But don't worry. This is really about it. I...I guess I travel—"

Light. Before he could finish, her eyes darted from his. "Wait a minute!" she exclaimed. Lowering her voice so only Shane could hear, she urgently whispered, "That's *my* bedroom."

It sure was. Fin and the boys had ignored the unoccupied guest bedroom across the hallway and were stacking Shane's boxes next to Lillian's closet door.

So this was her lair. Shane sidled closer, his pale hawk-like gaze piercing the interior. The door had been shut earlier today, but now he could see private quarters that were as Southern in decor as the rest of the place. He ignored his faint discomfort. Yeah, the woman's trim suits and professional composure couldn't conceal a nature that was decidedly more wild. She was so innocent-looking that an unguarded man could easily forget, but beneath prim blond Lillian still lay the much darker devilish Delilah....

She was the woman Shane needed to lure out.

And this was where she slept.

Shane's watchful gaze scanned the red-fringed shade of a bedside lamp before taking in the four-poster bed, with its thick mattresses and pillows piled high against the headboard. A patterned wool rug hid much of the hardwood floor and a small table was crowded with candles, incense burners and bottles of aromatic massage oils. Lillian was obviously big on scents and the room, which was filled with hers, hampered his concentration. New York's usual traffic sounds were absent; air rustled softly, swirling down from a ceiling fan.

Realizing he'd been holding his breath, Shane slowly exhaled as he stared into a mirrored bathroom beyond. The blueprint of the apartment he'd studied hadn't exactly shown the sumptuous details. There was a nondescript shower stall, but it was the huge round black sunken tub that commanded his attention. It had to be at least three feet deep. Steps led into it, past crystal fixtures and whirlpool jets, and thick white towels hung along the walls, over crystal-knobbed racks. The whole room was obscenely well-appointed. Shane could hardly believe Lillian wanted a baby so much she'd let both him and Lone Star move in.

Tamping down his vague discomfort at the blatant opulence, he wondered if Jefferson Lawrence had really paid for these furnishings, as she claimed, or if Lillian had...with the money she'd taken when she'd fled from the Mob in Louisiana. Shane couldn't wait to research all her personal financial records and find out.

Feeling silken fingers close around his biceps, he

turned and before he knew it, his own rebellious hand wound up grazing Lillian's waist. She felt hot—like a thousand summers combined—and since current weather predictions were calling for a storm to break the city's heat wave, Shane found himself wondering if anything could ever appease the ceaseless unwanted heat he felt for this woman. He'd do anything to get rid of it.

"Shane—" Her insistent hushed whisper was still low, so the movers wouldn't hear, and the soft panic-tinged drawl tampered with the regularity of Shane's heartbeat. Wincing, he controlled his reaction.

"What?"

"You…uh, can't stay in *here,* you know. I mean, we've got to tell these guys to move your things into the other bedroom. The *guest* bedroom."

"Sorry," he whispered back. "But we've got to make sure people think we share this room." Even though he'd arrest Lillian long before they were married, or before a caseworker actually came to interview them about adopting a baby, Shane had his own agenda. If his things were in her bedroom, he'd have the perfect excuse to search it at will.

"What about the rest of the stuff?" growled Fin from the hallway.

Shane glanced at the box on Fin's shoulder which contained a collection of classical music CDs. "The living room. Near the stereo."

When Fin and the agents left again, Lillian stared at the boxes. "I'm not sure I'm entirely comfortable with all this."

Since the thought of him in her bedroom caused so much obvious distress, Shane figured Lillian had picked up more of his male scent than she was letting on. "I'm not entirely comfortable, either," he assured, even as he leaned lithely, ripped open a cardboard box and started lifting out his clothes by the handfuls.

"Well, maybe we'd better talk some more…"

"At least set a few ground rules," he agreed, ignoring how her eyes bored into his back as he headed for the chest of drawers. He began tugging the heavy carved handles.

Her voice was strangely flat. "That's my underwear drawer."

Ignoring the sudden quickening of his pulse, he gingerly pushed aside multicolored silk bras and panties. As he shoved a wadded handful of boxer shorts next to the delicate garments, she released an uncharacteristic giggle.

He shot her a quick glance, feeling suddenly, unaccountably testy. "What?"

"They're pink."

"Pink?"

"Your underwear."

Shane swore he felt heat in his cheeks, and he damned her for both that and the fact that his voice came out sounding faintly edgy, almost terse. "I washed my shorts with a red union suit. The color in the suit ran. That okay with you?"

"Fine," she said lightly.

But now the woman was beaming at him. Damn. If there was one thing Shane found truly loathsome, it was when women were charmed by his innate inability to deal with clothes. He stained them. Lost buttons. Bought the wrong sizes. Mismatched them. You name it. So much for the image of the world-weary ex-detective.

Those guys were always pin-neat, austere as hell, and slept on beds you could bounce quarters on. Not Shane. He'd ironed something once—he couldn't remember what—and burned a hole in it. The button-down shirt he'd worn here earlier had been brand new.

"Here," she said. "Take them out. I'll bleach them."

He very calmly shut the drawer. *Stay out of my shorts, lady.* "No, thanks," he said mildly. "I like them pink." Finding his robe and toiletries, he headed for the bathroom.

The click of her footsteps followed, and he knew if he looked into the mirrored wall above the sink, he'd meet the dark brown eyes against which he had such little resistance. Reminding himself he was undercover, on a government sting, he kept his gaze trained on a zippered black toiletry bag and started unloading the items.

"My, you certainly are businesslike," she said.

He ignored her. He unloaded a cologne that was so cheap she wouldn't approve of it. A manicure kit he'd never used. A straight razor. He suddenly glanced up.

She was scrutinizing his belongings. "What's that?"

He stared down. "Handcuffs."

This seemed to amuse her. "You carry them in your toiletries?"

"Apparently," he said, having no idea how they'd gotten mixed in, and still feeling thoroughly distracted by her presence behind him.

"One more thing," she said.

"Hmm?"

"Please…do me a favor and keep your gun out of

sight. I want it unloaded, and put away somewhere safe."

"Fine." After another long moment, he turned and pierced her with a sudden aggravated stare.

She blinked. "What?"

He bit back a sigh. She looked so incredibly poised— her regal back straight. Her slender arms were long milky lengths of bone and satin skin, and as his eyes trailed over where they crossed at the waistline of her navy skirt, he was plagued by that bothersome tightening of his chest again. "No offense, but the way you're just standing there, watching me, reminds me of my Aunt Dixie Lynn."

"Your Aunt Dixie Lynn?"

"Yeah. Don't misunderstand, I love her. But when I visit, she always follows me around the house. Watches me pack and unpack." *Grills me about my love life, which she says is nonexistent.* "Except for Lone Star," he admitted, "I guess I'm not used to having people in my personal space."

"This is *my* personal space," she reminded, smiling. "My, my, you really are a lone wolf. How long's it been since you lived with anyone?"

"Years." He'd been seventeen. He hadn't liked it then anymore than he was going to like it now. His frown deepened as he realized what a strain this was going to be on him.

She tilted her head. "Don't you ever get lonely?"

"No." He caught her amused glance in the mirror. "Mind telling me what's so funny about that?"

"Oh nothing, you're just so…so…" She shrugged her delicate shoulders. "Lone-wolfish."

As he dropped a new toothbrush next to hers, he

tried to tell himself she'd settle down. She'd been more reserved this afternoon. No doubt, she was just overly excited about the changes taking place in her apartment. Unrolling copies of various news magazines, he arranged them near her makeup bag. Then he stood back and surveyed the artful effect. "Think it looks like a man lives here?"

Lillian's tone was dry. "It's certainly messy enough now."

"Men are supposed to be messy."

She didn't look convinced. "Seriously, Shane. I think we should discuss those ground rules…"

Shane knew if he conceded to a cleaning schedule, he was doomed. Fin had warned him of that. Shane was as undomesticated as Lone Star, and they would remain that way during their stay, which, Shane reminded himself again, would be blessedly brief. His eyes drifted to the bracelets on Lillian's slender wrists. Imagining they were handcuffs improved his mood. At least that's what he told himself.

"I'm *really* sorry, Lillian," he apologized. "I don't have any intention of intruding in your home. But if you're going to adopt Brandon, we need to make sure our cohabitation looks authentic. It'll be uncomfortable—" Realizing his eyes were fixed on her lips, Shane glanced abruptly away. "But we've got to convince people we share the bathroom. The messier it is, the more obvious it will be that I live here."

"Why, Shane," she chided. "Are you sure your motive isn't just laziness? Or a general lack of hygiene?" When he didn't rise to the bait, she said, "Nevertheless, I suppose you're right."

"Of course I'm right."

"Why? Because men usually are?"

Her backdoor way of challenging him was brought on, he decided, by her nervousness at having him move in. He started to say something to soothe her, but when his eyes settled on skin that was as creamy and silky as her blouse and stockings, he changed his mind because he felt the same need to challenge. The desire to exert his power over her came swiftly, and he imagined plundering her delicate mouth until she was so bewildered she couldn't even stand up anymore. He'd like to give her that kind of abandon, that relief from her own control. He softly said, "You really don't like men much, do you?"

"No." The quick, insincere smile she flashed said he'd hit a raw nerve. "And since our marriage isn't real, I don't have to."

"Prickly, aren't you?"

"Sometimes."

So was he. He gave her an accepting nod, but he was thinking about her dead husband. Sam Ramsey had been a rotten bastard. What had he done to her? Years ago, when Shane first saw her, she'd looked so shamelessly carefree....

He sighed as he hung his terry robe on the back of the door. Since he'd washed it with the shorts and union suit, it was pink, too, and it looked ridiculous next to hers, which was of white silk. Eyeing the robes, he decided if a caseworker was really coming, they wouldn't stand a chance of convincing her they were married. A woman like Lillian wouldn't be caught dead in bed with him, much less marry him. Next to his roughness, she was all silk and fragrance. Besides, she was too young for him, anyway. "I guess we'll have to tell everybody it's a love-hate thing," he suddenly muttered.

She was staring at the robes, too. "You mean where we're opposites, but very passionate?"

As if she didn't know a damn thing about men and women. He thought of Sam Ramsey, the criminal who'd been her lover and husband. "Yeah, people have to think we're passionate lovers, Lillian," he murmured distractedly, heading for her walk-in closet, feeling her behind him. His eyes pierced the interior, looking for...*something*. Maybe a safe or a strongbox. Somewhere she could hide anything that was left of the three million bucks with which she'd fled Louisiana....

"They've got to think I'm—" When Shane's eyes met hers, his heart tripped in a way he was loath to recognize, and he was suddenly unable to speak at all because the words were really his secret—and, he once again assured himself, unwanted—fantasies about her.

"That you're?" she prompted.

He forced out the words trapped in his chest. "Sleeping in that bed with you every night. Dressing in clothes from this shared closet. Wearing those robes while we make breakfast together. That I'm bathing with you in that tub..."

Faint color stained her cheeks and she clasped her pearls in her slender fingers. "Well, it's an unfortunate necessity," she said vaguely. "But I'm sure we'll manage."

Shane wondered why he was torturing himself by having this conversation. To escape the pull of her eyes, he glanced away—only to have his eyes land on the massive bed. It increased his discomfort, reminding him it had been too long since he'd shared himself with

a woman physically. Which was the only way Shane
ever shared himself with women. Fortunately, his voice
stayed steadier than his heartbeat. "Well, if we're going
to fool a caseworker, our supposed relationship can't
embarrass us. We've got to seem…" He turned abruptly,
hanging a battle-scarred black leather jacket next to her
conservative red wool coat. "Completely accustomed to
each other physically."

She chuckled. "I'm not the one who was embarrassed
over my pink underwear."

He was beginning to suspect she was intentionally
goading him. "I was not embarrassed."

Her lips twitched. "Of course not."

He wished he could remind her that he was the cop
and she was the robber here. Instead, he said, "I don't
get embarrassed, Lillian."

"Yes, well, anyway…" She blew out a quavering
breath, opening her arms slightly in tremulous invitation. *"Mi casa, su casa."*

Despite her fleeting smile, she looked as if sharing
the apartment was akin to a death sentence. "So, you
really think you can act like we're lovers?" he said,
dumping an extra pair of cowboy boots next to her prissy
spectator pumps and stiletto heels and marrying his
plaid flannel shirts in with her silk blouses.

"I can pretend, I think."

This, he thought, *from a woman who may have witnessed my uncle's murder and who's stolen three million in cash from the Mob.* "Will it be *that* difficult for
you?"

"No—no, of course not," she quickly said in apology.
"You're an attractive man." Realizing what she'd said,
she swallowed hard. "I—I mean objectively…"

He tried not to notice that her admission smoothed his ruffled feathers. "Objectively?"

"I mean I'm not personally attracted."

"Thank you for clarifying that." Suddenly afraid he was pushing his luck, that she would change her mind and back out altogether, thus ruining his—and the FBI's—chance of bringing her down, he persuasively continued, "I know the situation's inconvenient, but we have to think of Brandon."

"Believe me, I am."

No doubt. Every time he mentioned Brandon her eyes grew misty. Shane tried not to project about the moment when she realized this was all a hoax and her dreams of mothering that baby boy were crushed forever. No, Delilah Fontenont, a.k.a. Lillian Smith, probably didn't have much of a heart, but when she didn't get that kid, whatever heart she had was going to break.

And Shane was going to be the man who kicked away the pieces like so much rotten debris.

Lillian cleared her throat again. "Well…just how far do you think we need to carry this charade?"

All the way to bed, Lillian. Staring at her, he'd never felt more torn between duty and attraction. "I'll just arrange my clothes and personal items in your bedroom for show, then take the guest room. There's another bathroom off the hallway, next to the nursery, right?"

"Yes. Well, I guess we understand each other."

"I promise. We've got a hands-off policy. Consider it signed in blood." *My uncle's blood.*

"My, my—" In the confining space of the closet, her drawl rustled as softly as the silk of her blouses. "Blood signatures? Sounds very serious, Mr. Holiday."

In a second, her tone had shifted. The veneer had

dropped, and Shane glimpsed the woman she'd left behind seven years ago when she'd fled. The cop in him responded. So did the man. And there was no holding back his need to lean toward her, drawing in another deep whiff of the scent he found so maddening. "It's been a long time since a Southern lady called me Mr. Holiday."

"Then maybe you've been up North too long."

Guess the declaration of your honorable intentions made her feel safe enough to flirt. He glanced around. "Well, I guess this is home for now." *Until I've gotten the information I want.*

Her voice was strangely unsteady. "Yes, I guess it is."

Their eyes locked, and Shane remembered the nights he'd lain awake reading files from work. How his bed back in East Texas had looked with her pictures strewn across the sheets. Had he really been on an FBI boat only this morning, watching her stride into the living room with this same blouse open to her waist? Right now, as much as he despised his own weak-willed lack of professionalism, Shane admitted he'd desperately been wishing for more. Just once, he'd prayed for a slice of real life to take into his dreams. Just once, he'd longed to see Lillian walk into his line of vision wearing nothing at all.

But of course she never had.

"Excuse me—" Knowing he'd better move, he brushed past her, got some shirts and returned, hanging them next to her suits.

"You put your T-shirts on hangers?"

"I don't work on Wall Street, Lillian. All men don't wear starched shirts." *Or move in a world of high rollers, money deals and power brokers where you feel so obviously at home.* He'd kept his tone light, but there was no help for the depth of feeling this woman kept wrenching out of him. *Shane, you're acting like you've never talked to a beautiful woman before. And you're not really playing house, this is an investigation. You're here to search the place and help arrest her. Where's your professionalism?*

Lost in Lillian's eyes, that's where.

"Here," she said. She held up a stack of pajamas, still in cellophane wraps. "Jammies."

He suspected she was doing everything in her power to make his male presence less threatening. But did she really think he wore long powder-blue pants to bed? He couldn't help but allow himself one piercing stare. "My Aunt Dixie Lynn gives them to me every Christmas. I don't wear them. I sleep naked, Lillian."

Her eyes widened. "Oh."

He offered a glimmer of a smile. "Just in case Ethel wants to know an intimate detail from our marriage."

"Right."

She sounded throaty, and tension was hanging in the air again. It slipped beneath the surface, hovered above, and slid between them. It was so strong he could almost shudder from it, and their eyes were still locked.

Fortunately, Fin growled, "And what about this box, mister? It looks like pans."

Lillian abruptly broke the gaze. Backing away, she suddenly whirled around gracefully, then took long-legged strides into the hallway. "Pans can go in the kitchen."

"Or maybe you oughta just throw 'em out, lady. These are bent, burned and made of aluminum. And this—"

As Shane entered the hallway behind Lillian, Fin lifted out a Dutch oven with flaking Teflon and shook his head in disgust. "It's just a good thing you two are getting married. This guy obviously won't survive much longer without a wife."

"So true," Lillian agreed.

"My wife wouldn't even boil water in these," Fin continued. "And she says cooking with aluminum can give you Alzheimer's."

Shane frowned. "Aluminum?" he muttered. "Is that bad?"

"Don't worry, I'll take care of the pans," said Lillian in a tone so matrimonial that Shane felt seriously unsettled.

Fin chuckled. "Judging from his old apartment, I guess he's one of the most committed bachelors I've ever run across. No evidence of roots, if you know what I mean."

"Well, he's put down roots now," Lillian said sweetly.

Once you gave her the ball, Shane thought, she sure ran with it. Fin nearly doubled with laughter. "Well, mister," he said, "at least you and your dog are now living in the lap of luxury."

Shane thought of his tumbledown cabin in East Texas, which hadn't been much better furnished than the studio apartment he'd just left. Was this all he owned? He glanced at the boxes. All his life amounted to?

"He was kind of a lone wolf," Lillian explained to Fin. "At least until I tamed him."

The talk of taming him made him feel edgy, but soon enough, the agents would be gone and then Lillian's cool self-possession, which roused his need to dominate, would fade quickly enough. He doubted she'd chance even the most subtle dare when they were alone.

"—Congratulations on your wedding plans, anyway," Fin was saying. "So, is he taking you out for a nice romantic dinner?"

"Great idea," Shane said smoothly, not about to let Fin rile him. "Why don't you let me take you to one of the waterfront places, Lillian?" Given her psychological profile, plying her with wine over dinner would probably loosen her tongue. He guessed he wouldn't mind having a candlelit table near the river, where they could gaze out at the boats…. Shane remembered one of the boats belonged to the FBI and snapped back to his senses.

"Really," Lillian whispered, as Fin disappeared into the bedroom with another box. "I'd rather eat here and get right down to the business of getting to know each other. I'll throw some dinner together while you finish arranging your stuff."

So much for an expense-paid meal on the FBI. He nodded. "Fine."

For an awkward moment, she merely stood there.

"Well, go on, wife," he forced himself to tease mildly. "Put on the victuals."

He tried to tell himself he'd get through this, that when she was locked up, it would all be worth it. But he still remained powerless over how much he wanted her. As she turned and strode across the living room, the almost painful tension in his body eased with her receding steps. The farther away she got, the less hold she had on him, but only when she'd entered the kitchen could he really breathe again.

Before she was gone, Shane figured she'd felt the steady burn of his gaze that swept down her because she'd turned back, just once, with a fleeting glance. Surrounded by the gilt-framed mirrors in the hallway, Shane reminded himself that's all she was—just an image. A careful reflection calculated to disguise the woman beneath. He decided he was going to have to try to lighten the mood between them during dinner. The casual flirtation he'd engaged in today was sure preferable to whatever he was feeling now, and she'd seemed more comfortable with it.

Fin came from the bedroom, chuckling softly. "So, the lone wolf's about to get hitched, huh?"

Shane raised a lazy eyebrow as if to say Lillian's beauty didn't unhinge him in the least. "Now, Fin, you're just jealous."

"Ah, is the bridegroom nervous about his honeymoon night?"

Shane couldn't keep the sudden edge from his voice. "You know we're going to arrest her before it comes to that."

Fin merely laughed. "You *sound* nervous."

Hell, maybe Shane was. After all these years, he'd gotten his wish—to penetrate Delilah's lair—but when he'd watched her vanish into the kitchen with Lone Star, her hips swaying and her navy skirt teasing the backs of her knees, Shane was suddenly sure it was he—not her—who'd just walked into the trap.

CHAPTER FOUR

"I CAN'T BELIEVE THIS, Ms. Lone Star!" Lillian scratched behind the scraggly dog's ear, feeling panicked. Jefferson had called about something at the office, so Lillian hadn't even started dinner yet. Right now, Shane Holiday was probably in her bedroom again. That was bad enough. But soon he'd be coming into the kitchen, looking for her.

"And you need a makeover, don't you, Ms. Lone Star?"

Lone Star thumped her tail on the kitchen floor.

"Ah," crooned Lillian. "I bet you'll need a whole spa week at the doggie Elizabeth Arden! But don't you worry. We'll get you a nice bubble bath and a hair trim. Maybe some pretty pink polish for those toenails and bows for your hair. Why, you poor thing. When it comes to what a little girl needs, Shane Holiday doesn't have a clue!"

Lone Star barked in agreement. But Lillian's pulse suddenly accelerated, breaking through her denial. Given Shane Holiday's good looks, he was probably no stranger to female needs. How had she convinced herself that she was only interested in him because he might be able to help her adopt Brandon? When she'd opened the apartment door this evening, she'd almost gone into the kind of old-fashioned Southern swoon for which her Grandma Fontenont had been famous.

He was exactly the same man, but somehow his mild blue eyes were now a strange, hard-edged silver. Staring from a tanned, craggy face, the pupils of those eyes pierced everything they touched, and the razor straight hair he never managed to get out of his eyes drew attention right to the disturbing gaze. He was older than she'd thought, and hard and taut all over. Uncompromising but with glimmers of rusty humor.

Lillian fought down pure panic. Oh, she couldn't quite pinpoint all the differences. But they added up to one big difference: the man couldn't sleep under her roof. Not tonight. Not ever. And yet without him, she'd never get the baby. When he'd arrived, she'd simple done her best to cover her shock. But now she wasn't even sure what she'd said for the past half hour. Had she goaded him? Gotten on his nerves? Flirted? He did have a hands-off reserve that brought out the worst in her, making her want to tease him.

"What did I just get myself into?" she muttered.

Sighing, she stared at Lone Star again, trying to get her mind off Shane. No self-respecting caseworker would let a newborn near this rangy mutt. "I'm sorry, sweetie," she murmured, frowning guiltily. "It's not your fault your daddy's been so negligent. But we'll fix you up."

Lillian opened the freezer door and stared inside at the stacks of TV dinners, then she opened the fridge's other side, considering. At least she'd bought pasta and vegetables. Not that she was much of a cook. Still trying to deflect thoughts of her sexy new roommate and upcoming marriage, she forced herself to bustle around—boiling water and throwing butter into the sauté pan. She began dicing, starting with garlic cloves and broccoli. Now, if she could just remember where she put those bottles of expensive red wine Jefferson gave her last Christmas. It was nearly a whole case....

"How's my fiancée doing in here?"

Determined to keep her composure, she turned and smiled. "Fine. Are you completely settled, Shane?"

"Yeah. Anything I can do?"

"You mean like tie rice bags?"

Shane smiled. "Just don't throw me the bouquet at our wedding. If I catch it, we might have to get married for real." He glanced around. "Sure I can't do anything?"

"Really," she managed. "Everything's under control." But it wasn't. The man's black cowboy hat was sitting on the marble-topped table next to the front door, as if it had found its permanent home. His underwear was in her drawer, and his shirts were in her closet. Oh, she understood the need to create the illusion that they were lovers, but it was unsettling. Besides, wasn't he taking it a little far? Surely, they could keep separate underwear drawers. But then, such things would make their supposed relationship more convincing. As she watched him set up Lone Star's dishes, she reconsidered serving wine with dinner. Shane might get ideas. And he couldn't. It was why she'd turned down his dinner invitation even though going out would have been more convenient.

"There, Lone Star," he said. "Have some grub. Mind if I turn on the radio?"

"Please."

Maybe that would break the tension. But it didn't. No more than the frisky dog that kept popping up between them. Lillian could have sworn Shane was as lumpy as the linen jacket he'd worn earlier, but he had wide shoulders and a strong back. Jeans that were faded to white molded over a tight behind and around extremely long legs.

He wheeled the radio dial until it was playing classical. That came as a surprise. "Classical?"

He shot her a quick sideways glance. "In case you want to start filing away facts about me, I like Debussy." He frowned. "I noticed relaxation tapes in with your CDs. You have trouble sleeping?"

Realizing her eyes had settled on his broad chest, she suddenly felt tired of the tension between them. Deciding to try a new tack and meet it head on, she shot him a sudden saucy smile. "Afraid I'll sleepwalk into your bed or something?"

"Who knows?" The gaze that swept down her didn't seem nearly as placid as his voice. "You look like you could be a dangerous woman."

Despite his smile, the words struck too close to home. After all, dark dreams did invade her sleep and awaken her with terror. Memories she'd buried resurfaced at night, bringing explosions and gunfire. She mustered a smile of her own. "Well, Shane, I promise not to bite. Now, if you don't mind checking those cabinets, I think there's a bottle of red wine…"

"Glad to."

"Thanks."

Feeling shaky, she threw some red onion into the sauté pan and began rinsing celery stalks, silently wishing she didn't want a child so desperately. Should she call this off? Could she really marry this man who'd just moved out of his apartment and into hers? Everything had happened so quickly that she felt strangely man-handled. Not that Shane had touched her. And he'd come at *her* invitation. Besides, Ethel Crumble had spoken so highly of him. It wasn't as if he was a *complete* stranger....

Still, that she'd invited him here was a definite testament to how badly she wanted to adopt Brandon. Her gaze slid to Shane again. The ease with which the man moved around her kitchen calmed her a little. He seemed less cagey now than he had when he was unpacking. He still moved with caution, but he didn't seem nervous, and he instinctively seemed to know where she kept things. It was as if he was already acquainted with the layout, or had been inside her apartment before. As if he belonged here.

"Excuse me," he murmured.

Before she could react, he reached around her and opened the silverware drawer. The fleeting sensation of his body—his chest grazing her back and his groin brushing her hip—was already gone by the time she drew a sharp breath.

"Sorry," he said absently, still standing so close she could feel his heat. Setting the wine bottle on the counter, he angled the corkscrew into the cork. "Any more garlic," he teased mildly, glancing over, "and you can bet there'll be no good-night kiss."

Waving a knife in his direction, she drawled, "Careful there, mister, or you'll be sleeping on a bench in Central Park."

He smiled. "Just testing your boundaries."

The exchange, which was more akin to the casual flirtation they'd shared earlier, made her breathe easier. She guessed it would take a while to readjust to the fact that he now lived here. "Testing boundaries is fine. Cross them and you'll eat elsewhere."

He popped the wine cork. "Well, if you wind up having to drink all this wine by your lonesome, I can't vouch for your ladylike behavior when I get back." When he waved the cork beneath his nose, his soft male grunt of appreciation teased her spine with a sudden, delicious shiver. His voice was husky. "Great wine."

She shrugged. "I wouldn't know. It was a gift."

"No classical music. No taste in wine." Shane's gaze caught hers, as he checked through the cabinets, shaking his head in disapproval. "For such a classy-looking woman, you sure don't get out much."

"And this," she drawled, noting how he easily he found her best wine goblets, "from the man with the three-legged mutt and pink underwear."

"Hear that, Lone Star?" Shane poured the wine and tasted it. "Whoever sent you this has excellent taste."

"It was Jefferson, my boss." When Shane held out the other glass to her, she lifted her hands, so he could see they were peppered with vegetable bits. "I'll taste it in a minute."

He swirled the goblet beneath her nose. "Just a sip."

When he came closer, the movement of his body swept away her breath. He brushed against her as easily as air, even though he was all lean, rock-hard muscle. He was tall enough that even she—no slouch herself—had to lean her neck back to look at him, which she did. And then she was utterly captured, ensnared by a gaze so steady she felt utterly weak.

When he thrust his free hand though his hair, distractedly forcing it off his forehead, his groin brushed her side, making her pulse accelerate. "C'mon. I won't bite. No more than you will."

She had to struggle against the florid heat threatening to flood her face. And against gravity, since her knees weakened. Who was this disturbing man who'd come so suddenly into her structured life? He strode in on these long, lean legs and now threatened every ounce of the control she'd fought so hard to achieve. Somehow, she found her voice. It was amazingly steady. "Maybe just a taste."

Amusement flickered in his eyes. "You look so worried."

Determined to prove she wasn't, she parted her lips. Only when Shane pressed the full goblet to her mouth and tipped, did her knees quiver. In a quick movement, she righted herself—and red liquid splashed down her blouse.

"Damn!" Shane swore. "I'm sorry!"

Swiftly, he set the glass aside, grabbed a wet dish towel and started mopping the stain. As he did so, his fingers reached around her neck, cupping it. "Hold still," he commanded.

Was he kidding? With his thumb nestled behind her ear, Lillian was frozen to the spot. At least the music covered the quickening of her breath. No man had touched her for years. Not so much as a hug or kiss. And then to have this sexy man… She fought the sudden urge to ask how old he was. And to inquire about his last girlfriend. But no, this was very definitely the wrong time for date questions.

"I'd better watch you carefully," he was saying grimly. "One sip of good wine and you're already out of control."

Her? He was soaking her thin silk blouse with the cold
wet cloth, making the fabric transparent. She quickly
reached up, clamping her hand tightly around his wrist
to stop him. "That's okay," she managed. "Really, Shane.
I think I can get this."

Too late, she realized the pressure of her hand had
brought his lower arm to her breast. Her nipple constricted against the dampened blouse, against his arm.

He didn't move.

And she couldn't. Especially not when she felt his
pulse. And met his eyes. His expression was unnerv-
ingly bland, offering no indication he was affected, but
his pulse was racing, drumming beneath her fingertips. She became conscious of the radio announcer, who
was saying, "We hope you're staying cool in the heat
wave…"

She suddenly remembered the whole left side of her
blouse was soaked with frigid water. Shane's tone was
impossibly even, almost formal. "That cold water ought
to take care of the wine, Lillian. It won't stain."

"Thank you," she croaked.

The ease with which he dropped his hand made her
feel off balance, and his glance toward her chest was so
mildly dismissive that she refused to give in to embarrassment and cross her arms. Tamping down the color
that threatened to flood her face, she decided he simply
couldn't be as cool as he pretended. And yet touching
women probably came easily to Shane Holiday. She
imagined many things did.

He casually leaned around her, lifted the sauté pan,
and expertly swirled the contents. "Why don't you run
along and change while I finish dinner?"

Run along? Damn if the man hadn't just dismissed

her from the room. She felt a sudden, unaccountable rush of temper, then realized with a start that she was still standing there in her blouse. "That was my thought exactly," she managed.

He nodded. "I'd like to let the wine breathe."

The wine? What about her? Every time she looked at him, she was fighting not to swoon. Not that she'd let him know it. Turning, she did her best to sweep regally from the room, hoping he noticed her even strides and the long legs that men so often whistled at. Most men, anyway.

In the bedroom, she debated longer than she should have, then decided she wouldn't stoop to putting on fresh lipstick. Besides, Shane Holiday had only moved in to help her adopt her baby. To chastise herself, she didn't even check her reflection in the mirror, but returned to the living room in a loose, not particularly flattering sundress—only to feel her distress heighten.

Shane had set a candlelit table on the terrace overlooking the river. Feeling a wistful twinge, she kept her voice steady. "Why, this seems so much like a date."

Shane shrugged. "Figured we could use the practice."

She could have kicked herself. Shane only wanted things to look authentic. He'd been an orphaned child. That's why he wanted to make sure Brandon found a home here. A candlelit dinner would help prepare them for Ethel's visit by making them more comfortable with each other.

Shane's tone was unreadable. "The candles were on the table. You have candles everywhere. You must like them."

What else had he noticed? Her love of silks? Of aromatic oils? Of incense? She managed a smile as he held out her chair. "I do," she admitted. "Candles. Bonfires. Falling stars. Whatever."

"A woman who loves fire—" When he seated her, he leaned so close that his breath whispered on her neck. "Is that a warning a man could get burned?"

"Truly, I'm beginning to think you're a little afraid of me."

"Completely phobic."

She wasn't sure if he was joking. "Really?"

As he circled the table, she noticed his strangely graceful way of moving, as if his body were simply the extension of things less tangible, his will and mind. "But don't worry—" he said, seating himself. "I believe in shock therapy for phobias."

As she began twirling her pasta, her eyes drifted to where his sleek raven hair glinted blue, touched by the candle flames. "How's that?"

His riveting gaze fixed on hers. "I always immerse myself in whatever I fear."

The words sent a thrilling ripple through her. Her voice was huskier than she intended. "So, you're ready?"

"To?"

Her throat felt dangerously tight. "To take the plunge and get to know everything about me, so we can ace the interview with the caseworker and bring Brandon home."

He nodded. "I'm ready. But are you?"

Surely, she was only imagining the dare in his eyes. "Of course, I'm ready to get to know you," she managed.

But she could still feel Shane's warm breath ruffling against her neck as he seated her, and how her body had responded to nothing more than an innocent little touch over some spilled wine. And Delilah, a.k.a. Lillian, knew she'd crossed the line. Already, she'd become far more acquainted with Shane Holiday than she ever should have.

CHAPTER FIVE

"Shane!" Lillian squealed, collapsing with laughter against the side of the deep black bathtub. "Oh, Shane, help!"

Countless times, Shane had fantasized about sharing the bathtub with Lillian, but definitely not like this. He shook his head in warning, his lips twisting in a wry smile. "Whoa. Careful with that water jet, lady." Tightening his grip on Lone Star, who was drenched to the bone, Shane felt where Lillian had clipped away the knotted fur. The dog had shrunk with the hair loss. Damn. Shane was undercover, not here to have a woman meddle in his life—or in his dog's. He blew out an exasperated sigh. "Half my dog's gone now, Lillian."

"Don't worry. In just a couple days, you're going to gain another half. A *better* half."

"How's that?"

"You're marrying me."

Shane shifted uncomfortably. The date was drawing close, but no way was he actually going down an aisle. Bracing his bare feet against the bottom of the suds-slick tub, Shane let his eyes drift over Lillian. She was heart-stopping—barefoot, her navy shorts, white T-shirt and endless legs peppered with foamy water drops. Blond tendrils escaped from her ponytail, curling on her neck in the humidity.

By the day, it was both harder and easier to live with her. They'd found they could make each other laugh and hit a domestic stride with uncanny ease. Shane had insisted on paying his share of the monthly bills, doing all the cooking and walking the dog. Lillian tidied up after him without complaint and was the only woman he'd ever met who could make coffee the way he liked it. They weren't morning people, so they always ran late, getting ready for work in rushed silence and saying a quick goodbye on Broadway, where he hopped the train to Big Apple Babies and she turned onto Wall Street. Nights, they studied each other's lives preparing for the caseworker's visit and Brandon's adoption.

Privately, he searched methodically through her apartment and office, and beneath it all hummed their desire—sometimes barely noticeable, sometimes so powerful Shane couldn't believe they hadn't wound up in bed. But he'd held back with an iron will and hadn't even kissed her. So far.

"There now, sweetie," she whispered.

Shane kept his hold on Lone Star and watched Lillian comb the water massager over the dog's back, her long slender fingers swirling in fur, forcing the last soap bubbles toward the drain. When she dropped the water nozzle and began lathering in conditioner, Shane decided the sensuous way her hands moved was entirely lost on a dog.

"That's people conditioner, Lillian."

"Ms. Lone Star's people," Lillian returned with conviction as she began another rinse-out. "*Good* people," she emphasized. "And mama's gonna turn her into quite the little lady, isn't she?" Lone Star, who was getting her second bath in a week, wagged her tail, thumping Shane's thigh and soaking his faded, rolled-up jeans.

Shane sighed. "Lone Star *liked* being undomesticated."

Lillian glanced up, her eyes sparkling with humor. "Why, Shane," she chided. "You're projecting your feelings onto her again. Didn't they teach you lone wolves anything about psychology at the police academy?"

"We profile criminals—" *like you, Lillian* "—not canines."

Lillian wagged a sudsy finger at him. "A little psychology can go a long way."

"Watch," he warned, "or I'll psychoanalyze you."

At that, Shane saw worried shadows darken her eyes. They came often; he hadn't expected that. And the loneliness and darkness mirrored something in him, touching him in places he'd never known he had. Now Lillian laughed anyway—that bright, warm laugh that reminded him of sunshine chasing away rain.

"Tough guy," she drawled. "Are you really jealous of my relationship with your dog?"

"Hell, no."

But Lone Star—a.k.a. Ms. Lone Star—was going through a female bonding phase. As near as Shane could tell, Lillian possessed something maternal that Lone Star desperately wanted—and that Shane never realized he was supposed to provide. Now his loyal mutt was thicker than thieves with Lillian. From the first night, Lone Star had slept in Lillian's bed, and to Shane's surprise, Lillian let her. Of course, Lone Star still raised a ruckus if Shane didn't crack open the guest-room door, so she could trot in to check on her master during the night.

Trouble was, by sunrise the mutt had usually pushed both Shane and Lillian's doors wide open. And because the doors were facing, Shane woke staring at a sleep-tousled Lillian with her lipstick kissed off and the strappy silk gowns she wore twisted around her calves. Shane wasn't sure which bothered him more—how she habitually kicked off the sheets, or the fact that she'd stolen his dog's affections.

But how guilty was Lillian of serious wrongdoing? Shane was beginning to wonder. Lone Star was more distrustful than Shane, and just as apt to sniff out bad news, but she adored Lillian.

"Arf!"

Outside, lightning flashed. Through the bathroom window, Shane could see crackling threads of electricity fray from a jagged white bolt like capillaries from a main artery. At a crash of thunder, Lone Star wrenched from Shane's grasp, lunged from the tub, then skidded across the water-slick floor, her nails scraping the tiles.

"Oh, I declare!" As Lillian spun toward the dog in frustration, the warm stream from the massage jet in her hand wetted Shane's jeans, dampening him right where it counted. In a flash faster than the lightning, he caught Lillian's delicate wrist.

She gasped. "What are you—"

When her gaze landed on his soaked fly, the words died on her lips. High excited color flooded her cheeks, and dark eyes that were alive and lusty lifted to Shane's. She gamely yanked her wrist from his grasp, leaving his heart stuttering. Backing away with a high-pitched devilish giggle, she very deliberately raised her arm and trained the nozzle again.

"Why, you little—" Shane managed as she squiggled a warm wet *S* down his shirtfront.

"*S* is for Shane," she singsonged.

Swiping the air, he caught her upper arm and, while she was still laughing in breathless protest, he hauled her against him.

"Little what?" she panted innocently.

"Vixen," he finished. "You're asking for it!"

Despite her uneven breath, her steady gaze held a smug nonchalance calculated to rile him. She stared up at him. "Oh, am I a vixen?"

"Yeah." *And if you don't quit toying with me, you're gonna to get it, too.* "Give me that, you hellcat," Shane growled playfully, and grabbed the nozzle away from her. Keeping it just out of her reach, Shane jerked back his torso. She swung, her hips slamming his, and he bit back an agonized curse. Quicker than the storm outside, his unwanted response came on him, electrifying him, hardening his groin. She had to feel it. But she kept stretching for the nozzle, moving like a thoroughbred— fast, with her head held high and her long muscular legs feinting right, then left.

She swiped the air for the nozzle. "Give it up, Shane!"

He chuckled. "Lady, I want to hear you beg."

"In your dreams." Her pulse was racing beneath his restraining hand; the spear of her tongue was pressed to her upper lip in concentration; her breath was hot against his cheek. Suddenly she slipped, her bare feet sliding in frothy suds. Her mouth grazed his biceps as he caught her elbow, hauling her to her feet. Their lips were just inches apart, their breaths ragged.

His voice was hoarse. "You okay, Lillian?"

Her skin was flushed, a deep glowing rose. "Yeah."

Suddenly, impulsively, he brought his mouth a fraction closer, knowing she was going to let him kiss her. *What are you doing? She's under investigation.*

Abruptly, he released her, reminding himself he'd hardly come here to seduce her. For a fleeting second, her dark eyes searched his, saying, *Why didn't you kiss me?* And then she recovered and loosed another peal of laughter. Rich and lusty, it rang in his ears long after she'd leaped madly from the tub, swept towels off the racks and fled after the dog. A second too late, Shane was sorry he hadn't grabbed her. He'd let those long legs scissor from his reach when he should have yanked her into the tub again. He wanted her that way. Excited and breathless. Acting more like devilish Delilah than prim Lillian. He wanted to glide his hands over skin that was slick with suds, in this room surrounded by mirrors.

"Little Ms. Lone Star!" he heard her gasp from the hallway. "My, my, you *are* a devilish woman!"

"Talk about projection," Shane muttered, snatching the remaining dry towel, his jaw setting stoically as he stripped off his soaked T-shirt, then slid the towel down his damp front, pressing it against his fly, trying his best to soak up the moisture. He scowled. Lillian was driving him crazy! He wasn't used to living with a gorgeous woman. God, he couldn't wait until she was in jail. Tossing the towel in the hamper, he tidied the bathroom. Not that he liked to clean. He loathed it. But he figured he'd best let his desire subside before he faced Lillian again.

"Now, aren't you a mess!" She was crooning to Lone Star as he entered the living room. Even though she kept drying the dog, her eyes widened when she noticed

Shane's bare chest. Good. Turnabout was fair play. Lord knew, Lillian was bothering *him* enough. He glanced from where she was seated in the floor, to the open terrace doors and the hard-driving rain.

"About time the storm came," she remarked casually, as she patted Lone Star dry and stared at a legal pad in the floor, clearly ready to get down to business, as they had every night since Shane arrived.

Shane sighed. "Yeah."

The air was cooling, but still so hot that sweat beaded on his chest, and outside, the rain fell in sheets that looked like tinted glass. Dark steamy breezes stirred the air, and the fragrances reaching Shane—flowers from the gardens below, sandalwood incense and peach candles from dinner—mingled with Lillian's scent. As she reached for a wine goblet, he frowned. He kept expecting the dinner wine to loosen her tongue, but she nursed the same glass all night. Somehow, he had to penetrate the woman—to get at her secrets, her hidden life. If she had one.

She was tapping a fingernail against a legal pad, looking frustrated, her mood now serious. "C'mon, can't you tell me anything more about your childhood, Shane?"

"Believe me, Lillian." He left the terrace doors and sprawled on the floor a few feet away from her. "You already know more about Shane Holiday than any other woman on earth." For days, she'd poked and prodded, drawing out admissions he'd never thought he'd share.

"But it's all so factual, Shane. Nothing...*intimate* that will convince a caseworker we're really in love." She kept tapping the pad, which was filled with details about Shane's life—where he'd gone to school, the make of his first car, his high school football jersey number.

Studiously, she'd memorized the facts of his life for a caseworker he knew was never really going to show, and the knowledge made Shane ache for her. It was that ache that told him he was letting himself get too close.

He watched her smooth a loose tendril of hair that had dislodged from her ponytail during their water tussle. Oblivious of the effect she was having on him, she murmured, "Your first kiss was with Ruthie Miles, right? She had dark hair, dark eyes—" She glanced up. "Hmm. You like dark hair."

He smiled. "Good thing you're a blonde."

Her eyes caught his. "My hair's dyed, Shane."

It was an invitation. The chemistry between them was obvious, and she wanted to know why he wasn't acting on the signals. He said nothing.

Lillian chuckled self-consciously. "Uh…well, so you kissed Ruthie in sixth grade. But no matter how much you begged, she wouldn't use her tongue."

Lately Lillian's studies had focused more and more on Shane's love life. "Wouldn't you call that intimate?" he asked dryly.

"Pretty intimate," Lillian conceded.

I'll show you intimate, he thought. But he couldn't. He was a professional. And intimate, for Lillian, could turn out to be a cell. He glanced away, into the rolling marbled clouds of the dark, lightning-streaked night sky. The storm was the kind that could make a man believe in vengeful gods. But what about Shane's vengeance? Night after night, he and Lillian had played out this charade, studying the facts of each other's lives, as if they were going to meet a caseworker together and adopt a child, but he'd been collecting other facts about her, too.…

Lillian suddenly giggled. "How Chrissy Winters's daddy caught you in the back seat when you were sixteen is intimate, as well."

So were countless other things Shane had wound up telling Lillian. "Like I said, no woman has ever known as much about me as you." Shane wasn't sure how he felt about it, either. He kept telling himself he was sharing his life with her because he had to. But deep down, he wanted her to know him.

"You know more about me than any other man," she murmured.

Shane nodded. He knew a lot. "Your favorite color's navy blue," he recited. "Favorite meal, red beans and rice. You miss the South. And your daddy's special homemade gumbo."

She looked pleased. "What else?"

"You wear silk, not cotton." He arched a lazy eyebrow. "Listen to rock, not classical. And you wish you were a morning person, so you could read the *Wall Street Journal* while you eat your toast."

And you have the hots for me. Even if he hadn't been trained to analyze details and nuances he would have noticed that. Frequently now, she found excuses to touch him, and her eyes had grown bolder when she thought he wasn't looking. He also knew this apartment did belong to her employer, that no safe or strongbox was hidden in it, and that all her financial records held up to scrutiny.

Maybe she didn't take the Mob's money or see anything that night. Maybe she only changed her name to make a clean break with the Ramseys. The possibility niggled. Or was Shane's long-standing obsession for her blinding him to the truth? Was her beauty making him bend his professional ethics? Making him see only what he wanted to see?

He realized she was staring at him. "Tell me about *your* childhood, Lillian." Night after night, he tried to coax out some sliver of information that might shed light on who exactly had killed his uncle.

She stared out, into the rain. When she looked at him again, her eyes were misty. "Like I told you, I grew up in a small white brick house, with ivy growing up the side…" She paused, rubbing a towel against Lone Star's fur. "It had a picket fence…" Her drawl was hypnotic, drumming against his mind like the rain on the terrace tiles. "Truly, Shane," she murmured. "We had a wonderful life. Blessed and rich. Simple."

"Really?"

"Oh, yes."

She was a good liar. He'd give her that. Maybe the best he'd met. She kept her roots in the South and didn't change inconsequential facts, which gave credence to the lies. But Shane knew she'd been raised on the old Fontenont plantation. That she changed that particular fact got to him. He could swear she was daydreaming about a life she wished she'd led. It was clean. Honest. Simple. The kind of life he wanted.

"Behind our house were rose bushes my daddy tended…"

The simplicity of her secret desires made Shane feel guilty. He fought the sudden impulse to gather her in his arms and tell her it was okay, that he already knew about her real life. He suddenly wished he could take her back down South, where they both belonged. Yeah, the big fish might eat the little fish. And Shane might be the big fish at the moment. But in New York City, both he and Lillian were fish out of water. Feeling edgy, he rose and headed for the terrace.

"Where are you going?"

"To look at the rain."

Leaning against the doorjamb, he listened to the steady drumming and stared where the winds churned the river below. Ghostly lights of anchored boats glimmered back like winking eyes, and then were lost in the deluge. Rain splashed on the interior tiles near the doors, just enough to dampen Shane's bare feet, but not enough to warrant closing the doors. In the darkened glass of the open door opposite, Shane could see Lillian's reflection.

She was still riffling through the legal pad. "Okay. So, you went to Kilbert Elementary, Camp Creek Junior High, Lundston High…"

He tried to ignore her now. He couldn't afford to forget that her interest in him was purely academic. No one had ever attended so diligently to the facts of Shane's life, but she didn't care about him. Knowing him was only important to her because it might help get her a son.

Brandon. Shane glanced uncomfortably down the hallway, toward the baby's nursery, sandwiched between the guest room and bath. It was a wonderful room, bright and cheerful, with a rocker next to the crib. Shane had never known a kid who had a room so nice.

Lillian glanced up, squinting. "How do you remember everything about me so easily, Shane?"

I've been studying for seven years. Nevertheless, it was hard to keep things straight. Truths mingled with her fictions. He shrugged. "Good memory."

"Oh, right. You said it runs in your family."

He nodded, staring down where the thirsty ground drank up the rain. He felt a slight chill—either from a slight drop in air temperature, or from the memories of the rains that had claimed his parents' lives years ago, back in Texas. Was this job with Lillian another he was about to screw up?

He thought of his Uncle Silas.

Aunt Dixie Lynn's husband had been a Louisiana cop. When Shane's rebellious spirit landed him in adolescent trouble, Uncle Silas had helped curb it, which was how Shane wound up joining the force. Seven years back, Uncle Silas had found out that a Western crime consortium headed by a man named Jack Ramsey was bringing crime into Louisiana—mostly drugs and money laundering—and that a large payoff was going to be made to Louisiana's dirtiest cops. Except for a longtime partner, Trusty Joe Beaujolais, Uncle Silas trusted no one. So, Shane had taken a leave of absence in East Texas and gone to Louisiana to help Silas, until they had enough evidence to involve the FBI.

That was where Shane had first seen Delilah Fontenont.

He'd been tailing her car, but he didn't get a good look at her until she stopped for a soda at a bait shack on the bayou. In a white sundress and sandals, she shone like a lamp on the dusty porch of the old store. Shane had watched her slake her thirst—drinking with none of the reserve she had now, throwing back her head, exposing her creamy neck and gulping. Her long hair was dark and wild, like her eyes, and her walk was sexier than any Shane had ever seen.

He'd wanted her. So badly his heart missed a beat,

and he'd simply stared through the windshield, his hands unusually still on the steering wheel.

But he knew he could never have her. She was engaged to Jack Ramsey's son, Sam. Even worse, she'd signed over her family home, the old plantation, to be used as the basis of consortium operations. She was obviously in deep with the Mob.

She was used to the high life, too. The Ramseys had fixed up the plantation—landscaping and painting. Bungalows and an airstrip were built and the waterways cleared near a boathouse and pier. Ostensibly, the place was a refurbished as a resort and spa, but the consortium was using it for business. Jack Ramsey was using it to this day, even after what happened on Sam and Delilah's wedding night, when things blew sky-high.

That night, Shane was in a car, watching the main exit to the property, when he heard gunfire. After that, everything happened fast and trickled down later in bits and pieces. Delilah had sped away with the payoff money, which was meant to make every dirty cop in Louisiana turn a blind eye to consortium operations. When gunfire hit the boathouse, where the gang stored ammo, the building and the pier both exploded. Sam Ramsey, who'd been injured somehow in the melee, stumbled too close and was presumed dead in the explosion. And Trusty Joe said Uncle Silas got caught in the crossfire. Shane reached his uncle's side just before he died.

I loved you like a son, boy. Like my own flesh and blood.

Those were Silas's last words.

Now, staring into the rain, Shane felt her—Delilah,

Lillian, whatever she wanted to call herself—come up behind him.

"My, my, you do look serious. What are you thinking?"

Shane turned. Gazing deeply into her eyes, he was still seeing her speed down a one-lane private road in the dark, glancing into the back seat at a bag stuffed with three million dollars in Mob money. It was unmarked. Untraceable. Blood money his Uncle Silas had died for.

But the longer Shane stared, the less he was thinking about Silas, and the more he was wondering about the truth. Badly as he wanted to know who'd pulled the trigger and killed his uncle, Shane trusted his gut the way Lone Star trusted her nose. And his gut told him that a woman like Lillian would never knowingly marry a bastard like Sam Ramsey. *Or is her beauty blinding you?* That was still the sixty-four-dollar question.

She looked concerned. "Talk to me."

He shrugged, the gesture more casual than his mood. "My dark, brooding side starting to get on your nerves?" Even he could admit that his moods sometimes got darker than this night.

Not that Lillian seemed bothered. "Most lone wolves have a dark side."

That again. "I'm not a lone wolf, Lillian. I'm a man."

She merely nodded as if she had him all figured out. "Are you thinking of the flood…" *That killed your parents.*

"Yeah," he lied. At least he thought he was lying, but maybe not. Dark, rainy nights usually did lead him to his own demons. He wasn't sure why, but he found himself telling her more. "My folks were sandbagging against the rising river that night. I thought I should stay and help sandbag, instead of my mother, but I got sent to the schoolhouse with everybody they evacuated. Mama told me to look out for my little brother, Doc. And that was the last thing she ever said to me."

Fingers curled around his biceps like satin, and at the touch, Shane felt a shiver—not a cold shiver, but a shiver of heat. Lillian was so close right now, in body and spirit. For days, they'd been getting closer, physically dancing around each other while sharing bits of their lives. He thought back to the first night, when he'd spilled that wine and nearly kissed her.

"Shane?" she said simply.

His eyes penetrated hers, seeking answers. Why was it so important that he let this woman know more about him than the simple facts? More than his favorite color, which was gray. Or that he liked classical music and had once kissed a little girl named Ruthie. Wanting a woman the way he wanted Lillian was so foreign to Shane. And because of who she was, he didn't want to rely on her for his needs. Not sexual. And definitely not emotional.

He had a sudden, powerful urge to push her away. His voice was rough. "Still looking for those intimate details that'll help you get Brandon?" he bit out. "That's why you want to know about my folks, right?"

She looked as if she'd been slapped. She whirled away, but Shane instinctively grabbed her arm and when he pulled her back, her face—her eyes, her lips—were far too close. Her gaze was steely. "Think what you want, Shane."

"I am."

For no reason he could discern, her brown eyes

suddenly softened, looking like liquid. "I want to know *you*, Shane."

He managed a soft derisive grunt. "Right." He abruptly released her.

"Like I said, believe what you want."

He shrugged. Maybe he wanted to believe her. But how could he, when she was such a practiced liar?

"Please," she ventured. "Keep talking to me. Don't push me away."

His eyes drifted over a mouth he wanted to utterly possess. And then something inside him gave. "Doc," he found himself saying, "my little brother...he was only three years old and scared to death. I held him all night. He slept while I stared into the rain." Years later, still staring into the rain, Shane could feel the fear come back, the power of the swelling river that took everything in its path. He finally said, "Only in the morning, when they came and told me our folks were dead, did I realize I'd slept. I kept thinking, if only I hadn't fallen asleep...."

"You were only eight years old, and you did everything you could," Lillian said gently. "You've always watched out for Doc, too. He's grown up, in love now."

At that, a slight smile touched Shane's lips. His little brother was head over heels in love with a New York woman who'd given birth to his child. Frankie's family had taken a shine to Shane, and of course, Shane had met the baby. Not that he'd held her. Babies were just too small. Too weak. And Shane had failed too many times to protect those he loved.

"Doc's done all right," he said. "I figure he'll marry Frankie. And he does love their baby girl." Shane shook his head. "I remember when medical school was nothing more than a dream for him. I worked two, sometimes three jobs to help him through, so he wouldn't have to carry the debt. I figured one of us might as well have a life…"

Lillian reached and touched his weathered cheek, making his heart hammer. He'd never felt so vulnerable with a woman, never told one so much. *Dammit, Shane, she's just getting to know you because she wants the baby.*

"You deserve a life, too, Shane."

Uncomfortably, he edged away from her touch, re-situating himself against the door. "I have a life."

"You could have more."

It was clear she meant a woman. He thought of her, back on the dusty porch of that bait shack in Louisiana, the skirt of her pretty white dress fluttering against her kneecaps in the breeze. His voice was almost hoarse. "Well, Lillian, I wouldn't worry overmuch about *my* needs. After all, I don't see you keeping many men around here." *Only me.*

She colored. "That's different. And I'm getting the baby." Her voice caught with excitement. "I just know this is going to work. Brandon and I are going to be a family."

There it was again. That statement of the simple life she wanted that nearly brought Shane to his knees. He could no longer believe this woman had fled a crime scene with dirty money, or been party to the gunfire that had killed his uncle. Something else must have happened that night.

His realized his eyes were raking over her lips again. Against his will, he edged closer, drawn by that delicate mouth, those changeable eyes that could be sad and yet still sparkle. Over her shoulder, he caught the reflection of her long bare legs in the glass door. *Wise up. The lady's all reflections. And you're lost in the funhouse.*

"It really is different for me," she repeated huskily.

"Is it, Lillian?" She'd taken a new name, started over from scratch. These past seven years had consumed her, just as they had him, and it was just one more of the many bonds they shared. He heard her breath catch, but she said nothing.

His next words came before he thought them through. "C'mon, Lillian, sometimes you must need a man."

"Need a man?" Her forced chuckle fell flat when she tried to make light of it, and her voice sounded strangely dry, given the wet, hard-driving rain just inches away. "What on earth for?"

"Dammit, Lillian—" His own frustrated warning curse should have stopped Shane, but his hand—both strong and yet so powerless—reached out. Rough fingertips that vibrated with need slid slowly down a satin cheek. "You need a man, Lillian," he whispered hoarsely. "For this."

He knew what he was about to do was wrong. But he leaned unhurried, his searing gaze burning on the mouth he was about to claim. He looked long and hard because he was used to looking. Because for seven years of torment, only his eyes had touched the slender neck she was now tilting back with tremulous uncertainty. She was going to let him kiss her, so he watched her eyes drift shut—knowing he was watching for the last time, knowing he was finally about to taste.

"For this," he said again softly.

And then his mouth—as searing as the summer heat

that sent perspiration rolling between her breasts—
brushed and stirred the air above her lips.

She gasped.

And that one sound told Shane what he'd always
known in his heart. That from the second she'd laid
eyes on him, she wanted him every bit as badly as he
wanted her.

He savored it—both the near kiss and the need. His
palm curled around her neck, and his lips grazed the air
above her mouth again, starting their physical relationship the way all life began—with nothing more than a
breath. And then a dry, blistering barely-a-kiss kind of
kiss came, a hot, tongueless, open-mouthed nuzzling
that was infinitely erotic, and that made her fingers
tighten and tremble on his arms and made his whole
body hot, his groin hard.

They were still barely touching.

Again and again, Shane's mouth passed. Even when
her thirsty lips begged, he still wouldn't give his tongue.
Way back in sixth grade, a little girl named Ruthie Miles
had taught him this trick. He withheld his tongue even
when Lillian's legs whispered apart, just a sweet breath
opening against his thigh.

When she moaned from sheer want, her whole body
trembling, Shane thought he'd burst. He licked her
mouth then, streaking her lips with his tongue's thirsty
damp fire. Suddenly, he dived, the tantalizing tongue
going deep, thrusting possessively as he dragged her
to him, her breasts cushioning against his bare chest.
When that wasn't enough, Shane staggered two paces,
dragging her into the rain, where the storm's raging
thirst matched his own. He wanted her wet to the bone.
Inside out. With his passion unleashed in the elements,

he thrust his hand up through her hair, tearing at the band that held it.

He could no longer see her. His eyes were shut. No longer the secret watcher, he knew her only by touch. And taste. She tasted of wine and rain, which he suckled as the deep kiss touched bottom. Her wet silken hair was rushing through his fingers like the rain, and as his mouth drank from hers, he wished her hair was still dark, its natural color. He wanted her so badly. But he wanted *her*. The real her. Delilah Fontenont.

Sliding his hands down her rain-drenched back and over a T-shirt that clung to her like a second skin, he pressed her closer, tilting his hips in his soaked jeans, urging her to feel how painfully, how powerfully, she'd aroused him. She rose to meet the thrust of his hips, straining with a moan.

"Yes," he whispered to his wild, dark, devilish Delilah.

"Shane," she gasped, wrenching away. "Oh, Shane!"

SHE'D ENDED THE KISS.

Whatever was left of Lillian's old self—her wild carefree self, which meant her true soul—hadn't wanted to end it. But she'd *had* to! She deserved a nice clean upstanding life. No complications. No complexities. She just wanted a baby. And she couldn't forget that was Shane Holiday's sole purpose in her life—to help her adopt Brandon. But Shane, with that wicked kiss of possession, was more threatening than a whole pack of wolves. More threatening than any man…

Including Lillian's husband.

Her *dead* husband.

Thinking of Sam Ramsey made Lillian clutch the

phone receiver in a death grip. She clamped her palm over the mouthpiece, then glanced nervously around her office. Through the glass wall to her left her boss, Jefferson, who was also on the phone, adjusted a carnation in the lapel of his gray suit and ran a hand distractedly through his thick salt-and-pepper hair. To Lillian's right everyone in the brokerage cubicles was working. Good. No one was paying attention.

She tried to concentrate on the conversation. It was risky, since her boss had no idea she was eavesdropping. Oh, he knew a woman was on the line, he didn't know it was Lillian.

Though the glass wall, she watched her boss's lips form the words that came through the receiver in his deep baritone. "Tilford," Jefferson was saying. "You scared me."

"That's why I'm making this conference call," said the judge. "I would have phoned sooner, but I had no idea…"

"No idea!" Someone exploded.

Lillian, c'mon. Quit thinking about Shane and Brandon. You've got to pay attention to what they're saying. The call concerned the Big Apple Babies adoption agency, and with Brandon still being kept at the agency, as well as other matters pending, anything that concerned Big Apple Babies concerned Lillian.

When she'd first begun working for Jefferson, Lillian had done some extra filing and accidentally found out about Big Apple Babies. Apparently, years ago, the seven secret philanthropists who were on the phone had anonymously donated start-up capital for the agency to Jake Lucas, who was now the head executive, not to mention Shane's boss. At the time, Jake had been a dedicated prosecutor in the family court system.

Lillian had quickly discovered that her own boss, Jefferson, was one of the anonymous New York millionaires who'd started the agency. It was Jefferson's secret charity that made Lillian decide to adopt from Big Apple Babies. When she'd announced her plans, she'd even hoped her wealthy boss might pull some strings, so she'd be sure to get a baby.

For all Lillian knew, Jefferson had. But Ethel had turned her down. And now she was about to marry Shane because of it. Her stomach fluttered nervously. The blood tests were done, and the next step was City Hall. Or Trinity Church. She'd decided a church wedding would lend credibility when Ethel asked about her and Shane's marriage. Of course, that meant people at work had given her gifts, Jefferson was planning a small reception party and walking her down the aisle….

Into Shane's arms. Those strong, hard, muscular arms that had made her shiver when he'd held her. Lillian could still feel the hard hot rain pelting her clothes, drenching her while he'd kissed her. And while she'd made clear she wouldn't give in to the temptation again, she was now haunted by fantasies. What would it be like to make love to a man like Shane? A man who, like her, denied himself so much of what he needed?

Would you pay attention to the conversation, Lillian?

Jefferson was saying, "Well, the next time you do something like that, Tilford, let us know."

Lillian frowned. The honorable Judge Tilford Winslow, the most unconventional judge in New York and another of Big Apple Babies' secret financial backers, had recently faked a heart attack in his courtroom. Lillian would probably know why, if she could manage to pay attention. She bit back a sigh, wishing they'd talk about why singles couldn't adopt. *You'll get Brandon, with Shane's help. Don't worry.*

Everything would be fine if she didn't pursue a physical relationship with Shane. But the kiss that had so thoroughly reawakened her would be impossible to forget. It had felt so right, as if Shane had been studying her intimately for years and yet her marriage to him was only to be temporary. Besides, he was a cop.

Her eyes strayed guiltily to Jefferson's office, lingering on a bookcase. Behind it was Jefferson's hidden safe. Only she and Jefferson had the combination, and Jefferson never scrutinized the contents.

At least Lillian hoped he never did.

Because in addition to his papers, she kept some secret documents of her own. Including everything pertaining to the three million dollars she'd taken the night she'd fled from Louisiana.

CHAPTER SIX

SHANE LEANED AGAINST the rail of the FBI boat that was docked at the Manhattan Yacht Club. "Lillian doesn't have that money. Other than living under an assumed name, I don't think she's guilty of anything."

Fin's subordinates—four fresh-faced agents—hooted and slapped each other on the back. "I tell you," one laughed. "That was a helluva kiss in the rain the other night!"

"And check out the pooch!"

Shane's jaw set. Lone Star daintily pranced past, sniffing at deck chairs. Star-shaped barrettes kept her shaggy bangs out of her eyes, a red bandanna was around her neck, secured by a sheriff's badge, and she wore red toenail polish. Shane would never live this one down. Or the kiss.

He'd been so caught in the moment, he'd forgotten there was a surveillance boat in the Hudson. Not that Shane gave a damn what the agents thought. They had no more right to spy on his private moments than he'd had to watch Lillian over the years. A cop could stake out a woman without completely invading her privacy. In the future, Shane would remember it.

Fin thankfully offered more sobriety than his assistants. "I'm sorry, Shane," he was saying. "But you're crossing the line. Thinking below the belt."

Shane found the comment offensive. He wanted Lillian. But there were emotions involved. "You're wrong. She hasn't gotten to me."

"Oh, Shane. Shane," crooned the agent in falsetto.

He willed himself not to react. "I've been undercover countless times," he said flatly. "I don't lose perspective."

There was a long silence.

As he stared around, trying to quell his frustration, he decided he hated Manhattan. As far as he was concerned, the Manhattan Yacht Club was even worse. It reeked of soulless men who reveled in money and power, thriving on the rat race and their own hostile games. Right now, the FBI boat was hemmed in between three mammoth yachts—named the *Titan,* the *Machiavelli* and the *Bossman.* Tired of torturing himself, he glanced at the skyscrapers; the miles of steel shot into the sky. Beneath them was the only place on earth where you could get vertigo from looking up, instead of down.

Unless you're with Lillian. Propped on his elbow in the floor of her living room, gazing up into her eyes, Shane had felt that same vertigo. His life was spinning out of control in a whirlpool of emotion and energy he didn't understand—or even *want* to understand—and which he was powerless to stop.

He tried again. "Our best bet is to come clean with the woman. We'll talk to her, assure her we'll protect her. She'll tell us everything she knows."

Fin merely stared at him. "What? Did you sleep with her?"

"You've no right to ask." Shane kept his voice calm. "I've done what I said I'd do. I've searched her apartment and office. The only place I haven't searched is her boss's office. It's too open. But I've found nothing pertaining to the mob's money."

"She lives awful rich."

"The apartment belongs to her boss. It's a real estate investment. You know it checks out."

"How can she afford those clothes?"

"Sales. She doesn't really spend much on clothes."

The agents rolled their eyes.

Shane had about had it. "You really expect me to marry her tomorrow?"

Fin said, "Yeah, I do."

Shane grunted softly in frustration. "I guess you think we should wind up with a baby, too." He glanced up the river promenade toward the apartment. Supposedly, he was walking Lone Star before the kids came, since it was Friday night and he and Lillian were baby-sitting. Not that Shane knew anything about baby-sitting. Or babies.

He thought of Brandon. Tomorrow's wedding could bring Lillian closer to getting the baby. But he couldn't allow it to happen. If she did get the child she so desperately wanted only to be arrested and have Brandon taken away, it would kill her.

"I can't marry her."

"If you back out now," Fin said, "she'll know something's up. And Ethel Crumble agreed to interview you two immediately. Just follow through. It's no big deal. It's your job."

Shane was about to explode. "No. Technically, I work for Big Apple Babies, as a security guard. That's who pays me, Fin."

"Don't you care about who killed your uncle anymore?"

That was a low blow. Damn right, Shane cared. And he wouldn't rest until the murderer was caught. His eyes narrowed with anger, but his voice was even. "If Lillian saw anything that night, we won't find out this way. We need to talk to her."

"You know, Shane," Fin warned softly. "I've already got enough evidence to grill her about her involvement with the Ramsey crime consortium. On lesser charges, I could jail her by this afternoon. Do you want that?"

Of course not. He really hated these big-city types. "No."

"The only way you can stay in the game is to marry her."

"She doesn't have the money."

"Then I suggest you use this time to prove it."

"I'll do that." There was nothing left to say. Turning curtly on his heel, Shane whistled, bringing Lone Star to his side.

"And Shane—" Fin yelled as the boat cast off, heading back out to anchor in the Hudson, in front of Lillian's. "Look at the bright side. If you're married to her, then you'd never have to testify against her."

Fin did have a point there.

LILLIAN PUSHED ASIDE the pizza boxes and leaned next to Shane at the island counter near the living room. The kids were all fed, and now they were playing with Lone Star.

"Guess she's the main attraction," Shane said.

"No, you are." The boys had been fascinated by Shane's law-enforcement and Texas ranch experience, and the girls were attracted to his good looks. Shane didn't mind the attention nearly as much as he kept professing.

She suddenly smiled. As she watched the kids, she noted that Benny and his twin, Jim, exhibited different styles despite their identical looks; Jim was riling the poor dog while Benny petted with slow deliberate strokes. Blond, waifish five-year-old Susan pranced around in a dazzle of bracelets and shiny nail polish, not about to dirty herself by petting anything less than a pedigreed champion, although her friend, Cass, gave her all, scratching Lone Star briskly.

Lone Star didn't look nearly as enthusiastic as Cass.

Feeling the heat and hard strength of Shane's body as he edged closer, Lillian glanced up, still smiling. Grinning back, Shane stretched his arm easily behind her. "So, you baby-sit Wall Street kids, huh?"

"Most Fridays. Though not for the past few weeks."

He sighed. "I'd say Benny's going to be the CEO, and Jim'll be his right-hand man."

Standing side-by-side with Shane, his arm draped casually around her, Lillian couldn't help but notice how perfectly their bodies aligned. "So Jim's the fall guy, huh?"

Shane nodded gravely. "Spurred on by nothing more than veiled suggestions, Jim'll go for the throat of Benny's enemies, vanquishing them by brute force."

Lillian nodded at Ben, who was quietly lulling Lone Star with soft strokes. "Gentle Ben might slowly sneak up on everyone and emerge victorious."

Shane raised an eyebrow. "*If* Cass lets him."

Lillian's shoulders shook with mirth. "So, you really think Cass's good-hard-scratch approach wins out?"

Shane's eyes settled on Lillian, flickering over the lace-edged scooped neckline of her floral sundress. "I'd say it's a fifty-fifty. But soft stroking's good. Depends on the context." He shrugged. "Besides, Susan might be right. Sometimes no petting at all is best."

Lillian arched an eyebrow. "It is?"

"Sure—" Shane's quick smile sent a delicious shudder through Lillian, leaving her body weak. "The absence of all petting whets the appetite."

Lillian's cheeks warmed as she thought about the kisses she kept withholding from Shane. Was she merely building their desire? Thinking of how he'd held her, a slow shiver teased the space between her shoulders. Her voice stayed steady. "Hmm. Should our fictitious company be bracing itself for some sort of takeover?" Even as she said the words, another tactile memory of how good they'd been together came rushing back.

"Definitely." Shane dragged a hand through his hair, but when he leaned and toyed with the lace edges of her dress sleeve, a wayward lock fell into his eyes again. "It'll be swift. Ruthless. A real power play."

She chuckled. "Will I get any warning?"

He smiled. "Maybe one real slow shiver."

She sent him a sideways glance. "What? No rumors of war?"

"Maybe a husky whisper."

"Sounds like I'm in for a whole restructuring."

Shane nodded. "I'm thinking in terms of a top-to-bottom rearrangement."

There was no help for the sudden catch in her voice. "Sounds as if you're very thorough when you take over."

"All Wall Street raiders are," he warned. "And we security guys are even worse…"

Lillian widened her eyes in mock terror. "You are?"

"Down and dirty. We open every door. Go for complete and total surrender of the company."

"I take it you mean *present* company."

"Yours alone."

When their eyes met again, his smoldered, burning the hazy, hot smoky-blue of ashes. Awareness flickered in the depths and said he wanted more from her than this casual verbal sparring. He wanted the deeper things they could share. The things he'd been ready to give the night he kissed her in the rain. She realized she was having a good time again—feeling *sexy* again. And safe. She'd come to anticipate so many things—Shane's presence, the warm comfort of sleeping with the dog, and this light banter.

She glanced over the playing kids, then leaning closer to Shane. "Tired of talking business?"

"Lillian, I was talking pleasure."

"It's not good to mix the two," she quipped lightly.

"No, it's not."

She was surprised to see something strangely dark flit into Shane's eyes. What was it—doubt? A warning? Lillian didn't understand it. Didn't Shane *want* to mix pleasure with their business-style marriage? Wasn't that the point of this flirtation? Not that he cared about anything lasting. From day one, he'd made clear he wasn't the marrying kind. Unable to follow his train of thought, Lillian glanced at the kids again.

They were so wonderful. Just watching them made her want a family. Her throat felt suddenly tight, and her

eyes strayed back to Shane. His gray-blue shirt matched
his eyes, and the dark stubble on his sculpted jaw made
him look tougher than he really was. Nestled against
him, she was keenly aware of the coiled strength in his
body. He was a trained cop—she'd be a fool to forget
it—and she sometimes thought he experienced his every
breath as dangerous. His suspicious nature was evident
in how his gaze periodically swept over the kids, and
while Lillian feared his acute powers of observation,
she also trusted him. At least, insofar as she could trust
anyone.

"Hmm," he finally said, staring at Lone Star. "I'm not
sure my newly domesticated dog likes being the center
of attention. Should I rescue her?"

"Not yet." *Stand here with me another few minutes.*
"You're getting a little more domesticated yourself."

"If you're talking about my cooking, I wouldn't read
too much into it." He shot her an easy smile. "It's that or
your TV dinners." He suddenly squinted at her. "What?
Are you thinking about putting barrettes in *my* hair
next?"

"It would keep it out of your eyes." Lifting a hand,
she brushed away the fallen raven strand. "As undomesticated as you claim you are," she couldn't help but add,
"I think you'd make a great dad. The kids like you."

"Lillian," he returned flatly. "I *hate* kids."

She smiled. "You do not, Shane. And I refuse to be
bamboozled by your lies."

"As if you know me so well."

"I do."

That shadow Lillian didn't understand filtered
through Shane's eyes again. He frowned. "What *do* you
know about me so far?"

A lot. You've never let yourself love a woman because you fear you're unable to protect the people you love. "I already know more about you than any other woman," she reminded. "You told me that yourself."

So far. Already. Did those words imply she and Shane had a future? She thought of the white lace dress wrapped in her closet in plastic and felt a twinge of panic. Everything was getting so complex, so involved.

Shane's voice was oddly gruff. "Well, I guess you know enough about me to marry me tomorrow."

But not enough to let me kiss you again. That's probably what he wanted to say. Lillian felt so torn. But if they kissed again, it definitely wouldn't stop at a kiss. She tried again to restore the lightness of their conversation. "Now, now," she chided. "Let's not take our upcoming marital roles too seriously."

"Keep teasing me—" He quickly grabbed a finger she only now realized had settled on his chest. "And I swear, I'll claim my marital rights tomorrow night."

The kiss they'd shared was so powerful and urgent that she knew better than to taunt him, but she just couldn't stop herself. "Oh, I'm so scared, Shane."

This time his gaze lasered into hers, packing real heat, and the sparkle snuffed from his eyes. His voice turned strangely gentle. "Why would you be scared? If I claimed those rights, we'd both be in heaven." His eyes drifted toward her lips. "You *do* know that. Don't you, Lillian?"

Nothing more than his eyes touching her skin made her hot all over. "Yeah—" The word came on a hard breath. "But, Shane, we can't get confused about what we're doing here."

"We're getting married tomorrow."

She forced a smile, determined to regain the light tone. "But just think, if we were *really* married, you'd have to deal with kids. And you just said you hate kids. So, when the baby comes…"

You'll leave. The knowledge hit her all at once. Already her heart wrenched at losing him, but she was excited, too. "Oh, Shane," she wound up continuing in a hushed tone, "I just hope this works. Marrying me to help me adopt Brandon was such a risky idea, but now I'm so…" *Afraid it won't work out. Or afraid we'll get caught. Or afraid I'll get the baby and not be a good mother.* She settled on, "So excited."

Everything had fallen into place. Right after the wedding, Ethel was going to interview them as a married couple. "Really, Shane, even if it doesn't happen, I can never thank you enough for helping me try."

Answering emotion was in his eyes. Against her instincts, Lillian dared to hope it was because he was coming to care for her. She'd memorized so many facts about his life, coaxing out family secrets, private hurts and dreams. At first, it was only because she wanted a caseworker to believe she loved him. But fact and fiction had blurred. The kiss they'd shared was real and more urgent than anything Lillian had ever known.

That Shane understood how much she wanted the baby had moved her from the beginning. Now she impulsively reached out. Beneath her fingertips, the rough whiskers on his jaw prickled. When he didn't back away as he sometimes did, she stretched and kissed his cheek. The kids, still occupied with Lone Star, didn't notice. "I mean it, Shane," she said simply. "Thanks."

She saw his throat work when he swallowed, and the

gravelly sound of him clearing it touched her. So did the sudden vague helplessness in his eyes.

"You don't have to say anything," she assured gently.

His voice was rusty, almost apologetic. "If…if I ever can help you, Lillian, remember I will."

"You are helping me."

He nodded, but everything in his eyes begged to differ. Afraid she was embarrassing him, Lillian turned her attention to the kids. "Quit batting Lone Star on the nose, Jim, or you're liable to get bit," she warned.

"I thought Shane was gonna show us how to arrest somebody, anyway," groused Jim. "He said he would after we ate our pizza."

"C'mon, Shane," Ben called out.

Lillian nudged Shane, then watched as he strode toward the kids, pulling a set of handcuffs from his back jeans pocket. As he began explaining arrest procedures, Lone Star escaped to flop at Lillian's feet, happy to be relieved of entertainment duties.

Staring at the dog, Lillian shook her head. Each night, Lone Star nudged open her bedroom door. And last night, when she'd awakened, roused by a nightmare, Lillian had finally given in to temptation.

Pulling on her robe, she'd crept to the guest room. Shane was so sensitive to sounds, she was surprised he didn't waken. But he didn't. And she stayed there a long time, wanting to slide beneath the sheet and lie next to him. Not for sex—though she wanted it—but to feel his strong comforting warmth near her after that horrible dream. Was she really going to marry him? she'd wondered. This man whose life she'd so carefully studied for the biggest test of hers—to get a son?

Shane slept naked, just as he'd warned, and her eyes had lingered on the powerful, commanding shape of his masculinity beneath the sheet. She'd never seen a man so sleek and beautiful. Fine black hairs trailed down his hard chest, and his long legs were endless. With sleep, the lines around his eyes vanished, making him look younger, and reminding her he really was a man. A man who'd never admit how much he feared love. An ex-cop who'd seen men die. An orphaned child who'd tried to raise his own brother.

Watching him, she'd wondered if he'd ever seen her sleep. She'd even imagined him looking at her—his assessing waterlike eyes swimming down over her silk gown. Maybe he'd seen more. Her panties or the slope of an exposed breast. Now the wild thoughts gave her a slow warm shiver. His words came back: *Keep teasing me, and I'll claim my marital rights.* Oh, she suddenly wanted very, very badly to tease.

"Lillian's gotta be the crim'nal!" she heard Jim squeal.

That snapped her from her reverie. The kids wanted Shane to arrest her? "Please," she began, "I really don't think..."

Shane shook his head. "No, let's not."

But Cass was clapping with utter delight.

And Benny waved a small white card Shane had given him. "I get to read the Miranda warning. Shane says I can!"

Another shiver—this time, pinpricks of fear—settled at the small of Lillian's back. Her last wedding night had been so devastating, full of crimson sparks and earsplitting explosions. She couldn't get married again....

She pushed away the images. *Get hold of yourself!*

The kids simply want to see a security guard in action! You're not actually getting arrested. Keeping her gaze trained away from Shane, Lillian forced a smile. "Ah," she said. "So, what have I done wrong?"

"Robbed a bank!" suggested Cass enthusiastically.

"No," argued Jim. "Everybody robs banks!"

The mention of money made Lillian blank out again while the kids argued over the nature of her crimes. *The nature of my crimes?* she thought bitterly. Was it so criminal to foolishly love the wrong man?

Her eyes met Shane's. He seemed to be watching her so carefully. She managed a smile, just a nervous twitch of her lips that never reached her eyes. He smiled back— she could swear—a second too late. In that second, she felt sure Shane Holiday could read her mind. He could see into her past—and knew all about the crimson fire in her dreams and the explosions.

But of course he didn't. Fortunately, the kids were making headway. "Maybe she's a jewel thief," Jim said.

"Diamonds," Cass specified.

"And in the getaway, she killed a man!"

The words echoed in Lillian's mind. *Killed a man. Killed a man.* Her heart was pumping so hard she could no longer hear at all, and she felt as if every molecule of air had been sucked from the room.

"Lil'yun's not mean," announced Susan. "She did somethin' like Robin Hood, where she stole from the rich and gave to the poor."

Everyone agreed. Her heart still pounding, Lillian tried her best to enter the game. Playing the suspect, she started running circles around the living room, wildly waving her arms while the "bloodhound"—meaning Lone Star—barked and nipped at her heels.

The kids screamed, shouted and gave chase. With every pounding footstep and every gasping breath, Lillian could still feel Shane's strangely pale eyes riveted on her. *It's just your imagination, Lillian! The man can't read your mind.*

Stopping in front of the windows, Lillian waved her arms wildly, then fled again. She ran around the room until it finally felt good to run. Until the game started to feel therapeutic. After all, she *was* winning—she'd outrun her past. She'd eluded the Ramseys and was about to adopt Brandon.

Shane came at her head on, and she feinted left, then lunged. He just missed her. A whoosh of air sounded inches behind her and the handcuffs he was waving clinked. All around her, the kids giggled.

"Arf!"

"Get 'er, Lone Star!" Jim shouted, sounding bloodthirsty.

"I almost got 'er, Shane!" shouted Benny.

"Gotcha."

This time the voice was low and sexy. Unmistakably Shane's. Caught, she fell to the floor as gracefully as possible—breathless, her heart pounding, her knees weak. For just a second, her past seemed a lifetime away. Because she was suddenly laughing with the kids and Shane…and wishing. If only she could share a home with a man she loved. She wanted to roughhouse with their kids, just like this. And share pizzas and secrets, grow gardens and learn to trust again.

"You got the right to remain silent, Lillian!" Benny

announced. The little boy stepped back and, in spite of his giggles, tried to read the Miranda warning.

Lillian could merely smile up at Shane. Smelling of soap and old clean denim, he was kneeling next to where she lay on her back on the floor. When he hauled her to her feet, their eyes meshed.

His voice was low and hoarse—maybe from the tussle, maybe from physical need stirred by her close proximity. "You're under arrest," he said, slapping on the cuffs.

The chuckle suddenly died in her throat.

Footsteps were pounding in the outer hallway, and a fist beat on her front door. A man shouted, "Open up! Open up in there!"

She whirled from Shane's grasp as more steps sounded. For a second, she thought none of it was real, that her innermost fears had somehow come to life. Both men were rushing her door. Outside, hard bodies thudded against the wood. She watched in shock as someone realized the door wasn't even locked and turned the knob. Men fell through, with guns drawn and badges held out.

Lillian couldn't move. Not even to look at Shane. She could only stand there, in a frozen stupor. What was happening? Gunman were rushing toward her, down the front hallway she traversed every morning in her bathrobe. As if in a dream, she watched Shane race to intercept them.

"Get back!" someone shouted. "There's been an arrest."

But no one got back. Everyone but Lillian was still moving. Susan had fled for Shane's arms and he'd caught her in midstride, swinging her into his arms.

Cass grabbed Lillian's hand, and Lone Star protected the boys, growling fiercely at the intruders.

"What's going on here?" Shane demanded. "Who are you? How could you burst in here like this?"

The men stepped back, looking uncertain.

"We heard there was noise. Screaming and yelling. Some neighbors called and complained, saying they thought there was real trouble here." The man glanced toward Lillian's handcuffed hands. "Uh…"

"We were playing a game with these kids we're baby-sitting," explained Shane, taking command and shooing the men back through the door. "I'm an ex-cop, a security guard, and I was showing these kids how to make an arrest. Sorry. Tell all the neighbors we'll keep the noise down."

Lillian was shaking as Shane gently removed the handcuffs. Had real law officers just burst into the apartment? They'd vanished as quickly as they'd come. Her heart was still hammering and her mind could barely catch up. Her lungs ached and burned—maybe from running, but more likely from what had transpired. "Where did they come from?" she gasped.

Shane's voice was calm. "They said a neighbor called."

"But we weren't that noisy. And they came so fast." Response time for the police in New York City wasn't exactly immediate. And they were in plain clothes, not uniforms. Were they already in the building for some other reason? Yes, that must have been it.

"Neighbors called," she finally repeated, assuring herself. She felt Shane's arm glide supportively around her back. *Something's wrong, Lillian. You're missing something here. Was it something to do with one of those men...*

But they'd come and gone so fast. What was teasing her mind? A memory? Had she seen one of the men before? She managed to shake off the paranoia and plaster a smile on her lips. "I guess that just took me by surprise." She glanced around. "Sorry, kids."

"Sorry?" Jim said in awe. "That was great!"

"I can't wait to tell my friend Tony," assured Benny.

Susan looked fine. And Cass was petting Lone Star again. Lillian felt Shane's hand gently rubbing her lower back.

"You okay?" he said gently.

"Maybe I'm just nervous about tomorrow," she managed. *Tomorrow.* What was she going to do about the wedding? Oh, she wanted Brandon more than anything. But what she and Shane were doing was wrong....

Even worse, she could feel her past nipping at her heels, closing in around her like walls pressing inward. After only one shared kiss, she was falling for Shane, too, and having fantasies where he stayed, becoming Brandon's daddy. But Shane couldn't be in her life. He was an ex-cop. He'd realize there were gaps in her past. Maybe he'd already guessed that the simple white brick house with the picket fence existed only in her dreams. She yearned for it, just the way she did a baby. Just the way she yearned for Shane.

"Lillian?"

She gazed into Shane's eyes. The kids were excitedly discussing their visit from the police, but she kept her voice low, anyway. "Shane, I've changed my mind. We can't get married tomorrow."

His face turned hard. The pupils of his eyes held an uncompromising intensity she'd never seen, and his voice was a command. "Don't get cold feet on me now."

"But—"

"No buts."

She stared back in mute protest. How could she explain to Shane that the police might come here for different reasons someday? And that next time, her arrest might be real.

CHAPTER SEVEN

"IT'S NOT LIKE YOU to fidget, Lillian—" Jefferson Lawrence gently urged Lillian down the aisle, coaching under his breath in a soothing baritone. "Now, now, you're just getting married."

Just getting married. Spoken like a true Wall Street financier. The last time the Dow Jones plummeted, Jefferson had chuckled, run a hand through his thick, salt-and-pepper hair and said, "No more bull. We're in a bear market now, so get ready to growl!" *Just getting married.* As if she was filing papers or fetching coffee.

Lillian stared down the aisle. Shane was at the dim, imposing altar, standing as still as the churchyard statues visible through a side door's leaded glass. Somehow, she felt glad of the veil that covered her eyes. Otherwise, he and everyone else would see her panic. From the front pew, a camera flashed. No doubt the photographer was another of Jefferson's touches. Poor Jefferson, Lillian thought, her grip tightening on his suit sleeve. Her boss would be jittery, too, if he had any inkling of what she and Shane were really up to.

The anxious sigh she blew out in an effort to calm herself was so deep it lifted her veil. She had a valid Social Security number, but she'd been sweating all these details—everything from the marriage license to Jefferson's giving her away.

Without moving his lips, Jefferson again chided, "Please, Lillian, quit trembling. You look lovely."

"Thanks," she managed.

She could feel Shane's appreciative eyes on the white tea-length lace dress. It had short sleeves and a lace-edged sweetheart neckline, and the manicured hand that wasn't resting on Jefferson's arm was holding a cascade of sweet-smelling pink roses. She'd insisted Shane not see the dress before the wedding. Even if they weren't marrying for love, she wasn't jinxing this.

Still, she was nervous. Couldn't people see through her duplicity? Each step brought her and Shane nearer to a marriage that had nothing to do with love. And yet, with each step, Brandon was closer to home. Warmth infused her when she imagined the baby sleeping cuddled against her, his tiny pink hands flexing in helpless fists.

If you can get through the vows, everything'll fall into place. You have to believe that. Surely, as soon as she got the baby—*if* she got the baby—she'd forget Shane. Of course she cared for him. She'd experienced the beginnings of rebuilt trust, and his kiss had devastated her. But it didn't mean anything, and neither did the self-indulgent ideas she kept entertaining about making the marriage real. It *is* real, she thought with renewed panic. They'd had blood tests, and gotten a license.

She really should turn around and simply stride through the bronze doors of Trinity Church. She'd hit Wall Street, her satin heels clicking, the breeze lifting the veil over her face. As she rounded Nassau Street and passed the stock exchange, the brokers on break would glance at her wedding attire while they crushed cigarettes butts under their heels. Maybe she'd toss them the roses.

She kept marching.

Trinity Church was a Gothic-revival showcase, and through her veil, the stained-glass windows that arched toward the vaulted ceiling looked as strangely opaque as the hallways that led to marble crypts and tiny chapels beyond the altar. Lillian glanced at the coworkers who smiled from the front pews. It was so sweet of them to come, especially since she'd never gotten close to them—both because she feared they'd find out about her past and because she was afraid to trust in friendships after Sam's betrayal.

Shane hadn't called his brother yet. He'd been too worried Doc might sense something amiss at the wedding. But maybe not. Apparently Doc had recently started having his own love troubles, fighting with his girlfriend, Frankie. Still, it seemed a shame he wasn't here since there were so many well-wishers.

Even Bennie and Jim, their baby-sitting charges, had offered gift; they'd taken Lone Star to their parents' apartment for the night. As if she and Shane needed privacy! Tonight, as always, they planned to quiz each other on the facts of their respective lives, since Ethel was coming tomorrow.

Still staring at her coworkers, Lillian's guilt became positively insufferable. They'd brought such lovely gifts to the office—personalized stationary for Mr. and Mrs. Holiday. Monogrammed tea-towel sets. An engraved tea service. The name Lillian Holiday and the initials LH now peered back at Lillian from all her cupboards and towel racks. She just hoped Ethel Crumble noticed tomorrow.

Not that it helped the here and now. Jefferson smiled benevolently, giving her away. As the minister began the service, Lillian's eyes slid to Shane. Nothing was more solid than the massive stone church, but as she looked at the man who was about to become her husband, everything seemed to shake. No wonder she kept wishing this marriage was real.

He looked gorgeous, although his suit was nothing fussy—just a plain dark suit with narrow lapels, worn with a crisp white shirt and dark tie. Clean-shaven and with his hair combed back, he looked very austere. He'd traded his cowboy boots for leather dress shoes, which he'd bought for the occasion.

He smiled—a quick flash of straight white teeth that seemed to make him shine in their dim Gothic surroundings. His eyes, too, were light in all the darkness— peering from tanned skin, and from sleek slashes of dark eyebrows and sparse rims of black eyelashes. What was Shane thinking right now? Did he share her doubts?

"Does anyone know why this couple should not be joined in holy matrimony?" the minister finally asked.

Lillian could think of countless reasons, beginning with the fact that her name wasn't Lillian. And that she and Shane weren't in love. Realizing she was holding her breath, she slowly exhaled. What had she been expecting? That the ghost of her dead first husband would protest? Or that *she* might voice her own reasons? At least a hundred nights, she'd awakened with nightmares, scared and alone and wishing she wasn't living a lie. She wanted to tell someone what had happened.

Now was definitely not the time.

When the minister continued, the words suddenly made Lillian's heart ache in remembrance. Seven years ago, she'd stood for this same service in the rose garden her father had so carefully tended. Although she'd lost both her parents in the preceding two years—her mother to cancer, her father to a heart attack—she'd felt their warm, loving presence in that special place on her wedding day. She'd known they were proud, since her marriage to Sam Ramsey had helped her restore the Fontenont family home.

Then, as now, a new baby was anticipated, since Sam promised he and Lillian, then Delilah, could immediately start adoption proceedings. They'd pull out all the stops, he'd vowed. Do whatever it took. He loved her so much, there was nothing he wouldn't do for her.

Only hours later, he'd shattered all her earthly dreams.

"Lillian…"

She stared through the veil as the minister said, "Do you take Shane to be your lawful husband?"

For an instant, she couldn't find her voice. Emotions crowded in on her: the heartfelt longing for Shane she was trying to fight; the anticipation of Brandon's powdery softness cuddled to her breast.

She swallowed hard. "I do."

"And do you, Shane, take Lillian…."

Shane's face, so stark and solemn, seemed to mirror the emotions in her soul. The sheer weight of their surroundings—the high arched stone ceilings and imposing windows—seemed to bear down on them, accounting for the seriousness she saw in the watery translucent depths of his eyes. She felt now as if he could see straight through the veil into her heart. Suddenly, she felt sure he'd always seen through her—and that he'd loved her anyway. He didn't, really. But it would be wonderful if such a thing was true.

He said, "I do."

The minister nodded. "I join you now as husband and wife."

She became conscious of her nerves again—her staggering pulse and shaky knees, and braced herself for the necessary touch of Shane's lips, assuring herself the kiss held no significance. It was only a performance. The altar was the stage; the congregation, the audience. Now if only her leading man would grin or wink, Lillian wished. If only he'd do something clownish or inappropriate, some damn cute thing to remind them they were playacting…

But Shane's gaze was more serious than ever as his fingers caught the veil's edge. Her lips parted in silent anticipation and her traitorous hands trembled on the flower stems.

Get it over with, Shane! her eyes pleaded.

When his dark hand paused on the filmy material, he seemed to hold a handful of Lillian's bunched, little white lies. Her breath caught—as if his lifting the veil could actually remove those lies. As if his kiss was something magical that could transform her, change her from Delilah Fontenont into someone who really was Lillian Smith. Or Lillian Holiday. A woman who had a real husband and a son named Brandon.

It couldn't. But right then, Lillian wished for it. Suddenly, her eyes stung. She should have known they would. She always cried at weddings. Gently, Shane lifted the veil and brushed it from her face. As he stepped closer, her breath caught as his roughly tender fingers slid beneath her chin. Cupping it, he lowered his lips. "Lillian," he sighed, simply.

Then his firm warm lips pressed hers, his supportive hands gliding down her sides, his languorous tongue flickering, then going so deep that Lillian felt the timeless kiss melt her; his mouth vanished and she felt only warm smoky tendrils curling inside her. Very definitely, this was more than wedding decorum allowed.

Leaning back, he stared at her. His eyes, sometimes so unreadable, now held desire that shook the core of her. This kiss never should have happened.

"Your performance was worthy of an Oscar," she murmured, her husky voice so low no one could hear.

"Well, for my acceptance speech," Shane returned softly, "let me tell you it wasn't a performance."

She was afraid of that. "You swore you wouldn't kiss me like that again," she whispered.

"I lied, Lillian," Shane whispered back.

"But I don't want you to do it," she said. And then she swallowed hard, because she was the one who was lying.

Everything in his eyes said he knew it.

"I THINK IT WENT WELL," Lillian managed lightly.

Shane lounged against the doorjamb, watching her wiggle the key in the apartment lock, his gaze trailing down her long legs. It was late. He felt heavy, full and faintly aroused—from the aged red wine Jefferson favored, and the oysters and caviar at the buffet arranged by Jefferson's private club, and from playing the part of Lillian's husband—cutting the cake and dancing with her for the benefit of the few wedding guests.

It went well? Was that all Lillian meant to say about their wedding? About the fact they were now legally husband and wife? "Yeah," Shane agreed, "I think everybody had a good time."

"I'm sorry your brother wasn't there."

Shane was, too. He hadn't phoned Doc, but there was something, well…*wrong* with that. Doc should have been best man. Their aunts should have been there, too. Aunt Dixie Lynn, especially, would skin Shane alive if she knew he'd gotten married. That the marriage wasn't for love wouldn't bother Dixie Lynn in the least, if she knew—no more than would Shane's working undercover. She'd just say, "Any woman fool enough to marry my nephew for any reason is good enough for me." And then Dixie Lynn would pump Lillian with questions, find out about the plans to adopt Brandon, and start calling Lillian "niece."

Lillian caught his gaze, a slight smile curving her lips. "What are you looking at?"

"The prettiest bride alive."

"You wear a suit well yourself."

"Thanks." He considered stepping over and embracing her from behind. He wanted her close right now; wanted his arms wrapped around her waist while he burrowed against her neck and pulled in deep breaths of her. His eyes settled where her lace dress hugged her lower curves, and he was conscious of the lazy heat teasing his belly, just a slow-circling spiraling push of arousal that Lillian's every soft breath seemed to stir. He leaned, almost impulsively, swiftly threading his fingers through hers. They hadn't been alone since he'd kissed her at the wedding, and for hours he'd wanted to pull her in front of him as he did now. "C'mere. I want to talk to you."

Their bodies weren't even touching, only their hands were linked, but her voice was oddly husky. "Yeah, Shane?"

He had no idea what he wanted to say. Oh, he knew how he felt. He ached for her—and he felt guilty. If he had a brain in his head, he'd phone Fin and end this damn charade before he did any more damage. Trouble was, he didn't want to leave Lillian even though he knew this had to end before tomorrow morning when Ethel came. Were the agents right? Was Shane too deeply involved?

His throat felt strangely raw. "You were a beautiful bride today, Lillian."

"Oh, husband of mine," she said lightly, "like I said, you didn't look so bad in wedding clothes, yourself."

Before he'd kissed her at the altar, he'd cupped the moist silk of her chin. Even as he did so again, he was remembering the agents bursting into the apartment yesterday. He'd called Fin; apparently the guys staking out Lillian's thought Shane was arresting her.

Now Lillian nodded toward the open door. "As good as we look, I guess we'd better change into jeans, go over our notes and make sure we don't forget any pertinent facts tomorrow."

"I've got a better idea." His eyes never leaving hers, he dropped a finger from her chin to her lace-covered shoulder. "What say, we take the night off?"

She smiled. Her eyes were slanted with drowsiness and, in this light, they looked lighter, flecked with almond. "Just what did you have in mind?"

What I have in mind every time I look at you. Settling

his palms on her waist, his eyes drifted over the up-swept hair he wanted to unpin. "Maybe seeing your hair down." He never had. At least not dry.

She chuckled softly. "Now there's a worthy activity. Any other ideas?"

Shane could think of nothing worthier. His eyes drifted to where her lace-edged neckline made dappled shadows on the swells of her breasts. "What about my carrying you over the threshold? Would that qualify?"

"Oh, Shane, we'd better not—"

"Why not?"

"Because we're married now."

"Exactly."

He lifted her easily, so quickly she couldn't protest, and held her against his chest—an arm around her back, the other under her knees. Finding her lighter than he expected, he took a step back to compensate, then he glided over the threshold. As he elbowed the door shut behind them, she wrapped an arm around his neck.

He headed down the long unlit hallway.

"No, Shane," she protested gently, sensing where he was headed. "I'm so worried something will go wrong tomorrow. I'm afraid I won't get the baby. We really need to study tonight."

"You're Lillian Holiday," he returned. "Previously Lillian Smith. You're five-foot-eight. Weigh a hundred and thirty pounds, but right now you feel lighter. You grew up in a little white brick house with ivy and a picket fence, and you like gumbo and raw oysters. When we kiss, you're going to taste of warm red wine, sugary white icing, tangy cocktail sauce, ice cream and—"

"But, Shane—"

"No buts, Lillian." His voice was low, his breath

lingering near her lips. "You live at 390 Liberty Terrace, work for high financier Jefferson Lawrence and
even though you profess to hate it, you secretly love to
be tickled—"

"Please, Shane—"

"Don't 'please-Shane' me. You also love kids and
reruns of bad television shows from the seventies. Besides that, you've got a body any man would kill to hold,
just the way I'm holding it right now."

His murmured recitation continued. But with every
step, his heart was wrenching with guilt. He knew better
than to try to take her to bed. He wasn't anymore truth-
ful than she. And if he answered Ethel Crumble's questions tomorrow, Ethel might actually decide they could
adopt. Not that they'd get the baby immediately. Surely,
they'd have to undergo weeks, maybe even months, of
waiting and red tape.

They? Where had that come from? His heart skipped
a beat. Quickly, Shane reminded himself it was Lillian
who wanted a son, not him. And that he might not be
staying here another day, much less months.

He heard her soft, near-silent catch of breath as he
entered the bedroom. Another as he flicked on the bedside lamp and laid her across the bed. Wordlessly, he
sat beside her on the mattress—their hips touching, the
lace of her pretty dress feeling rough when his warm
palm resettled on her hip.

Delilah Fontenont, a.k.a. Lillian Smith.
Lillian Holiday.

Shane never guessed he'd get this close to her, much
less become her legal husband. He'd never imagined
her looking this gorgeous, lying in bed on their wedding night. The red lampshade's dim glow had turned

her dress and the poreless skin of her cheeks pink. And seeing how red highlights danced in her hair nestled on the rose-touched pillows, Shane forgot everything: that she was a fugitive and he was a lawman. And that she sincerely thought he would help her adopt Brandon.

He reached, removing pins from her hair and setting them on the bedside table. When his eyes swept past the open bathroom door, the quick glimpse he caught of his reflection in the mirrors reminded him he had no real rights here. He was deceiving her. Maybe it was he—not she—who was all smoke and mirrors.

Her smile was too flip. She was trying to make light of what was happening. "Excuse me? Did I miss something? Did you just put me on the bed, Shane?"

He didn't smile. His unflinching eyes settled on hers. "Isn't that where a man puts his bride?"

A tremor shook her voice. "C'mon. What exactly are we doing here?"

"This." He drew a last pin from her French twist, then raked a hand beneath her nape. Loving the touch of the silken strands between his fingers, he fluffed her hair across one of the myriad pillows, then toyed with a stray lock, where it brushed her shoulders. Like him, Lillian was torn between common sense and desire. He could read that plainly in her seductively slanted eyes.

"We're not *really* married, Shane."

His eyes pierced hers. "Things have changed, though, haven't they?" They'd exchanged vows. His voice hit a rough, hoarse patch. "Look, Lillian, I never guessed getting married would mean anything, but..." It did.

So did the laughs they'd shared, and the long nights they'd spent talking about their lives. He thought of lines Lillian had spoon-fed him, so he could tell Ethel why he'd be a good father: *I want to share the things I love with my son, Brandon—woodworking, fishing, hiking. I want to take him to see Texas and Louisiana, all the places where I grew up.*

But suddenly, those didn't seem like rehearsed make-believe lines anymore, and Shane craved the boy and family that would never be his. As his gaze swept down the bride he wanted to possess, he felt the familiar seven-year ache that hurt both his body and heart. It was a hollowness he'd felt while watching her through windows, or following behind her, feeling like her love-slave as he tailed her at a distance.

Oblivious of his thoughts, she nodded slowly. "I guess it's hard to make wedding vows without…" She paused, swallowing hard. The room was warm without air-conditioning and suddenly very still and silent; her eyes darted downward, as if she'd just become conscious she was lying in bed with him leaning over her. "Without the vows meaning something," she finished.

He murmured, "Everything means something, Lillian."

Her smile was gentle. "How wise. What else do you know?"

"About you?"

She nodded.

"A lot." The slight, faintly lopsided turn of his lips made his eyes crinkle. "You're Lillian Holiday," he recited again. "Very recently married. Five-foot-eight. One hundred and thirty pounds. And when I kiss you—"

"I'm going to taste like cocktail sauce."

"Don't forget the wine, icing and ice cream."

Her voice was a near whisper. "What's a kiss without ice cream on top?"

Shane leaned closer. "A whole lot hotter."

She chuckled, then her throaty drawl turned as soft as the restraining hand she lifted to his shoulder. "Really, Shane, I…I don't think we should pretend anymore. It's not right to carry me over the threshold, or to kiss me the way you did at the church." *Or to make love to me the way your eyes say you want to.* She might as well have said it out loud.

"But I did."

She must have seen something timelessly male flicker in his gaze then, some feral light or predatory awareness, because a soft plea infused her tone. "Shane, we can't forget we only got married because of tomorrow…"

His hand tightened possessively on her waist; the slow firm rub of his thumb caressed her side, teasing the white lace. "I don't care about tomorrow," he said. It wasn't true. He cared a lot. But as he tilted his head down, hoping she'd let him kiss her, he found himself saying, "All I care about is right now, Lillian. Just you and me. And the present moment."

"Shane…"

Once again, she'd only huskily murmured his name. Did she fear talking more—and admitting too much? Would another kiss threaten her control? She was definitely threatening his. He was so close that her breasts brushed his chest and their breaths mingled. He barely recognized his own voice; it had roughened to the point of hoarseness. "Why shouldn't I kiss you?"

"Like I said, we're married now."

"Like *I* said," he whispered back, descending the last inch separating them, "that's exactly why we should." As he captured her mouth, he did taste wine and sweet icing from their wedding cake, but Shane's heart had a taste of a claiming he'd never known. She was his wife. Something had happened to him in that church. Shane didn't know what. But in the eyes of the law, he and Lillian belonged to each other now. And if there was one thing Shane believed in, it was the law.

Against his mouth, she murmured, "Really, Shane, there's so much we don't know about each other."

"You're Lillian Holiday. You're five-eight, a hun—"

"But you don't understand…"

I understand better than you think, Delilah. But one look at you—and I'm swept away, drowning. He leaned back a fraction, his eyes suddenly blazing into hers because he knew she wanted him, and her denial was starting to gall. She made him feel so many things he wanted to fight. Hadn't she guessed he was used to being alone and feared needing anybody—especially her? Didn't she know the emotions he was feeling didn't come easily to him? "I've wanted you a long time, Lillian. Can't you understand that?"

"We've only know each other a few weeks."

He had no answer for that, so he grasped her hand—roughly in gesture, softly in touch—and curled it against his chest, whispering, "I've dreamed about being with you."

And he wanted to say more. To confess those dreams had haunted him for years. Feeling her trembling hand against him set his mind spinning and flooded his groin, making him throb with frustrated need. It was unbearable—the way her most innocent touch could arouse him so thoroughly.

Her lips suddenly parted, and the hand that wasn't against his chest found his shoulder and clung. The soft rasp of her voice, the sweetness of her breath, undid him.

"Shane, I admit I've…thought about this, too. About making love with you."

Breath eluded him. "You want to…?"

She nodded. "Yes. Yes, I do."

He felt he'd waited a lifetime to hear it. He moved his body on top of her, his tongue parting her lips. He'd wanted so much more than this kiss—his emotions demanded it—but what exactly he ultimately wanted, he couldn't quite admit. So, he gave with his tongue— diving deep in a wet possessive kiss, thrusting.

After a long time, he leaned away and saw her jaw was slack, her eyes dazed. She looked utterly beautiful in the wedding dress that had risen above her knees. His eyes never leaving hers, he removed his tie, then his jacket and shirt. When he was bare-chested with his belt open, his heated gaze strayed from her face to her toes.

Delilah.

He almost said her real name aloud. He could see hints of the dark wild woman he'd wanted so long ago. Determined to coax her out of the primmer Lillian, Shane leaned and cupped her face, sending a searing stare deep into her eyes. It was meant to pierce her soul—and did.

"Undress me," she whispered.

Hearing the soft catching sigh of her voice, he felt a crushing tenderness for her that he knew he could never fight. Somehow, some way, he'd help this woman out of whatever jam she was in. And he'd bring her the release she was begging for with those glossy dark eyes.

Gently, he drew the delicate wedding dress over her head. Seeing her underwear—a fancy silk bra, bikini panties and garter belt—stripped away anything remaining of his common sense or professionalism. Shane's heart thudded dully as he molded his hands over her thighs and calves, pulling the white stockings from her endless legs like veils.

"Here," she murmured, sitting up and tremulously unhooking the back of the bra for him. With a dry pant, he helped her edge the lace straps down the creamy lengths of her arms, until his eyes were on her full breasts—his warm gaze flitting over the milky mounds, the dark aroused distended tips.

He quickly filled his hands. "You're the most gorgeous woman I've ever known." The words were matter-of-fact, but his voice came in a slow-rolling husky drawl as he molded his palms over the mounds, then slid the smooth backs of his hands under and around the curving slopes. He stopped, brushed his thumbs back and forth across the hard nipples, and then slowly, deliberately, leaned and curled his tongue, like a burning lick of fire, around each taut tip. Leaning back again, he kneaded her with his hands while he watched her face. Arousal made his voice low. "Look at me, Lillian. Into my eyes."

She met his gaze. But when he saw her eyelids flutter anxiously, he felt a flash of temper, such as he'd never before felt in bed. It came on him fast and hot, like his physical craving for her. Suddenly, he was reminded, not so much of the lie she lived, but of the fact their marriage wasn't real. Even now, he could hear how her voice shook when she said her vows today. As if it meant something. *Don't kid yourself, Shane.*

She was fighting him with her will, afraid to lose herself, even though her hips had begun twisting, wrenching to seek a greater pleasure. He tried to tell himself he was too old for this—too old for games, too old for her, and too old to look for love in her eyes. But he still looked. And he wanted her to look back at him.

Her voice was hoarse. "I'm really sorry, Shane. But can we turn out the light?"

Hearing the sincerity in the simple request, he felt his anger vanish as abruptly as it had come. His eyes trailed over her a final time—over what the rose glow of the lamp did to her pale breasts and panties. His breath caught, and he fought the urge to ask her to take off the panties for him. He'd love to see her completely naked right now.

But he turned off the light.

And in the dark Shane's dreams returned. She was the woman who'd haunted him since he'd first seen her on the porch of a bait shack years ago, long before she'd run to this city they both hated, where she had no roots, no home, no family. Her hair was wild now, not blond, but dark, the color of dark molasses in the Southern sunlight deep in the bayous.

When his lips settled over hers in a claiming kiss, he realized the dark allowed her to let go. Over and over, he kissed her, his mouth shameless. While he used his tongue to coax out the lost girl from Louisiana, his roaming hands drew out her sighs. Powerful, pungent scents started rising from her skin like hot steam, eliciting his most unbearable response, making his voice ragged.

"You're so beautiful." Somehow he said it again—as if he wasn't speechless when his hand dipped inside silk, touching where she was as damp as the humid summer night, and as if he could actually see in the inkiness of the room. Imagining her not as blond where he stroked, but her natural color, sleek and dark, he groaned and then he stripped away the last veil of silk, dropping her panties to the floor. Raising her knees, he tongued her thighs, and bringing his palms under her smooth bottom, he urged her up to his mouth, opening her with a long slow stroke of his tongue.

"Shane!" She sobbed his name as he parted her again and again. "Oh, Shane!"

Share yourself with me now, Delilah.

And, oh, she did.

Lost completely, she arched with his suckling, crying out. His mind plummeted into the dark, pulled down by her scents—all fragrant oils and musk. Turning his long legs, he drew down his zipper, and she reached out immediately, her hands seeking where he most ached for her. Gripping the powerful evidence of his need, she strained wildly to his mouth, her thighs shuddering with climax.

"Shane!"

The reckless way she shouted his name made him feel that she, not he, had waited these seven years. He pulled her into his arms, and as she released a last whimper, he mindlessly stroked her face. Her hair was damp and wild and tangled now, and he senselessly kissed it, his heart pulling with intimacy.

When she was ready, she simply lay back, opening her arms to accept him. He quickly stripped off his slacks and came to her, bracing against her heat. His full weight was behind the first unbroken thrust that brought him to her womb. He went taut, absorbing the power of it, and he gave her time to feel what he'd dreamed of for so long.

And then he withdrew and thrust hard into her—

wrenching gasps from her, filling her, shooting hot rippling pleasure through her until she twisted her head away, sucked greedily for air and rode him while he feasted on the neck she offered. His need for release was fierce. Holding it back, Shane had room for no thought. But when she shattered, his mouth caught her final cry. And as he spilled into her, he realized this act made their marriage real.

CHAPTER EIGHT

SHANE UTTERED A SOFT curse as he paced up and down the hallway, stark naked and feeling cornered, with Lone Star on his heels. Ethel Crumble was due any second. When Shane awakened, he'd slid naked from bed, coming straight out here, hoping for a quick flash of brilliance. Or the return of the logic he'd lost seven years ago, the day he'd first seen Delilah.

"Lillian," he murmured in correction.

Lillian, who'd studied the facts of his life, coaxing out feelings Shane never guessed he had. Last night's intimacy had shaken loose the last of his remaining locked-up places. He'd hidden none of his tenderness and he hadn't bothered to shield her from the intense physical hunger she aroused in him.

Turning, he headed toward the living room again, his eyes darting around as if the walls held answers about what he should do now. Once last night, in a broken voice, she'd said, "Nothing like this has ever—*ever*—happened to me, Shane," and he knew she'd been thinking of Sam Ramsey, whom they'd never even talked about. Not that Shane was proud of his need to erase the traces of her husband. Her *previous* husband. But he was glad she thought he was a better lover.

Reaching the living room, he turned, heading back in the direction of the front door and the grandfather clock, glancing toward the bedroom door. The image of Lillian, still in bed sleeping, made his heart squeeze so tight that he lifted a hand and kneaded the spot. He wanted to make her breakfast, then get back in bed with her.

But he had to think. He had to find out what she'd done with the Mob's money. Soon, Fin was going to give up on finding it, and bring her in for questioning. At that time, she'd be officially booked for fraud charges relating to the false identity she'd assumed. Unfortunately, Shane's repeated searches of her apartment and office were turning up nothing. And yesterday, he'd phoned Uncle Silas's partner, Trusty Joe, who was retired now. Trusty Joe said the money was definitely in the car she was driving that night. So, where was the evidence of what she'd done with it? And why had she run?

She had to have good reasons. Shane loved her so much he couldn't believe otherwise. He knew that now. Which meant he couldn't tell her why he'd really moved in with her. Feeling betrayed, she might throw him out, rejecting his help when she needed him most. It was a risk he wasn't about to take.

"What a mess," he muttered. He just wished he knew what to do about Brandon. Shane's heart seemed to stretch inside his chest. Not that he really wanted a baby, of course. But he *did* want to make Lillian happy…

She's my wife.

Shane stopped in midstride, absorbing that, then he resumed pacing. Yeah, this morning, he was about as married as any man could be. How had he so seriously miscalculated the depth of his own passion? Been so blind to his own motivations? How long had he been denying his fantasies about adopting Brandon? Or his jealousy of Sam Ramsey?

For years, Shane knew he felt...*something*.

But until last night, he'd never called it love.

He'd really thought his obsession with Lillian stemmed from the case. He'd said, "Sure, she's beautiful." It was a simple fact. Any red-blooded man who had her under surveillance would have had fantasies. But all along, he'd thought his sole motive was to eventually punish whoever pulled the trigger of the gun that killed his uncle. Lillian was the key to that mystery.

It was a mystery Shane still intended to solve, but that hardly explained why he'd been living and breathing nothing but Lillian for seven years. Fact was, he'd solved a number of crimes without getting married. Or becoming a father. "You're *not* a father," Shane whispered.

He just wished he could call his little brother for advice. Doc had more experience than Shane with long-term relationships. But Shane had been lying to Doc for weeks, by omission. Every day at Big Apple Babies, he and Doc lunched together, but Shane hadn't even mentioned Lillian. Now Shane thought of Doc's baby girl, Astrid. With her spray of black hair, she really could be Brandon's cousin.

Of course, Shane wasn't adopting Brandon.

But he'd fallen in love with Lillian. And she wanted a baby. He'd nearly reached the living room when a sound intruded on his thoughts. Someone was knocking, probably Ethel. Only when the door started swinging inward, did Shane realize it hadn't shut securely last night. He was getting as bad as Lillian about relying on the building's internal security. And Shane knew better than to ignore standard safety procedures.

"Wait!" Maybe it wasn't Ethel. He bolted down the hallway, determined to catch the door. He almost made it. His fingers swiped the air, brushing wood just as it opened.

"Shane!" Ethel gaped—her jaw slack, the rest of her frozen. Only her round owlish blue eyes moved, dropping to...

He was naked. He'd reflexively sprinted for the door, forgetting. Holding his hands in front of him, Shane edged a pace backward, thinking, *Poor Ethel.* Despite her old-fashioned name, the virginal caseworker was only in her twenties, and her face was as now as dark red as the blunt-cut bob that swung around her shoulders.

"Shane, so good to *see* you!" she suddenly tittered, her eyes sparkling in a way that said she meant to thoroughly enjoy his discomfort.

Shane's jaw set. Suddenly, he felt ridiculous, standing there like Adam. Adam—he wished! About now, he'd kill for a fig leaf. Not that her embarrassed girlish giggles bothered him. Hell, he was an ex-detective. A security guard. He owned a gun. "Good to see you, Ethel," he managed dryly, edging back another step, his eyes searching the hallway for something he could wrap around himself.

"Is this symbolic?" She sagged against the door, still laughing with embarrassment. "Like, you're in your birthday suit because you want a newborn? Get it?"

He got it all right. But why wasn't she turning around? "Look, could you just excuse me while I get some pants?" He guessed he could turn and simply walk back to the bedroom. Yeah, that's what he'd do. So what if she saw his butt? Right?

She was still grinning at him, her face bright red.

His eyes landed on the marble-topped table and his Stetson. Of course, to get it, he'd have to unclasp his hands... He reached quickly. The hat wasn't much, but it would have to do. Grabbing the brim, he turned the interior so it cupped his unmentionables.

"Gee, that really helps!" Ethel chuckled. "My hat's off to you!" she added shrilly.

Shane glanced over his shoulder. The bedroom looked miles away. "You know, Ethel," he said levelly. "*You* could turn around now."

Her laughter had tempered to a wicked grin. "Not on your life, Shane."

"Shane?" Lillian's gasp came from the bedroom doorway where she stood, clutching a sheet to her chest. Obviously, she wasn't wearing a stitch more than Shane.

"Naked," Ethel announced. "Save for matching mortified expressions."

"Before today, Ethel," Shane said levelly, "I thought you were a nice woman."

"Oh, Ethel, I'm so sorry—" Lillian's flustered, upset voice called from the other end of the hallway. "Please, seat yourself in the living room! We'll be right in!"

Maybe. Shane was still staring at the far-off bedroom doorway. Well, it was now or never. Pressing the Stetson firmly to his groin, he started walking backward again. "Do go away, Ethel," he managed.

"Go away? And miss this fashion show?" Ethel loosed a gasping laugh. "No way. Believe me, this is better than anything this side of Madison Avenue."

LILLIAN WANTED TO CRY. Not that she would. But the power of Shane's lovemaking had left her completely shaken. And now, before she could even process it, Ethel had arrived. Lillian stormily swept past Shane in an uncharacteristic emotional display, pulling on her robe and grabbing underwear from the drawer. "How could you do this to me!" she burst out.

Shane glanced up, his eyes widening in slight surprise as he stepped into jeans and buckled his belt. He studied her a long moment, then he simply reached out and grasped her elbow. "Whoa. Hold on, Lillian."

His voice was so soothing she wanted to scream. How could he be calm at a time like this? Ethel was here! And wasn't he even affected by what happened last night? She jerked back. "We don't have time to talk right now!"

"Ethel's waiting another minute won't hurt."

"She saw you naked!"

"And going off like a rocket won't help."

Feeling totally unbalanced, she strode to a mirror. Pursing her lips, she tried to roll a French twist, but her fingers were shaking so much she made a mess of it. Escaped strands of hair fell against her neck. "I'll never get Brandon now." She was so sure it wasn't going to happen that her heart was breaking.

Even worse, she could feel Shane staring at her back with that calm self-restraint that, on any other morning, might have been reassuring. He said, "Is this really all you have to say to me this morning, Lillian?"

She caught the last escaped tendril of her hair, tucked it into the twist and secured it with a pin. Squaring her shoulders, she regally swung around to face him—bracing herself against the irrational anger rushing through her. And against what this man had done to her last night. In a few hours, his dark kisses had swept her away like a rushing current, and she'd been flooded with a storm of emotions she hadn't felt for years—or ever before.

How could she have let it happen? She'd sworn she'd never let herself be vulnerable again. She couldn't afford to be open, trusting and reliant—like the foolish, blushing, gushing bride who'd once believed in the husband who said he loved her. After all, that's how she'd been on her first wedding night—right up until Sam Ramsey destroyed her. Just how long would it take for Shane to do the same thing?

Right now, she felt as furious with Shane as with herself. In fact, everything about him was making her angry, including his feigned mild manner and the ease with which he sometimes teased and joked with her. Not even his icy reserve had expressed his true self. No, last night, Lillian had finally met the real Shane Holiday. And the introduction was something she'd definitely never forget. Wrapped in his naked arms and the sheets, she'd become highly acquainted with why fiery explosions periodically punctured his reserve: because the molten core of him was all hot passion and raw tenderness. All love. And she was scared to death of it.

"Well?" he finally said.

It took everything she had, but she kept her voice from trembling, and gave a quick toss of her head. "Just what did you expect me to say to you this morning, Shane?"

His lips compressed and those all-seeing eyes searched hers. "Please, Lillian," he said levelly, even though dealing with emotions wasn't exactly his strong suit. "Just share with me whatever you're feeling."

Her heart tugged with the need to love him, even as

fear, masked as anger, continued pouring through her. "I don't think what I feel right now matters," she was powerless but to snap. "Everything's ruined. Ethel knows we're not a punctual couple and that you go around naked with the door open."

The set of his jaw said he was above gracing that with a response, and that he knew she was unreasonably taking out her nervousness on him, but trying to soothe her, he said, "I'm sorry."

"I'm sure you are." She strode for her jewelry box. He was sorry. Great. She wished he'd scream and yell. Or give her that cold reserve that could freeze the room. Or melt it, she thought, a lump lodging in her throat, as she stirred her earrings with a finger, blindly looking for a match. She forced herself to go on, "Not that you care about anything." *About the baby. Isn't that what you really want to say, Lillian? Aren't you trying to goad him into saying he wants to have a baby with you?*

Shane's voice came up behind her, as did his body. The voice was gruff with temper he was tamping down. The body generated heat, reminding her of the fevered dampness of his skin last night and how much his mouth had made her burn. "What don't I care about, Lillian?"

She whirled around again, now rapidly blinking back tears. Didn't he know she didn't want to get involved? That she didn't want to fall in love? Hadn't she told him that, the day they met? The day he'd completely lied to her, assuring her he was an untouchable lone wolf. She could still hear him saying, *I'm not the marrying kind.*

Well, guess what, she thought. *We're married now, Shane. In every sense of the word.*

"The baby," she found herself saying aloud. "I'm the one who wants a baby, not you! You don't care what happens today!"

His tone was even. "I care."

About what, Shane? Me? The baby? About what happened last night? She tried to tell herself she didn't really want any answers, that she didn't need them, because she had absolutely no intention of falling in love with him. And yet she knew she'd already fallen. Hard. "If you care, then why did you answer the door naked?"

"I didn't."

Of course he hadn't. At least, not intentionally. She knew better. Whirling away from him, she took long strides toward the walk-in closet now. Once inside, she pulled the door shut, slamming it, then she stared at the outfit she'd chosen for today—a navy A-line tent-type dress. Her heart beat wildly as she dragged on a slip, then realized it was inside out. A dry sob escaped her as she took it off, then put it on again. Last night, Shane had made love to her in ways she'd never even imagined. Next to it, Sam Ramsey didn't even come close. And she'd married Sam. *You married Shane, too.*

But it wasn't a real marriage. And she had to forget last night happened. *Focus on this morning,* she commanded herself, conjuring an image of Brandon—his smooth skin, strands of black hair and angelic eyes. She hadn't even offered Ethel a soda. No coffee was made. And the A-line dress was… "It's not right!" she burst out. "It's just not right!"

"What's not right, Lillian?"

She hadn't even heard him open the door. Ignoring him, she raked at the hangars. "This stupid dress. It's the wrong dress. I hate this dress. It's too—too—" As she ran her hand madly over the rack, searching for another dress, she realized Shane had made her different last night, reigniting her emotional spark, changing her back to what she used to be—quick to love, quick to tears. Too bad her more emotional side was something she'd wanted to forget.

Warm broad hands settled on her shoulders, and Shane slowly turned her to face him. "The dress is perfect, Lillian." Those devastating, unwavering, silver-blue eyes fixed on hers. "And so are you."

Her eyes suddenly stung, feeling gritty. If he only knew. What was she supposed to do now that they'd made love? Tell him her name wasn't really Lillian? That she regularly carted around three million bucks she'd taken from the Mob? That seven years ago, she was pretty sure, she'd witnessed a murder—but hey, it was a dark night, and the details, which still remained mysteriously buried in her mind, were a little blurry?

No. The only thing she could do was back away from Shane. And right now, she needed to train her mind on Ethel and the baby. She'd spent so many nights getting to know Shane and preparing for this. She swallowed hard. "After Ethel leaves, we really need to talk about last night…"

No doubt he knew what that meant: she was going to back away from their physical relationship, but he merely focused that penetrating gaze on her, and she had the sudden premonition she was caught. No matter what she said or did, Shane wasn't about to let her go. He eased her blue tent dress from the hanger. His voice couldn't have been milder as he handed it to her. "C'mon, Lillian. Ethel's waiting."

Her eyes drifted over him and she realized he was already dressed—in his best jeans and a nice shirt. He looked good. He was trying. He really did care about her getting the baby. She should have given him that much credit. Her eyes suddenly filled with tears that hovered in the rims. She really didn't want to hurt him. "Everything's just going wrong. I was going to serve..."

He was peering at her kindly through a lock of fallen raven hair. "Serve?"

"Muffins," she managed. "And cinnamon buns."

"Just finish getting ready and I'll take care of it."

"You will?"

"Sure."

A tear suddenly fell. "I'm sorry, Shane."

His voice was gentle. "Please. Come on over here, Lillian." With that, he pulled her into his arms, and in spite of her overwhelming fear, her arms wound up wrapping tightly around his waist. Pressing her cheek to his clean shirt, she exhaled a shuddering sigh. Slowly, she'd gotten close to Shane, and with each new gesture of intimacy, she thought she could take another step.

Until last night.

"Oh, Shane," she whispered miserably, able to say only part of what she felt. "I'm not going to get Brandon, I just know it."

Leaning back, he cupped her chin and lifted her face. "C'mon," he coaxed, leaning and offering a quick, soothing kiss. "It's not over yet."

But where would they be when it was over? she wondered, still tasting his lips. Was it possible that she, Shane and Brandon would be a family? And if she didn't get Brandon, would she still have Shane?

Or was she too afraid to love again?

PANTS DIDN'T HELP, Shane decided.

Ethel still snickered every time she looked at him. Lillian, of course, was completely poised now, and being the perfect hostess. Shane just hoped her worry about the baby had caused the outburst in the bedroom, and that she wasn't considering backing away from their physical relationship. Had Sam Ramsey hurt her in some way? The mere thought made Shane want to go at the man with his fists. Not that he could, since Sam Ramsey was dead.

Shane glanced at Lillian. She was remarkably cool under fire. Right now, the only proof of her nervousness was the slight dampness of the fingers she'd threaded through his as she told Ethel about their love affair, describing how she and Shane had been involved years ago, and how they'd met again and enjoyed a wonderful whirlwind courtship. She was brilliantly threading through all the facts of Shane's life—somehow managing to mention Ruthie Miles, Chrissy Winters, and the fact that he'd been number seventy-two on the football team at Lundston.

Shane still hadn't decided how to handle the situation. It would kill him to make a further bad impression—he couldn't stand to think about intentionally undercutting Lillian's chances of getting Brandon—but helping a fugitive, even Lillian, adopt a baby didn't sit well with him. Besides, if she was arrested, the baby would be taken from her. *Not if, Shane. When. The woman's carrying a falsified Social Security card.*

He eyed Ethel, who was sipping iced tea from a monogrammed glass he and Lillian had received as a wedding gift. "Well," he found himself halfheartedly venturing, "you know Lillian grew up in a…redbrick split-level—uh no, it was a…"

"Little white house with a picket fence, wasn't it, Lillian?" Ethel said.

Lillian shot him a look that nearly broke his heart. She knew he had an excellent memory. Her eyes pleaded with him, saying, *Why are you doing this to me? You're supposed to help me, Shane! You said you cared about the baby!* It ripped out his damn heart. If he pretended to forget her supposed past again, the disappointed expression in her eyes would kill him.

"So you both miss the South?" Ethel asked conversationally.

It took everything he had, but he gave it another try. "Lillian more so than me. She loves the food. There was a dish her daddy used to make…." Feeling crushed under the weight of his own self-loathing, he squinted as if trying to recall. "I think her daddy made some kind of pot pie…"

"Gumbo," Lillian stressed. She stared at him again, her eyes bugging. He could all but hear her voice. *Please, Shane! What are you doing? Are you trying to hurt me? The whole point of your moving in was to help me get this baby. We studied so many facts about each other— how could you forget?*

"Ah," Ethel's cup clinked again her saucer. "That amazing gumbo. You gave me the recipe, remember, Lillian?"

Of course she did. It was the reason Shane had been instructed to bring it up. Lillian's grip on his hand tightened. Her voice held a faint protest. "Shane knows I love that gumbo. He even made it once, himself."

Ethel merely smiled. "So, you're looking forward to the baby, Shane?"

Shane knew exactly what lies he was supposed to tell Ethel now—the ones about teaching Brandon how to woodwork and fish. And how, when Brandon was older, they'd take long summer road trips to Texas and to Aunt Dixie Lynn's on Bayou Teche. Except, Shane thought, his heart suddenly squeezing in a way that made him feel strangely unsettled, maybe those things weren't lies anymore. "Well, Ethel…adopting's really Lillian's idea." Even though he trained his gaze away from Lillian's, the raw betrayal he knew was in her eyes pierced him like a knife.

Oblivious, Ethel smiled pleasantly. "Yes, Lillian wanted a baby before you two even met again."

Lillian's voice quavered. "But Shane wants the baby, too. He really does. When we're alone, it's all he ever talks about. He's always coming home from work with things he's bought for the baby on his lunch hour…."

Her fingers were clasped so tightly through his now that his hand actually hurt. Staring down at her white knuckles, he knew he couldn't take much more of this.

"Shane, c'mon," said Lillian. "Tell Ethel how much you want the baby. Remember how, just the other day, you were saying you wanted to teach him woodworking? Remember, you want to take him on some road trips?"

Even though his few fumbling responses had been calculated to ruin their chances, there was no denying the pain of loss he felt over possibly not getting the baby. And what was he going to say to Lillian when this interview was over? How could he explain the errors he'd made? How could he deal with her devastation? *And what about your own disappointment, Shane? Can't you admit this woman's making you want a family?*

Shane bit back a sigh. There was only one solution. *If* he wasn't able to help Lillian, and *if* she was arrested, then he'd simply have to take responsibility for the baby. Hell, he didn't know anything about babies, but maybe he could hire someone to help. Shane would…well, he would *act* like a father. Just a surrogate until Lillian and the baby were no longer separated. It was the only right thing to do. His responsibility, really. If the adoption went through, the boy would be his—legally.

The words seemed to come from outside himself, and Shane's drawl sounded unusually thick to his own ears. "Maybe I'm not making myself clear, Ethel. I want the baby a lot. I've…really been looking forward to fatherhood."

But his words had come too late. Ethel merely listened politely, smiled and thanked him and Lillian for their time as she rose to go. His lips parted in angry protest, which he almost voiced when he saw Lillian's wounded disbelief.

"But Shane and I are so in love," Lillian protested as they walked Ethel down the hallway. "We want a child to share that with. We've had our hearts set on it."

Ethel merely smiled. "I can see that."

"Well, then?" Lillian pressed when they reached the front door, her strained voice indicating she knew it was a lost cause.

Ethel turned at the threshold, uttering a soft laugh and clapping a hand to her forehead. "Oh, I'm sorry. I thought the answer would be so obvious to you." She blushed. Reaching, she took Lillian and Shane's hands.

"I admit I was suspicious of you two at first. I mean, you'd be amazed what lengths people will go to in order to adopt. We've even had people pretend to be married. Or actually get married, even though they're not really in love."

"No kidding?" Lillian murmured, looking distressed.

"Oh, yes. So, when you called for another appointment, I thought that maybe—" Ethel's guilty color deepened. "Well, that you two were pulling some such stunt. But—"

Lillian's voice was urgent. "But?"

"But—" Ethel colored and loosed another giggle. "Given the fact that your husband appeared at the door stark naked this morning, it's pretty obvious you're the genuine article. That cinched it for me. I know you're nervous, Shane," she continued sweetly. "But since we work for the same agency, I'm already acquainted with your background. I didn't talk to your brother—he'd be biased—but I know you two have a great relationship. And Jake Lucas was more than helpful while I was researching your work record."

"You talked to Jake Lucas?" Lillian said.

Ethel nodded. "As you're probably aware, he's the head executive at Big Apple Babies. Both Jake and I love the idea of placing the baby with people we know, where we'll get to see him grow up. Jefferson Lawrence sent me a formal letter of recommendation, too. And..." Ethel wagged a finger at Shane. "You may act like a tough guy, but I've noticed how frequently you go to the nursery and look in on the baby."

Lillian turned to him, surprised delight in her

gaze. "You go to the nursery and check on the baby, Shane?"

Ethel chuckled again. "He goes at least five times a day."

Shane assured himself that was an exaggeration as Lillian's silken fingers curled around his biceps. It was hard to believe that hands so slender and soft could feel like iron.

"So we're approved?" she asked in wonder.

Ethel edged over the threshold. "Absolutely. And if you'll be home, I'll have the baby here tonight."

Shane's eyes widened. *Tonight?* It was so quick. He hadn't expected that. "But what about all the red tape? The final paperwork…"

Ethel shook her head. "No, Lillian's taken care of everything. All she needed was a husband. And she's apparently found one who loves her very much."

"But…" Realizing his lips were still parted in mute protest, Shane managed to close them as Lillian shut the door. She'd barely turned to him before she threw back her head and laughed, lunging into his embrace with such an uncharacteristic lack of reserve that he could only catch her in his arms, feeling stunned.

"Oh, thank you, Shane—" She sprinkled his face with quick kisses. "I know you were so nervous for me that you couldn't remember everything. I can't believe you said pot pie, instead of gumbo. But I forgive you. I can't believe this worked. I've never been so excited! Can you believe this is happening?"

"Not really," he managed. Not that he was sorry about how things had turned out. The sudden lightness of Lillian's bearing and the warmth of her smile meant too much to him. He knew she hadn't experienced much joy these past few years. Her parents were gone; she had no siblings. Coworkers admired her, but she wasn't close to them, and while parents of the kids she baby-sat often extended invitations, she always declined. As far as he knew, she didn't have so much as one real friend, except for Jefferson Lawrence. In fact, Shane might be one of the few people on earth who even knew her real name. Or cared. That Lillian wasn't better loved was a personal affront to him, too. She deserved so much.

As his gaze drifted over her, Shane decided that giving love was more important than taking it. All his life, he'd had his little brother to worry over, and now Shane guessed the love he'd showered on Doc had helped him more than Doc. But Lillian had no one to love. Which was why she wanted the baby so much.

Her gaze had turned solemn. Lifting a finger, she traced his lips tenderly. "Shane," she said. "I'm sorry I exploded earlier. But I do want to talk. With the baby coming, things are different, and maybe it's not the best time for us to get involved."

"We're already involved." He very much doubted the baby was the real reason she was backing away. He shook his head. "C'mon—" His low drawl carried faint chiding. "Do you really think I'll let you get away that easily?" Surely last night taught her more about him than that. Or had she used him to get the baby? Made love to him so he would be caught with his pants down this morning? Sudden anger flooded him as he remembered how she'd arched to take his intimate kiss, and the sheer relief he'd felt at being all the way inside her. "What?" he said with a calm he hardly felt. "Did you make love to me so we'd look more convincing to Ethel this morning? Is that why you slept with me?"

Lillian gaped at him, her dark eyes instantly sparking with temper. "How could you think that, Shane?" she demanded hotly. "How could you even suggest such a thing?" Before he could respond to the string of questions, she was blinking back tears.

"Oh, God, I'm sorry, Lillian—" Swiftly, he slid his hands over her back, bringing her a step closer, so she molded against him. Her body still vibrated with anger, but the arms that circled his waist held him with a quick rush of forgiveness he hardly felt he deserved. "I don't know what got into me. I've got a suspicious nature." *And the fact that I don't know everything about you hardly helps.*

"It's not as if you haven't warned me, Shane."

Holding her, he guessed he had. Every night, he'd had told her about his brooding side, about his inclination to buck authority, his dark moods, and occasional displays of temper. He had a lifelong habit of walking the razor's edge, just as he was walking it with her. "I guess I figured you deserved to know what you're getting yourself into." His voice lowered a husky notch. "And you've got to admit, we've gotten into something good, Lillian. Last night was amazing."

"Last night was so good, Shane," she murmured against his chest. "*Too* good."

He pressed a kiss to her hair. "There's no such thing as too good."

"Yes, there is," she countered, sounding certain. "And I'm afraid." She lifted her gaze and shook her head solemnly. "Shane, I've made some…well, some mistakes in my life. And with Brandon coming tonight…"

"I still want to be with you," he said softly. He had no answer for the questions in her eyes. He didn't know how he really felt about the baby, only how he felt about her.

Her voice was heartbreakingly sincere. "Then can we slow down, Shane? Just see how things go with the baby here? Maybe not make love again right away?"

He lowered his head, bringing his lips almost to hers. "Sounds good to me." As his eyes drifted over her face, he knew he'd stop the world from turning for this woman. "And congratulations on getting Brandon, Lillian."

"Thank you," she whispered, happiness shining in her eyes.

"You're welcome," he whispered back.

And then, right before his lips closed, warm and firm, over hers, he thought, *I'll protect both you and your son however I can.* And as he pressed his mouth to the loveliest lips he'd ever seen, Shane tried to forget the people he hadn't protected in the past. And he hoped things would be different now. Because he'd fallen seriously in love with this woman. And by tonight, she would have a child.

LILLIAN GLANCED UP. "You ready to hold the baby now?"

Shane doubted he'd ever be ready. "No, you go ahead."

"You can hold him in a minute, Shane, I promise."

He managed a nod, his chest feeling unbearably tight. "Take your time."

Shane had just returned to the nursery with a bottle, only to find the baby had fallen asleep again. Which was just as well. He'd been worried about the temperature of the milk, since instead of doing it the way Lillian showed him, he'd tested it against his wrist too long. It had gotten stone-cold, then he'd had to put another bottle in the warmer.

His eyes drifted over Lillian, who was sitting in a rocker, cradling the sleeping baby. Somehow, now that Brandon was in the nursery, he looked even smaller to Shane than he had when he was at Big Apple Babies. Scrawny, with fisted hands, he was wearing only a diaper and a tiny white shirt. Lillian gazed lovingly down at him, her face glowing and her dark eyes looking unusually serene. From the second Ethel had nestled the child into her arms, a noticeable peace had seemed to descend on Lillian.

She'd called Jefferson immediately; she was technically on maternity leave now. And Shane had called Doc, figuring he'd better, before his brother heard about the marriage and baby from Ethel or Jake. Doc might be having love troubles, but he clearly suspected something was amiss, since Shane wasn't exactly the marrying kind. Not that it put a damper on Doc's heartfelt congratulations. The only reason he hadn't raced over was because he wanted to give Shane and Lillian time alone to bond with Brandon. That's what Shane got for having a pediatrician for a brother.

"Are you okay, Shane?"

Shane glanced up. "Hmm?"

"You're pacing."

Realizing Lillian was right, he leaned against the wall and tried to relax.

"C'mon, Shane, why don't you sit down in the rocker?" she suggested, rising. "I'll hand him to you."

"Really, I'm fine." But he wasn't. Shane had never even held his niece. Or any baby, he realized as he edged toward the rocker. In fact, truth be told, he'd always avoided babies, and the only reason he sat down now was because Lillian asked him to. Once he was seated, Lillian leaned toward him, and as she gently settled the child against his chest, Shane was drawing in a heavenly breath of her musk fragrance.

Shane glanced up at her. "Like this?" His arm had curved into a cradle, and now he curled a supportive hand under the baby's head.

"That's exactly how you should hold him," Lillian said.

When Brandon started wriggling, Shane suddenly, reflexively lifted the baby. "No. Look…he's waking up."

"That's okay," she whispered with a smile.

Shane stared back down. He remembered Lillian telling him about the first time she'd held Brandon. She'd said in that one instant, they'd formed a bond. Now, his chest swelling, Shane knew exactly what she meant. He'd never wanted to protect anyone more in his life. His eyes lingered on the small mouth. It was puckering and moving with a gumless chewing motion. "I think he's going to cry."

"He's just hungry," Lillian assured. Kneeling next to the rocker, she lifted the bottle gently, guided Shane's hand around it, and brought it to the baby's mouth, showing Shane how to hold it. As the baby's mouth closed over the bottle's nipple, Shane felt a lump form in his throat, and when Brandon suckled hard, waving his arms with seeming pleasure, Shane touched a tiny palm, to steady it. With firm pressure, Brandon's fingers curled around Shane's and everything inside Shane seized up. "Well, look at that," he murmured.

"Yeah." Lillian chuckled softly, sending him a long sideways glance. "Have you ever held a baby before, Shane?"

He shook his head. "I've got to admit, this is a first for me."

There was a long silence.

"Shane?"

He said nothing. He couldn't. His attention was still riveted on the baby's suckling mouth. He felt, rather than saw, Lillian's hand as it trailed over the rocker's armrest. As she gently rubbed his forearm, Shane glanced over to find her smiling into his eyes in a way that brought softly shining light into hers. She whispered, "I'm going to rename him."

Shane frowned. "You love the name Brandon."

"I do. But I thought of a name I like better."

"What?"

Leaning, she pressed a kiss to Shane's cheek that undid him with its tenderness. "Shane," she whispered. "You helped me get him. So I'm going to call him Shane."

CHAPTER NINE

BECAUSE THE BABY needed to be in the bedroom with his mother, Shane had moved the crib, changing table and rocking chair from the nursery to an area near Lillian's bed.

Now he smiled grimly down into the crib. He'd felt uneasy since the day before yesterday, when the baby arrived, but now Shane knew he had cause for worry. Apparently, the photographer at the wedding—a man he and Lillian assumed Jefferson had hired—had been one of Fin's men. And now Fin had run a wedding picture of Shane and Lillian, along with an announcement, in half the newspapers in the country. Since Lillian's workplace was mentioned in the announcement, any fool could find her.

That Lillian and the baby were being used as bait filled Shane with cold fury. How long would it be before Lillian found out? How could the bastard do it? No doubt, Fin was hoping someone from the Ramsey crime consortium, maybe even Jack Ramsey himself, would see the picture, hunt Lillian down and try to get back the three million bucks. And then, of course, Fin would be there to collect. For days, Shane's relationship with Fin had been strained, but even now Shane had managed to keep it professional, so he'd be kept in the loop where Lillian and the Ramseys were concerned.

Glancing from the crib to the closed door of the bathroom, Shane listened to the shower run. He was tempted to tell Lillian what was happening, but with the wedding picture circulating, he couldn't risk her being angry with him. Besides, she'd waited so long for a baby that he couldn't bear to ruin this special time for her, either. And anyway, Shane was used to coexisting with—or silently bearing the burden of—danger. While he didn't see a lot of action in his current position, he'd been a detective for years.

Genuine humor suddenly touched his eyes. "Happy with yourself, kid?"

Little Shane yawned and squirmed.

Tugging off his T-shirt, Shane shrugged his faded bathrobe back on over his bare chest and boxers without tying the belt. "Lil?" As he called out the name, he vaguely wondered when he'd started calling her Lil, in addition to Lillian. "When you come, could you bring me a clean T-shirt?"

"Sure. Is everything okay in there? Having trouble dressing the baby?"

"A little."

"Try to do a better job than you do on yourself."

"He's not wearing anything faded," Shane said, defending himself.

As Lillian's light, soft laughter floated from behind the closed bathroom door, Shane felt his spirits lift. It was good to hear her sound so happy. Wistfully, his eyes passed over the bed. The past two nights, he'd tried to share it, but Lillian stopped at kisses that left them both wanting more. Otherwise, they'd been completely occupied with the baby.

The baby, Shane thought. He sure was a handful.

Gently, Shane scooted an outfit under him, then grasped the baby's fist and coaxed, "See? Little Shane's legs go here." The baby's lips peeled back in what Shane told himself was a smile. He started fumbling with some overly small snaps. "If we keep this up," he said with a sigh, "you might be dressed before the year 2000."

They'd begun at the changing table, but the baby had spit up on the first outfit, then dirtied a diaper when the second was in place. While Shane changed the diaper, Little Shane had wet on him. Which meant moving the baby to the crib again. After that, Shane tried to leave, to wash himself in the bathroom Lillian wasn't occupying, but the baby began screaming.

Shane had paused at the threshold. It was ridiculous—he'd just needed to leave for three minutes to wash up—but those tiny screams of terror had stopped him short. Lone Star, who'd taken to protecting the crib from a distance, seemed to suspect Shane had hurt the baby, and she'd growled so ferociously that Shane hadn't been able to get past the baby gate again until he'd brought Milk-Bones from the kitchen to bribe the dog.

And then Shane had called Fin, which had utterly destroyed his peace of mind. "Look here—" He tugged Little Shane's arms into place. "This is where Little Shane's arm goes."

"Know where Big Shane's arms go?"

Shane turned from the baby and leaned against the crib rail. "Around Big Lillian?" he suggested, his gaze drifting over her. "Don't come any closer," he suddenly added.

She stopped in her tracks, squinting. "Why?"

Because you look so gorgeous, baby, that's why. She was so heart-stoppingly beautiful that it almost hurt, and

Shane was half sure he'd kill any man who threatened her for so long as a heartbeat. His voice was throaty. "I just wanted to take a gander at you."

Slightly flushing, Lillian turned a graceful full circle, then stood there smiling. The morning light was shining yellow in her loose blond hair, and after her shower she'd thrown on fresh nightclothes, instead of dressing. Beneath the white silk robe, he could see hints of an aqua silk shorts-style pajama. The lounge-wear top had spaghetti straps that lay on the upper swells of her breasts.

Her smile broadened. "Shane, can I please move now?"

Looking at her had brought a slow pull of arousal, but her sleep-tinged voice was even more of a torment. Despite all the worries plaguing him, he smiled back at her. "Say pretty please."

"Pretty please."

He didn't say anything more, and she didn't move. And the longer he looked at her, the tighter his throat got. "Sweetheart," Shane finally murmured huskily, "why don't you just come on over here for a kiss?"

She came, and as soon as she was close enough, Shane grasped her hand and pulled her into his arms, turning her so they could both look into the crib at Little Shane.

After a few silent moments, she gazed up. "Sorry, Shane—" Her husky teasing drawl flooded his lower body with sweet warmth. "I thought you said you were going to kiss me. But now I'm not sure I want that kiss, after all."

"Teasing me? Why, you naughty girl."

Her dark drowsy eyes sparkled. "Well, if I'm so naughty, what are you going to do about it?"

He was sure he'd think of something. He'd never been so intimately aware that there was nothing between him and a woman save shorts and a silk pajama. His eyes drifted over her face. She still looked sleepy, since the baby had kept them up, and she wasn't wearing a hint of makeup, but Shane had never seen anyone look better. The baby had utterly transformed her. There was a new hope in her eyes now and a lightness to her step. She was in her element, loved and being loved.

Maybe it was his proximity, or the underlying seriousness of his tone, but Shane felt a slight shiver move through her as he suddenly confessed, "Lillian, in all honesty, I'd have trouble stopping at a kiss right about now."

She met his gaze, swallowing hard. "Then maybe you're right, Shane—" She glanced at the baby, then edged back a pace. "Maybe we'd better not get started…"

"I'm afraid it's too late," he said, coaxing her close again and tenderly brushing her wispy bangs from her forehead. Right now, they were both barely dressed, vulnerable from their dreams, and the air the around them was turning as hot and clammy as August.

She sighed, relenting with a soft smile. "Well, maybe just a kiss."

"Damn right there'll be a kiss," he whispered, his mouth firmly settling over hers with a pressure that opened her lips, so his tongue's soft flickers could taste her. When she leaned back, her eyes were the color of toasted almonds in the warm morning sunlight, her lips reddened and damp. She gazed over Shane's shoulder at the baby, clearly trying to regain her equilibrium. "So, he's been fussy, huh?" she asked, sounding a little shaky.

Shane smiled. Much as he wanted this woman, he also liked simply being with her. "Fussy?" he returned. "While you were taking a million hours to shower and brush your teeth, he was the kid from hell, Lillian."

"I did not take hours," she retorted.

"Did so. And all the while I was left parenting alone." *Parenting.* The word felt strange in his mouth, but Shane wanted to try it on for size. And he was glad Lillian didn't protest. Truth was, he enjoyed playing daddy— and she knew it. He liked how the few people who'd phoned yesterday—mostly his and Lillian's coworkers— were calling him Big Shane, to differentiate him and the baby. The people from Big Apple Babies who'd seen the dark-haired boy said that he already looked exactly like Shane.

With a start, Shane realized he was merely smiling down at the baby. He glanced at Lillian. "You hungry, sweetheart?"

"Not quite. Are you cooking?"

His mouth curved in a wry smile. "Guess so. Unless Little Shane and I want to split a TV dinner for breakfast."

She chuckled softly. "Maybe Little Shane could cook?"

"Maybe." Shane glanced into the crib again. In the baby, he saw so much raw potential, so much promise. What lay ahead for the baby? For all three of them? Shane tamped down another spark of temper at what Fin had done. "Well," he said dryly. "Little Shane doesn't exactly look like the Galloping Gourmet—yet."

Lillian lifted an eyebrow. "Maybe the crawling gourmet?"

"Crying gourmet," Shane countered. "When *will* he crawl?"

"In a few months."

"A few months." Shane sighed, trying to imagine the baby growing up. Would Shane and Lillian be together then? What of this baby's life would they share—if anything?

Gently disengaging himself, Shane leaned and lifted the baby. Every time he did, he wondered why he'd avoided holding babies for so long. In no more than a day, he'd come to love how the kid sprawled, warming his chest and cuddling those tiny fists on his shoulders. "C'mon," he said to Lillian or the baby, he wasn't sure which. "Big Shane wants to at least start thinking about our morning grub."

Looking for all the world like a family, they padded down the hallway. Lillian sighed behind the two Shanes, tidying as she went—picking up sneakers, socks and slippers that Lone Star had dragged out of the bedroom. Lone Star, staring longingly at the "toys" now in Lillian's hands, brought up the rear.

Just as they reached the living room, the baby emitted a strangled sigh that meant he was about to start wailing, so Shane began pacing between the terrace doors and windows overlooking Rector Park, bouncing the baby and cooing, "There, now. Don't you start crying."

He came to a halt. The longer he stared down from the window, the more he couldn't deny the premonition of danger he always trusted. His eyes scanned the terrain, taking in where Liberty Terrace opened onto Rector Park, a small green with a few benches and center landscaping, but nothing seemed out of the ordinary. He decided he was just feeling paranoid because of the wedding photo Fin was circulating. He started pacing again, telling himself no one was out there.

Besides, if they were, trained agents were watching. As was Shane. He was taking time off from work, at Jake Lucas's insistence, since Jake strongly felt Shane needed to be at home with Lillian and the new baby.

Well, maybe Shane was getting somewhere. Yesterday, when he'd gone to Lillian's office to pick up some work she wanted to complete, Shane had snooped around some more. This time, he had found the combination to a safe. Could be nothing, could be something. But where was the safe itself? he wondered now. In Jefferson's office? If so, did Lillian make use of it? Was it possible that Jefferson Lawrence knew about Lillian's past?

"What are you looking for, Shane?"

He gently bounced the baby. "Looking for?"

Lillian frowned. "You keep pacing."

"Sorry," he murmured vaguely. But he did feel unsettled. While he couldn't believe Lillian was hiding three million dollars somewhere, Uncle Silas's partner, Trusty Joe, swore the money had been in the car she was driving when she left Louisiana. That meant countless people could be looking for her.

Shane realized Lillian was still gazing at him and the baby, now with the same bemused expression she got when she watched him fumble with domestic tasks to which he wasn't suited. Shane squinted at her. "What?"

Her eyes turned solemn. "You really like him, don't you, Shane?"

Shane glanced at the baby, his voice lowering, touched by emotion. "I like him a lot." It was an obvious understatement.

A long silence fell, a quiet observance of the possibility that they could become a family, and when Shane's gaze suddenly swept over the Hudson, he truly wished he could take the surveillance boat out of the landscape. Fin had sure rustled up a lot of manpower for an investigation that wasn't official. But that was to be expected. Fin had wanted to bring in the Ramsey family's crime consortium for years.

As Shane lifted his eyes from the river, Lillian came up behind him. Shifting the baby and reaching with a free hand, he fluffed her hair, running a finger under it. He watched as the smooth, soft strands fell over his fingers like a waterfall. "I want to make love to you again," he said simply.

The way she reached out and grazed a finger down his cheek was both tender and intimate, but now Shane had come to crave such touches. How, in all these years, he wondered, had he stopped himself from loving a woman like this? *Because there's never been a woman like this.*

For years, his little brother had been his sole responsibility, and Shane had feared that any distractions might hinder his ability to fulfill the promise he'd made to his mother: to watch over Doc. But now Shane's little brother was a man, with a baby of his own. Maybe now it was Shane's turn, Shane's time…

The tender way Lillian kept touching his face stole his breath, making it too shallow. Thinking into the far past, he remembered the night of the flood again—the sound of the ghostly, howling winds, and of the hard rains slashing the windowpanes. To calm himself that night, he'd fantasized about the sunny days to come, when the swollen river would recede and he, Doc, and their daddy would fly-fish in the tame waters.

Even as Shane had indulged those simple daydreams, his daddy had been dead. And Shane hadn't even known it. But now, maybe it was finally time to let the past go....

Lillian's velvet finger crooked on his cheek; somehow, it seemed to beckon him, calling him back to love again after all these years. He suddenly knew that wild horses could never drag him from this woman and child. Should he tell her everything now? Maybe ask for her help in figuring their way out of this? *She really could push you away because of it. And then she and the baby'd be on their own, with no one to protect them. Is that what you want?*

"Shane?"

"Hmm?"

"You seem so worried."

"I'm fine."

Sighing, she stretched on her toes, and with a gentleness he'd never felt and would never forget, she kissed his cheek. Shifting the baby again, he turned his head and found her lips. He'd shared deeper kisses with her, but this was the most satisfying—with the baby cradled in his arms, and her mouth so warm and soft beneath his own.

She smiled. "There. Did that calm your nerves?"

Not really.

Suddenly, his heart jump-started. His body tensed. Sensing the changes, the baby gave a strangled sob, followed by a deep gasp, then a wail. Shane barely noticed.

That green van, he thought. It had been parked out-side ever since the baby's arrival. He'd never seen it on the block before. Maybe that's what kept bringing him back to this window. Now he saw a glint of light flash from it, maybe from a camera lens or binoculars. Was it another FBI agent? Or someone who worked for Jack Ramsey?

"Here." Shane gently moved the baby into Lillian's arms.

Her eyes narrowed with concern. "What?"

"Just take him. I'll be right back."

Shane headed down the hallway with long strides, then summoned the elevator. Once inside, he stared at his reflection in the mirrored interior, suddenly wishing he was wearing something other than the robe, or that he'd at least gotten shoes and his gun. But he hadn't wanted to waste time dressing. And the gun, which he kept out of Lillian's sight at her request, wasn't accessi-ble. It was hidden in the guest-room closet, unloaded.

Downstairs, he hit the hallway running.

"You realize you're wearing a robe outside, sir?" called a desk clerk, as if he were long accustomed to eccentric tenants.

"No, I didn't realize that," Shane returned without missing a beat. "Thanks for telling me." That was the one good thing about New York, he thought, heading through the front door. A man could streak stark naked down an avenue without anyone noticing; sometimes it came in handy.

Leaving the high-rise, Shane rounded Rector Park, then he turned left, circled South End Avenue, and doubled back, approaching the van from the back.

It had New York plates. Since the driver's window

was open, he considered knocking on the metal beside it. But feeling sure the person inside was watching Lillian's apartment, he decided a surprise approach was best. He'd rather accidentally scare somebody innocent than lose a skirmish with someone watching Lillian and his son.

His son.

As he crept toward the back of the van, Shane's heart thudded, both from the possibly impending danger and the admission of how he really felt about the baby. Not that Shane's feelings mattered. Face it, the boy *was* his—legally. Maybe Shane hadn't protected his parents. Or his Uncle Silas… But he'd protect Lillian and Little Shane.

Shane took quiet, shallow breaths as he silently flattened his back against the side of the van. The metal, heated by the sun, burned his skin through the robe while the pavement blistered the bottoms of his bare feet. Squinting against the sun's glare, he inched along the van, toward the open window, until he reached the driver's side door.

Swiftly, he grabbed the door handle and tugged. Reaching inside, he grabbed the person's shoulder— realizing too late that brute force wasn't necessary. The person who tumbled out was slight of build, but wearing a hat in spite of the heat. Shane swiped at the hat.

Red hair cascaded down.

"Ethel," Shane said with a frustrated sigh. Didn't she know how close he'd come to possibly hurting her?

Her wide blue eyes blinked owlishly and her blush made Shane suddenly remember he was barefoot and bare-chested. His robe was undone, flapping in the summer breeze and exposing his ridiculously faded pink boxer shorts. "I promise, Ethel," he muttered, retying the robe. "One day we'll meet when I'm fully dressed."

"Sorry," she murmured guiltily.

You should be. "Ethel, I kept seeing this van out here. I thought it was…" He could hardly tell Ethel he'd suspected she was a member of a dangerous crime consortium. "Uh…some crazy person." In New York City, such an admission passed for reasonable.

Ethel's face had turned crimson. "I should have known you'd catch me, Shane! When I called your ex-boss in East Texas, to check you out, he said you were an absolute guru when it came to surveillance. That's a quote. He said you don't miss a thing."

Shane could merely stare. "You called my ex-boss?"

"Sure. I'm your caseworker. It's my job. I had to check out your work history."

Shane bit back a sigh at the reminder that this woman still had the power to take away Little Shane; she was due to return for follow-up visits. He kept any trace of real worry from his voice. "What were you doing out here?"

"My job." She suddenly wrung her hands. "See, Shane, I've had some trouble at work. Everybody says I'm a soft touch. But I love to see deserving couples get kids. Anyway, in your case, I was afraid people would say I was too hasty. So, I just wanted to make sure everything was fine."

"We're fine," he managed. And they were. Finding Ethel out here instead of a mobster relieved Shane tremendously. It was proof he was overreacting.

Ethel's eyes drifted over him. "Well, I can see that. And," she joked awkwardly. "I do hope to see you in clothes someday." After another moment of conversation, she got back into the van.

When Shane reached the apartment building, he looked back. The van hadn't budged. He guessed Ethel still meant to watch their every move. With his luck, she'd notice the FBI surveillance. Or Fin would decide to arrest Lillian.

"Great," Shane said with a sigh, heading inside. All he needed was another person in this crazy mix to worry about.

SO THAT WAS Delilah's latest husband. Or Lillian's.

Seven cars behind the van, a man in a tan Chevy shrugged out of his white linen suit, then raised binoculars to his eyes. He'd figured out a lot in the past twenty-four hours. Delilah had gotten herself the baby she'd always wanted, the redhead was the caseworker, and the new husband looked as if he'd make a worthy adversary.

Shane Holiday was a professional tough guy. A security guard, apparently. Not bad-looking, tall and well-built, with black hair. Attractive if a woman liked the dangerous type, which Delilah obviously did. But Holiday had an unfortunate fatal flaw—he leaped before he looked. Otherwise, he wouldn't have run outside in that raggedy bathrobe and confronted the caseworker.

But who was Holiday expecting? The man in the car wasn't sure, but he figured he'd better leave before he was spotted. Besides, he had all the information he needed now. The next step was talking to Delilah. Alone. Without her tough-guy watchdog around. Of course, he needed to give Delilah a good scare first. Just so she'd know he meant business. Seven years ago, she'd taken three million dollars in cold hard cash. And now he wanted it back.

Taking her by surprise would be simple enough. After all, Delilah thought he was dead. In fact, she thought she was the one who had killed him, however accidentally.

Sam Ramsey laid the binoculars beside him on the seat, next to a Glock 9 mm pistol and Panama hat, and stared down at the newspaper picture of his wife, which was on the seat. She was wearing a white dress—the one in which she'd married Shane Holiday.

"Married her," Sam Ramsey muttered. *Well, I guess that makes you and me both, Shane.* "Seems the woman's got one too many husbands at the moment. Now, what are we going to do about that?"

LILLIAN'S HEART was racing, pumping adrenaline. She cradled the baby more closely against her. "Shane, what's this all about? Why's Ethel out there?"

He quickly, calmly, related what the caseworker had said.

Lillian still couldn't believe it. "I saw the whole thing from the window. Is…is she thinking about trying to take away Little Shane?" Carrying the baby, she followed Shane as he headed for the kitchen. "And who did you think was in the van?" she continued. "I mean, why did you go crazy like that?" She attempted a laugh. "Not that I didn't enjoy the display of brawn, of course."

In the kitchen, Shane gulped down a glass of water, then set aside the glass, leaning against the counter. He shrugged. "Sorry. I'm trained as a cop. Sometimes my instincts just go on overdrive."

Still bouncing the baby in her arms, Lillian leaned

and dropped a kiss on his forehead. "So, Ethel's been watching the apartment since she gave us the baby?"

Shane nodded, drawing both her and the baby into his arms.

"And you just had a hunch?" she clarified.

"Yeah. I felt like there was somebody out there watching us. And there was. But it was only Ethel." Now that Lillian was calmer, he repeated everything Ethel had said again, this time more slowly. "Ethel's just worried," he finished. "She's just doing everything she can to be thorough."

Lillian managed to nod. Ever since the baby came, she'd been wondering if she should risk telling Shane the truth about her past. He was an ex-detective. And a trustworthy one. He'd know what to do. Maybe he could help her. Of course, there was always the possibility that he'd turn her in...

Leaning against his chest, she gazed down, her eyes roving over the baby—the wisps of dark hair, the small pink bud of his mouth. It had been years since she'd first set her heart on getting a baby, but she'd never have initiated the proceedings if she hadn't been sure it was safe now. Still, seeing Shane in action had made her past come racing back. What if someone other than Ethel *had* been out there?

"It was Ethel," she murmured aloud, drawing in a deep breath to steady herself. No one from her past was outside. Sam Ramsey was dead. His father, Jack Ramsey, would never find her. The only thing Lillian needed to think about was whether or not to tell Shane what had happened to her seven years ago.

With his thumb, Shane traced her silent lips, then delivered a kiss to the spot his thumb had touched. Even that unassuming touch of his mouth made Lillian's limbs heavy with wanting him. It was pointless to fight it. Especially right now, when she wanted nothing more than all his strength and comfort.

"Still want to make love?" she found herself whispering.

"You know I do."

Moments later, in the bedroom, they put the baby down, then Lillian shut the blinds and curtains against the light, slowly opened her robe and lifted her pajama top over her head. A second later, Shane pulled her into his embrace. And then they were tumbling together into the still-messed covers, rolling—and rolling fast— toward whatever might come.

CHAPTER TEN

"SHANE, I'VE BEEN TRYING to call you! I forgot to turn on the phone this morning. Where are you?"

Even though the baby was asleep in Shane's arms, something in Lillian's voice compelled him to lift his as he rose from the rocker. "I'm in the bedroom, Lil."

He'd awakened this morning to a note saying she'd run to Big Apple Babies, to sign another paper concerning the adoption, and he'd been worried ever since. Now the front door slammed, footsteps pounded, and Shane fully registered her panic as she neared. His voice rose another notch. "What's happened?"

"What's happened is that Jake Lucas got shot!"

"Got shot?" Shane's body tightened reflexively, going utterly still except for a sudden quiver of his chin and the thickening of his blood. As he carefully laid the baby in the crib, his pale eyes went wary. He turned from Little Shane just as Lillian rushed into the room. Despite the circumstances, Shane's breath caught as his eyes swept over her, taking in the heightened color of her flushed face, the twining loosened tendrils falling from her French twist, and the spot where the hem of a white sundress touched her long legs. No matter what else was happening, Shane's whole world stopped every time she entered a room.

"Oh, Shane, I can't believe it!"

With her frightened exclamation, the world started turning again. Breathlessly, she barreled forward on sheer momentum, and he caught her—cupping her bare shoulders that were still warm from the sunshine outdoors. Even as he registered her soft fragrant muskiness, he was reminding himself not to fly off the handle, the way he had yesterday when he'd confronted Ethel. He kept his voice calm. "Is Jake all right? Did it happen at Big Apple Babies?"

Lillian gulped down air, her head bobbing up and down. "Right outside."

He wished she'd awakened him. Between their love-making, and getting up for the baby's feedings, Shane had wound up sleeping like the dead. Usually, any change in a silent room roused him. "The shooting occurred right outside?"

"They think it was random."

"They?"

"The police."

"And is Jake all right?" Even as he said it, Shane knew the question was ridiculous. His boss had been shot.

Lillian drew in a deep quavering breath, then slowly exhaled. More calmly, she said, "I think so. They took him to Saint Vincent's Hospital. It's only a couple blocks from the agency."

"How many shots were fired?"

"One, I think. It hit him in the shoulder, or maybe the arm. I saw it."

Shane drew in a sharp breath at that piece of information. His eyes scanned her again, this time to reassure himself she was unharmed. "You saw it?"

The pulse was ticking rapidly in her throat. "I was on the sidewalk, about twenty feet from Jake."

She'd been that close? Shane's arms tightened around her back. She was still in shock, too, he thought, as he freed one hand so he could make a call. Turning over the bedside phone, he flicked on the ringer. No wonder she couldn't get through. At least he'd disabled the FBI phone tap, so he could keep his and Lillian's conversations private. Shane punched in the number for the hospital while his mind shifted through the scant facts Lillian had just given him about Jake. As the phone rang, he kept a strong arm braced around Lillian and his eyes fixed on hers.

"Oh, Shane," she said simply.

"Thank God you're all right," he murmured in a soft understated drawl, shoving the phone receiver between his shoulder and jaw, so he could use both arms to hold her again. She squeezed back, her quick tight hug saying she relied on him now, and bringing back all the love they'd shared last night.

How could he have let this happen? he wondered, stroking her hair. It hardly mattered that Jake had insisted Shane take time off to be with Lillian and the baby. Protecting people at Big Apple Babies was Shane's job. He should have been there. Now he had to find out who would shoot Jake. And why. Was this really an act of random violence?

"This is Shane Holiday, chief of security for Big Apple Babies," he said when someone finally answered the phone. "I just got word a man named Jake Lucas has been shot. Can you give me more information?"

He was put on hold. Leaning back slightly, he peered into Lillian's eyes, then used a gentle, probing thumb to pull down the skin beneath them, checking the dilation of her pupils. Good. She was calming down. "Now, start from the beginning and tell me everything."

Lillian took a shaky breath. "Wait—" She disengaged herself from him, long enough to go to the crib. Securing the baby in the protective curve of her arm, she rocked him as she leaned against Shane again. "I'd already signed the papers," she continued, "and I'd stepped out for a muffin at that little café—you know, the one across the street. I was going to come home after that, but then I decided to go back inside Big Apple Babies and introduce myself to your brother. I mean, I know he's coming over later this week, but since we hadn't even met..." Her voice trailed off. "Anyway, I was right under the agency's sign when it happened. Jake and a man whose name I don't know, a heavyset guy who looks like Lou Grant from *The Mary Tyler Moore Show*—"

"James Sanger."

"James Sanger," she repeated. "Well, James and Jake were coming into the building, carrying cups of coffee. They'd just crossed the street and they weren't but twenty feet from me." She was trying to be brave, but her voice broke. "Oh, Shane—"

"It's okay, baby," he whispered, tightening his arms around her. Slowly, lovingly, he brushed his mouth back and forth across the top of her head. While her skin smelled of musk, the scent of her hair was harder to name—it was just something fresh and sweet—and under Shane's lips the strands felt excruciatingly soft.

She made a soft, barely audible sound—half sigh, half whimper—that made his chest constrict. "I'm so sorry you were there," he murmured. Leaning, he found her lips, offering the gentlest pressure of his mouth as reassurance.

"Shane, I was scared," she confessed. "More than anything, I wanted to be home with you and the baby."

"I know." Ducking his head, he kissed the baby's forehead, then smoothed a loose strand of Lillian's hair, tucking it behind her ear. Had his relief over finding Ethel in the van made him overlook precautions? Should he have gone after Lillian this morning? He'd started to when he saw the note, but he hadn't wanted to take the baby outside. Damn. It was bad enough Jake had been injured. But what if something had happened to Lillian? He shoved the phone receiver more firmly under his jaw. "You say you were only twenty feet away from Jake, Lillian?"

She leaned back in his embrace again, nodding as she rocked Little Shane. "Yeah. I—oh, Shane—" Her voice cracked. "I was so close." She glanced down, comforting herself by cooing to the baby. She looked as if she'd run all the way to Wall Street from Greenwich Village to get home.

"How'd you get home, sweetheart?"

"Cab." She drew in a sharp breath as if only now realizing what a close call she'd had. "I can't believe I saw the whole thing. Shane, I didn't even know what was happening. Jake suddenly spun around and fell. James ran inside. I...I feel bad about it, but I didn't even move. I couldn't. I think I went into shock. And then your brother came racing out...."

"Doc?"

She nodded. "When he first ran out, I didn't know it was him. But after he left with Jake in the ambulance, everybody on the sidewalk said he saved Jake's life. I immediately started trying to call you, but I couldn't get through…."

Shane was still on hold. Should he give up, hang up, and call back? "Did you see anybody suspicious leave the scene?"

She shook her head. "The police started canvassing the street, asking the same question. Somebody said a tall blond man who was wearing a white Panama hat walked away quickly, looking suspicious. They said he was near Jake, which means he wasn't any more than twenty feet from me. I gave a statement to one of the uniformed men. But why would anyone shoot Jake Lucas?"

Shane rubbed soothing circles on her back. "I don't know." *Yet.*

Lillian shook her head, trying to make sense of this. "Jake and I haven't been formally introduced, Shane, but from everything you and Ethel told me, he's a highly unlikely target for violence."

"He is." Jake Lucas was a family man. He had a wife, Dani, and two kids. He worked hard, went to church and paid taxes. But Shane's years on the force had taught him that senseless things happened all the time. Not that it was right. Men such as Jake Lucas deserved nothing but the best. So did women like Lillian. And yet she'd somehow wound up married to Sam Ramsey.

"So, do you agree it's a random attack, Shane?"

"Possibly."

She was wearing high heels, which meant she was nearly eye level with Shane, and right now, her eyes looked big and brown. Doe-like, they were full of unspoken questions, and her obvious shock over the senseless violence tugged Shane's heart. Gazing into her eyes, he

realized she was far more trusting than he. She'd deny
it, but whatever had really happened in her past hadn't
robbed her of innocence. By contrast, he was a closed
book. Without even intending to, Shane always kept his
cards close to the vest.

She shook her head again. "Why?" she asked
simply.

As if Shane knew. He did his best to answer her.
"This is a big city, with a lot of random crime. Otherwise, Jake runs Big Apple Babies. Maybe one of the
parties in an adoption wasn't satisfied. Maybe a parent
wanted a child back after they gave it up." When Shane
first took his job, he and Jake had discussed the countless possible security risks at such an agency. It was why
Shane had installed a new state-of-the-art alarm system,
as well as outdoor and indoor surveillance cameras.

He frowned, again considering hanging up the phone
and redialing. He didn't. Law enforcement work always
meant waiting. Cops and their ilk had the patience of
saints. He sighed. "I just wish I'd been there."

"Shane—" Lillian stretched, nuzzling her face against
his cheek. "I should have guessed you'd think this was
your fault. It isn't. You know that, don't you?"

He didn't know any such thing. "I should have been
there for both you and Jake."

"You were with the baby. You can't be in two places
at once."

No, he couldn't. And now he was going to have to
leave Lillian and go to work. He was still furious at Fin,
but at least he knew Lillian would be fine in the apartment, since the agents were watching. They were all
highly trained and competent. The crème de la crème.
Shane would give them that much.

The line suddenly clicked on. "Detective Sean Mc-Sween from the Thirteenth Precinct speaking. Is this Shane Holiday?"

"Yeah."

"Sorry it took me so long. We're questioning potential witnesses. A lot of the Big Apple Babies staff came over to the hospital."

"No problem. How's Jake?"

Lillian's eyes were now wide with worry, so Shane tipped the phone, letting her listen. As she and the baby snuggled closer, Shane lifted the coiled phone cord from between them, draping it more conveniently behind Lillian's back.

"Jake's all right," the detective said. "There's a doctor with him, Winston Holiday—" The detective paused.

"Yeah," Shane said. "Same Holiday. He's my brother."

"Well, you ought to be damn proud of him. He saved Jake Lucas's life. Mr. Lucas lost a lot of blood, and it's a rare type, but the hospital found a donor, and now the patient's seeing visitors. He's weak, but otherwise fine."

Shane sighed in relief. Even if he hadn't been there, the way he should have, Doc was on the scene. He imagined how Doc must have felt, running into the street to help his boss and friend. *Good work, little brother,* he thought.

Squeezing Lillian's shoulder again, Shane tried not to think too much about the fact that she'd been on that sidewalk, too. He repositioned the phone more comfortably under his jaw. "So, it really looks like a random shooting, detective?"

"Call me McSween. We're a hundred percent sure

it was. The shot was fired by a pedestrian on Waverly Place. We traced him to the subway on West Fourth Street."

"West Fourth," Shane murmured. The station was a hub, with seven trains heading through Manhattan and into Brooklyn and Queens. Times Square station, where every train in the city was available, was only a stop away. "From West Fourth, the guy could have gone anywhere."

"You got it," said McSween. "I doubt we'll catch him."

Shane nodded. "I'm headed over there."

"I've got an assistant with me. We'd rather hook up at Big Apple Babies, if you don't mind showing us the tapes from the surveillance cameras trained on the street."

"Not at all. We can watch the tapes in my office." Hanging up, Shane decided he'd call Doc later and get his take on the situation.

Lillian's voice was heartbreakingly brave. "You've got to go to work, right?"

He nodded grimly. Lifting a hand, he ran the back of it down her cheek; it lingered, stilled by the power of sheer touch, then his fingers gently stroked. Seeing the worry in her eyes, he spoke the next words before thinking them through, "Lillian, do you think you could ever really live with a cop?" What was he doing? he wondered, his heart suddenly thudding. Proposing to the woman he'd already married? He'd never even told her he loved her.

A slight smile touched her lips. "I think I already do live with a cop, Shane," she returned, and then doubt clouded her eyes. "Still, you're an ex-cop. And I...I don't want you in danger. Frankly, I'd rather you did anything else for a living."

He couldn't help but smile, a slow twist of a smile that crinkled the corners of his eyes. "What would you rather see me do?"

She shrugged. "Buy a fishing boat?" she suggested. "Sell ice cream to kids. Run a self-service laundry. Anything safe."

"I'm usually not in any danger."

She didn't look entirely convinced. Still, he wasn't usually in danger at his current job. But what about his future? Gazing at her and the baby, he realized he hadn't even thought about the career path he'd take when all this was over. Two years ago, he'd been so anxious to trap Delilah Fontenont that he'd given up his badge in East Texas, along with a much better salary and benefits package. He always figured he'd become a full-time detective again.

But maybe not. Maybe he'd rather keep himself safe for a family he loved. For Lillian and their son. He would if Lillian wanted him to. Suddenly, he felt an overpowering urge to simply grab their bags and head south. He really felt he wouldn't rest easily until he saw Lillian and the baby calmly rocking on the porch of his cabin in East Texas. Or sitting in his Aunt Dixie Lynn's warm yellow kitchen on Bayou Teche. "Lock the door behind me, Lillian," he found himself saying. "Don't leave it open the way we do sometimes."

"I won't. I promise."

He loved watching those words form on lips he had the swift urge to capture in a kiss. *I promise.* He wished he had time right now to talk about other kinds of promises...commitments. "I'm taking my beeper." He leaned and scribbled down the number he should have given her before now. "You call immediately if…" If, by some crazy off-chance, trouble winds up on our doorstep. The Ramseys, for instance. "…If you need anything."

"I promise," she repeated.

Once again, he reminded himself that agents were outside, ready to descend faster than angry hornets. The recollection of how they'd burst into the apartment when he and Lillian were baby-sitting now came as a comfort.

Her voice was throaty. "You be careful, Shane."

"You don't need to worry. Jake's already out of danger."

"I didn't say I was worried about Jake," Lillian returned tenderly. "I said I'm worried about *you,* Shane."

He smiled, leaning down a fraction. Right before he kissed her goodbye, he said in a husky drawl, "I never knew it could feel so good to have a woman worry over me."

"So, a man could get used to it?" she'd murmured back.

As his lips closed over hers, the words were almost lost. "This man's already used to it, Lillian."

SHANE LIKED Sean McSween immediately. The detective was a big Irish guy, with razor-short black hair and bottle-green eyes. He looked smart. So did his assistant, a redhead named McNutt, who had alert eyes and let his boss do all the talking. After the three shook hands, McSween sent McNutt to the café across the street for three coffees, saying, "Holiday and I'll wait on the sidewalk."

"He seems sharp," Shane commented, resettling his black Stetson more firmly on his head, then shoving his hands in his jeans pockets while he watched the young man hustle across the street, through traffic.

"Smarter than a whip," McSween agreed with a chuckle that made his green eyes sparkle. "Every morning, I fear I'm training my replacement."

Shane smiled. "I doubt it."

Apparently caught off duty, McSween was wearing khaki shorts and a T-shirt that said World's Best Dad. Now he glanced down. "Got the shirt for Father's Day," he explained.

"Kids?"

McSween nodded. "Boy named Romeo and a little girl, Colette. Wife's name's Britt."

Shane nodded. As much as he wanted to get down to business, small talk was protocol, at least until they got inside. Shane wasn't sure how much information he wanted to share, anyway, since he was close-mouthed by nature. But was it wise to continue hiding so much from Lillian? Shane guessed only twenty-twenty hindsight was going to make clear whether he was making the right decisions. Maybe he was holding a flush. Maybe he'd take a hit. Maybe he should fold.

Pushing aside the thoughts, Shane drawled, "Nice to have a family, huh?"

McSween cracked another smile. "I didn't come by fatherhood naturally, believe me. Britt dragged me into it kicking and screaming. Now, I love every minute of it."

Shane's heart tugged. "My...wife and I just adopted a little boy from here. He just came home the other day." *My wife and I.* The words echoed—warming Shane, making him feel he was a part of something. Making him feel, he realized, loved.

McSween's eyes had widened in surprise. "You and your wife adopted from Big Apple Babies?"

"Yes, we did," Shane returned, still trying on the words for size.

McSween merely gave the cursory, satisfied nod of a man long accustomed to family life. "Good for you. How old's the lucky kid?"

"Newborn."

McSween loosed another chuckle and shook his head. "Crying up a storm is he?"

Shane couldn't help but smile back. "Yeah."

"Not sleeping nights, huh?"

Shane let a telltale pause elapse, then he succinctly said, "Hell, no."

The two men shared a good laugh.

It was the genuine icebreaker they'd been looking for. Now Shane glanced around. The adoption agency was down in the Village, on Waverly Place, which was a pie-slice of street wedged between Sixth and Seventh avenues. Right above Shane's head was a catchy sign, designed by Grantham Hale, an advertiser who, like Shane, had gotten children from the agency. Hanging over the street, the sign was fashioned to look like a huge diaper pin, and through the bottom metal rod of the pin was a white banner, presumably of diaper cloth, on which the agency name was written.

McNutt was coming across the street, carrying bags. "All they had was cappuccino," he apologized.

Shane shook his head. "C'mon, you guys. Don't they sell plain old coffee anywhere in this town?"

McSween laughed. "You've got a helluva drawl. Where are you from, anyway?"

"Mostly Texas. Spent time in Louisiana."

McSween squinted with real concern. "I heard all the coffee down south tastes like river water."

Shane merely shrugged. "One man's poison is always another's pleasure." He led them inside, passing murals in the downstairs hallway depicting gold, red and green apples. Beneath the murals ran the agency's motto: Big Apple Babies are babies of all kinds!

"Mr. Lucas's office," McSween murmured.

Shane nodded as they passed a frosted glass door, on which black block lettering said Jake Lucas: Director. At the end of the first floor hallway was the sealed records room, where Big Apple Babies' confidential files were stored. Shane hung a left, headed into his office and turned on the lights.

He dropped his hat on a desk, then nodded toward the chairs in front of a TV. "Have a seat. I'll get the tapes."

As soon as he returned, Shane quickly dumped four sugars into his cappuccino, grabbed the remote control and popped in a tape. It showed a high-angle view of Waverly Place, shot from a camera attached to the Big Apple Babies sign. The street was crowded; people walked in and out of the shot. At the bottom of the screen, in white digital numbers, was the date and time.

McSween said, "It happened about nine."

Shane hit fast-forward. Later, they'd go back and watch all the tapes. It was boring work, but there was a chance Jake had been intentionally targeted, and often a perpetrator came to a crime scene days, even weeks, before committing a crime. For now, the law officers would start by viewing the crime itself.

Shane stared intently at the screen, feeling oddly bereft when Lillian appeared. The black-and-white videotape was grainy, and seeing her through the eye of a camera seemed impersonal. He'd loved the woman intimately, but now he was watching her as if she were a stranger.

Impulsively, he rewound. Watching Lillian come into the frame again, he saw what he hadn't the first time—how much she'd changed since he'd moved in with her. Sure, he'd noticed that her eyes had become a little less haunted, that her steps were lighter. But now, in the eye of the camera, he saw the changes for what they were—staggering. *The baby and I have made her happy,* Shane thought with a start. *She trusts me. She loves me. She's not really afraid anymore.* He shifted uncomfortably, pushing down guilt, and thinking of the agents watching her. He could no longer deny that this whole situation had gotten beyond him.

He heard McNutt say, "Now, there's a gorgeous woman. She's got legs that don't quit."

Shane almost said, "She's my girlfriend." But that wasn't the truth. Hitting the play button, he said, "She's my wife. Lillian."

"No kidding?" said McSween.

Shane nodded. "No kidding. She was here signing papers having to do with…our baby." *Our baby.* He liked saying that so much.

"Your wife was on the sidewalk during the shooting?" McSween repeated, mulling over the information.

"Yeah, she gave a statement. She—"

The conversation ended abruptly.

On the screen, Jake and James Sanger appeared behind Lillian. Over the traffic sounds came a loud pop. Jake's left arm flew out wildly; his whole body spun and he fell. Quickly, James leaned over his friend, saw the severity of the injury, then fled for the doors and help while the crowd in front of Lillian parted like a river. Lillian's stunned eyes searched the faces of people coming toward her. From this camera angle, Shane could only see their backs, but he could imagine their eyes widening in warning. He could almost feel the beginnings of Lillian's fear—her increased heartbeat, the race of her pulse. Suddenly, someone broke ranks and ran.

Lillian turned, gaped, then stood stock-still. She'd just now realized a man behind her had been shot, and she couldn't move.

She looked so terrified and beautiful, merely standing there, with her white sundress blowing in the breeze, that Shane couldn't take it. He wanted to turn back time, swoop down and carry her from the sidewalk.

As he punched still, and then rewind, Shane felt Mc-Sween's hand clamp down on his shoulder. McSween squeezed. "She's okay, buddy."

"Yeah," Shane managed. "It just kind of shook me up." He blew out a sigh, nodded toward the TV, and hit play again. "Here. This time maybe I'll notice the suspect."

But as the tape rolled, Shane watched Lillian come into the frame again. Once more, she was standing there. Terrified. Frozen in time.

In that second, Shane was sure he'd give his life to save hers. He'd simply never seen beauty so compelling. As soon as he could, he was taking her back down

South, if she'd go. Sure, bad things could happen any-where and, per capita, some smaller U.S. towns were more dangerous than New York City. But he wanted to give Lillian her little white brick house with the picket fence. He felt he wouldn't rest until they—him, her, and the baby—were all piled into a U-haul truck.

"Finally," McSween said.

Shane lifted his gaze from Lillian and focused on the suspect. The picture was black-and-white, and the man's face was obscured by a hat brim. Shane watched him draw a pistol from a jacket pocket and fire the shot. Shane registered two facts at once: first, some-thing about the suspect—maybe the way he moved—reminded him of the deceased Sam Ramsey, whom he'd tailed years ago. And second, Lillian had been far closer to Jake and the gunman than she'd thought—more like five feet, not twenty.

Which meant she, not Jake, might have been the target.

"LILLIAN?"

"In here."

He set his Stetson on the marble-topped table and followed her voice, which sounded strangely muffled, to the bedroom, then leaned in the doorway. The room was dim. Silent, except for the creak of the rocker and the rhythmic pad of Lillian's bare feet as she pushed off. For a moment, she kept her head bowed over Little Shane, and Shane took in how, as she rocked, the light of the red-shaded lamp played on her dark, knitted eye-brows and the escaped waving blond strands touching her neck.

She glanced briefly up at him. "Hey, Shane."

"Hey." He'd called her periodically, to check on her, so she already had all the updates on Jake's condition and knew he'd be fine. It had turned into a long day, and now the bedside clock read nearly midnight. Shane felt bone tired. After watching the tapes, he'd returned to the hospital with McSween. Pushing aside his worries, he'd turned his mind to business, ceaselessly reviewing all the possible angles. In the strangest turn of events, it was found out that Lillian's boss, Jefferson, had stepped forward, claiming to be related to Jake Lucas. In fact, it was Jefferson who'd offered the rare blood Jake had needed to survive.

"Who would have guessed your boss was Jake's father?" Shane murmured now from the doorway.

Lillian smiled. "I told you Jefferson's an angelfish. Since he spends all day looking for good causes to fund, it doesn't surprise me in the least that he's been secretly contributing to Big Apple Babies all these years."

Shane could merely shake his head. "I knew Jake was adopted and that he'd been looking for his birth parents, but…it just seems so coincidental that his biological father would turn out to be your boss."

Shane had definitely expected Lillian to be more surprised. Of course, Shane was well aware of how Big Apple Babies had gotten started. He even knew who some of the previously anonymous secret backers for the agency were—Judge Tilford Winslow, whom he'd first met at a Big Apple Baby party, and the ad man Grantham Hale, who'd designed the Big Apple Baby logos. Now he frowned. "Did you *know* your boss was Jake's biological father?"

She didn't answer, only bent her head low, over the

baby again. "Oh, nothing surprises me," she offered mildly.

He nodded. "Well, truth's definitely stranger than fiction."

"It really is."

Now Shane mulled it over, trying to imagine how Jake had felt, years ago when he'd been a burnt-out prosecutor, and when he'd received an anonymous check to start Big Apple Babies. Who would have thought that opening the agency was Jefferson Lawrence's idea? A way for Jefferson to offer a new job opportunity to a son he'd watched grow up from afar—while Jake was being raised by his adoptive parents?"

"It's kind of magical, isn't it?" Lillian murmured.

Shane nodded. There might be senseless violence in the world, but there was plenty of good, too. How Big Apple Babies got started was a reminder of that. "My brother made up with his girlfriend at the hospital, too." Shane added. "I didn't have a chance to tell you that on the phone."

Lillian's voice hitched. "Doc and Frankie Luccetti made up?"

Shane nodded. "Yeah. Frankie showed up outside Jake's hospital room." He suddenly grinned. "Doc didn't waste any time, either. He proposed."

"And she accepted?"

"Yeah."

"How wonderful."

For a moment the dim room seemed overly quiet. Lillian quit rocking, and Shane could swear the silence was begging for his own proposal. He thought of his and Lillian's lovemaking, of how yesterday and last night it was even deeper—so deep it scared him. *Maybe the rest of your life could be this way, Shane.* Like Jake Lucas, or Sean McSween, maybe he could work hard, pay his taxes, and come home after a hard day's work to a family he loved.

His gaze drifted over them. The baby was in a T-shirt and diaper, and Lillian hadn't yet changed from the sundress. Its white fabric reminded him of her wedding dress, and how he'd laid her across the bed, awash in this same rose lamplight. His breath caught when he remembered turning out the light, how he'd savored her in the dark.

He'd never yet made love to her in the light, only at night or with the blinds and curtains drawn. Now, thinking of their lovemaking, he felt awareness in the heaviness and heat of his groin. But tonight he didn't want sex so much as love. And really, he was content just to watch her and the baby like this…to feel these strange new emotions that were touching him. He needed so much to keep her and the baby safe. And to give this woman his body. He craved her response to him—the assurance they belonged together.

Maybe tonight, she'd speak the words: I love you, Shane. Or maybe he would say them. He silently practiced as his gaze drifted over her. *I love you, Lillian.*

As if she'd read his mind, she raised her head, looking directly at him. With a sudden surprised start, Shane realized she'd been crying. Her head had been lowered and the lights so dim, that he couldn't tell before now.

He took a quick step forward. "Lillian?"

There was a hitch in her voice, and when she spoke, she said the last thing he ever expected.

"My name's not Lillian."

CHAPTER ELEVEN

"PLEASE JUST LISTEN and keep an open mind," Lillian continued.

Only when Shane spoke did she realize she'd been holding her breath, expecting an explosion, instead of his softly voiced, "All right." She watched as he came silently across the room, casting a long shadow, his boot heels nothing more than soft clicks on the hardwood floor that muted when he reached the rug. He sat on the bed's edge, not a foot from the rocker, and her eyes took in where the lamplight had deepened the shadows on his chiseled face, and where rose threads seemed to glimmer in the dark strands of his hair.

She peered at him. *All right.* Was that all Shane was going to say? "Didn't you hear me?"

He leaned, a lock of hair falling forward as he brushed a thumb down her tearstained cheek. When his hand dropped, it grazed the sleeping baby. "Yeah, I heard you."

All the years she'd been hiding out, Lillian had expected the world to come crashing down when she finally voiced that simple sentence: *My name's not Lillian.* She swallowed hard. "How could you be so...calm?"

He tilted his head, as if to say she should expect more of him. "How should I know what to feel? I want to listen, to hear...whatever you're going to tell me."

For years, she had watched her coworkers longingly, wondering which could be trusted if she divulged the secrets of her past. She'd considered telling Jefferson the truth. And more recently, Shane. Now the words came in a rush. "I didn't grow up in Mississippi, Shane. I'm Delilah Fontenont and I'm from Bayou Laforche in southern Louisiana."

She paused again, waiting for the explosion.

A bright, watchful intensity gleamed in Shane's pale eyes now, but nothing more. His features didn't betray any feelings. Was he going to hate her for lying? Turn her in?

He said, "I'm listening."

The low timbre of his drawl moved through her, bringing an answering ripple that pulled inside her like a current. What did he really think about her? About the baby? How deep were his feelings? Anxiously, her arm tightened around Little Shane, who stirred, but didn't awaken.

Finding her voice, she quickly continued, "Shane, I know you well enough to know you'll at least be fair. See, I'm in trouble. Real trouble. And since you're an ex-cop, maybe you can help…"

"I can try."

"I don't know where to start."

"Anywhere."

She took a deep breath. Her voice still scratchy from tears she'd shed through the day, she told him how her parents had died within two years of each other. "Everything seemed even worse because my father…" She interrupted herself. "Oh, Shane, I've told you about him. I loved him so much." She paused, a fledgling smile curling her lips. "I know you would have liked him.

He was such an old-fashioned Southern gentleman. He called me Lilah. And when I was little, he was always drying my tears with his fancy monogrammed handkerchiefs. He whistled all the time, and he wore linen suits and a tie, even if he was only driving his big old Cadillac down the road to the store…."

After a moment, Shane gently coaxed, "I know you loved him."

"So much," she repeated. At her father's memory, she felt the sting of tears. "Daddy loved life more than anyone I've ever known. But his heart was bigger than his pocket and he was more charitable than we could really afford, always helping people from our church or poor families further down the bayou…

"When he died, I quickly found out he left no money and more debts than I could pay." It pained her to say anything bad about her parents, but she forced herself to continue. "Maybe they let me run wilder than I should have. They didn't want me to become a Fontenont snob, but I wasn't exactly trained to be much else."

She gave a soft dry chuckle, as she shook her head and gazed down at the baby. No doubt, all parents, no matter how well-intentioned, made mistakes. "Contrary to what accountants told Daddy, he remained convinced to his dying day that our family money was endless. But it wasn't. And I'm the end of the line."

"Little Shane's the end of the line now, Lillian."

She guessed Shane wasn't going to call her Delilah. "Yes," she murmured, glancing from the baby to Shane again, fruitlessly searching for emotion in Shane's eyes. She thought he'd come to love her and the baby. But he'd never said… The nights they'd gotten to know each other, in preparation for Ethel's visit, his interest seemed so genuine, and his lovemaking could be excruciatingly tender. And while he'd never so much as held a child before Little Shane, he barely put him down over the past two days. Whenever he looked at the baby, Shane's pale eyes warmed and softened.

Eyeing him, she wanted to ask: *Are you starting to love me and feel like this baby's ours? Do you want to try to make it that way?* But she knew that, perhaps, it no longer mattered. She forced herself to continue, "Well…after my parents died, I met a man."

She thought jealousy sparked in Shane's gaze, but he merely nodded. She didn't feel right talking to him about another man, but she had to make him understand. "Sam Ramsey…seemed like everything I wanted. He told me he was a land developer. He really was building shopping malls on the East Coast, even if that was only half the truth. I didn't care that he was rich, but the way he courted me was like something from a movie. He brought flowers, took me out for fancy meals and dancing."

Shane's words were guarded. "I'm not like that."

"No," she returned. "You're not." Tears suddenly threatened. "And I'm glad you're not, Shane." He'd never know how glad.

"But you loved him."

"I loved an illusion. Everything about Sam was an act. All smoke and mirrors."

Lifting her eyes from the baby again, she pleaded with him to understand. "I thought my life was falling into place. I wasn't even twenty yet, I was alone for the first time, and I was about to lose our family home. Daddy had left it untended. The house needed structural work, the grounds were overgrown."

"And Sam Ramsey said he'd help you fix it up?"

Humiliation arrowed through her. Was what happened to her that predictable? How many people had been on to Sam's real agenda? She tamped down her fury and tried not to wonder if people had had a good laugh at her expense. Or even worse, if they'd guessed at Sam's deception, turned a blind eye and simply felt sorry for her. She hoped not. That she might have been pitied tweaked her considerable pride.

"Sam had me sign some papers, saying they'd allow him to hire contractors," she continued. "I signed, like a fool. Later, of course, I found out I'd sold our family home down the river." Her voice caught. "That house was in my family for generations."

Shane was squinting. "The papers were deeds?"

She sighed in frustration. She was getting ahead of herself, but unable to stop the outburst. "I trusted him! He had a wonderful idea to turn the plantation into a resort. And now—" Her voice broke and her eyes darted helplessly around the room.

"Now?"

"It's a resort, all right. Run by his father, Jack Ramsey, who hangs out there with a bunch of his mobster cronies..." Taking a deep breath, she forced herself to backtrack, telling Shane about the plantation's new airstrip, stables and guest bungalows. "The place is gorgeous. I thought my parents would be so proud, since my father was always talking about restoring it." As she shifted the baby in her lap, her trembling chin shot up. "Now, I'm just glad they didn't live to see the travesty."

Shane reached over, squeezing her arm reassuringly. He seemed to understand. The Fontenonts had that land for nearly two centuries, since a time when land, not machines, was the great engine fueling the country. Shifting the baby, she lifted a hand and tucked the escaped tendrils of her hair back into her French twist, as if that might restore her dignity. Her voice shook with barely suppressed fury. "Our land and home meant everything to us, Shane."

"I can imagine."

Gazing into his eyes, she knew he really could. Swallowing hard, she forced herself to tell the next part, the worst part. Quickly leaning, she nuzzled the baby, taking comfort from his softness and scent. "Well, Sam and I got married…" She paused, suddenly feeling she couldn't go on.

Shane's drawl was gentle, reminding her of the home she'd lost. "Go ahead and tell me all of it."

She blew out a long shaky sigh. "The evening ceremony was lovely." She could still recall the startling red sunset over the bayou and how she'd thought it portended good things to come. "We'd been trying to have a baby—" Warmth flooded her cheeks and she held Little Shane closer. "I know we should have waited for the wedding, but I wanted kids so badly…"

"You were that sure of his love," Shane murmured.

She nodded. "Oh, yes. Especially when we found out I couldn't get pregnant. He was wonderful and said that, after the wedding, we'd immediately adopt." She'd been so moved when Sam offered to accept another couple's child. Of course, it was nothing more than lies. Now, she wondered if Shane could love someone else's baby….

"And then what happened?" he said.

"Only the worst thing in my life. After the wedding reception—it was at the plantation—I overheard Sam talking on the phone to a woman."

"You know it was a woman? You were on the phone line?"

Did Shane really think she'd intentionally eavesdrop? "Of course not," she returned, taken aback. "I was in the hallway."

"Then how did you know it was a woman?"

She should have guessed her story would bring out the cop in Shane. "For starters," she managed, "he was flirting. He called me his 'little Southern trophy wife,' and he assured whoever it was—" feeling a sudden, sickening rush of vertigo, she drew in a quick, steadying breath "—that he was only adopting to appease me. He said he hated kids, that his father pressured him to marry me, wanting my family connection. And then… then he said to the woman, 'Tonight, we're paying off all the cops. Look out, girl, because my family's taking over Louisiana.'" Her eyes caught Shane's. "Taking over. That's exactly what he said."

"He said he'd paid off the cops?" Shane repeated.

"That he was going to. I wasn't sure what it meant then. I was still in shock at finding him speaking intimately with a woman." There was no help for the temper in her voice now. "It was my wedding day, Shane! And worse, for the first time, I realized Sam Ramsey was one of the Ramseys from out West."

She'd felt so duped. "I always read newspapers, Shane, but I…I never made the connection until that moment. The Ramseys are linked to a Western crime consortium, but they've never been convicted of anything. I've looked up articles about them since coming here. Have you ever read about them?"

"Yes."

Most people had. She realized her heartbeat was rapid

now, pulsing too fast in her throat. Only the baby in her lap kept her from hopping up and pacing off the nervous energy. "Apparently, the Ramseys felt my historic home and good family name would be an asset when they settled in the area. Feeling confused and betrayed, I ran. We kept all the car keys in the garage, and I got into the first car I came to, a big black car. The few wedding guests had left by then and it was dark out.

"I guess someone saw me running." She shuddered now, remembering how badly her foot was shaking as she tried to press the gas pedal. "I'd almost reached the end of our private road when I...I ran over my husband."

Shane gasped. "You what?"

It was the first real emotion he'd shown. "Shane, Sam came running toward the headlights!" She'd seen nothing more than a shadow darting from the trees before she heard the sickening thud. "I jumped out, felt for his pulse. I couldn't think straight. I thought his father would try to kill me for revenge or something. I was so scared. I was only eighteen years old, and my mind was running wild. I even thought people would say I'd killed Sam on purpose because of how he'd betrayed me with another woman."

"So, you kept driving?"

She nodded. "I drove all night." There were no words for the terror she'd felt. "I didn't even know I was going North. I was so scared I wasn't even watching road signs. When I stopped at dawn, I simply left the car in a ditch and got a bus ticket here. Later, I changed my name. I...I just started over."

He was staring at her, taking it in. "Why didn't you go to the police?"

Her lips parted in silent protest. "Well, apparently the
police were in Jack Ramsey's pocket," she finally said,
in her own defense. "And I was so afraid no one would
believe…" *My hitting Sam was an accident.* It was so
horrible, she couldn't even say it again.

"What else?"

She started to confess the rest. It would help if Shane
knew about the strange papers she'd found in the car,
and the money. Sam's infidelity and death almost paled
in comparison with what she'd found. So did the fact
that she'd signed away her home to a crime consortium.
"That's it."

"Are you sure?"

She nodded. Heaven help her, but she had her reasons
for keeping quiet about the money. If one good thing
ever came from the past seven years of her life, it would
be from her silence. "I don't know exactly what happened after that. As I pulled onto the main road, I heard
an explosion. Behind me, the pier and boathouse went
up in flames. I…saw two men in the glare. But…"

Shane leaned forward intently. "But what?"

She narrowed her gaze, trying to recall, but to this
day, the memory remained a blur. "I think…one of the
men may have shot the other."

Shane's voice was deathly calm. "What did they look
like?"

Why couldn't she remember? Had she not seen
clearly? Or was it so horrible that she'd simply blocked it
out? She shook her head again. "I really don't know."

"Try," Shane pressed.

"I've tried for years. I think it was just so traumatic
that…" She'd banished it to her deepest nightmares.
Couldn't Shane understand? Everything had happened

so fast. Within minutes, her dreams were shattered. Her marriage was over. She'd been betrayed, accidentally killed her cheating husband, given her home to a crime boss who had the police in his pocket. Even the realization that she possessed such dangerous naiveté was completely devastating. She'd been so innocent that she'd never seen so much as a warning sign. In the snap of a finger, she'd gone from being a blushing bride to being on the run.

"I don't know what happened," she said again. All she knew was that she was stronger and braver now than she'd been that night. "But somewhere, locked in my mind, I think I have the face of a killer. And the man he killed. So today," she continued, "when Jake Lucas got shot, I had to consider that maybe my past had caught up with me. Maybe that bullet wasn't meant for me, but I can no longer pretend my past doesn't haunt me. I…I still have dreams."

His voice was low. "I know. I've heard you in the night."

She gazed at him, seeing the concern reflected in his eyes. And none of horrible judgments she'd feared. Had she really thought this man would handcuff her and haul her into the nearest precinct? Her voice caught. "The whole thing just makes me feel so…*dirty*."

There was no other word. She glanced down at Little Shane, his face so hopelessly innocent, then she looked at the skirt of her white sundress. Earlier, she'd been too distraught to change, and now the dress seemed limp from the long day. "Shane," she continued bravely, "because of all this, I want to do something. And because I'm unsure of your feelings about me and the baby, we need to have a serious talk about it."

He sounded faintly alarmed, and she couldn't blame him in the least. "What do you want to do, Lillian?"

"Take Little Shane back to Ethel."

TAKE LITTLE SHANE BACK?

In spite of the room's warmth, a bitter chill gusted through Shane, making his chest constrict and his lungs burn as if he'd sucked in air on a cold winter day. "We can't do anything tonight," he managed.

"Someday," she returned fiercely, "just because of who I am, he could be hurt."

Maybe so, but Shane couldn't bear to take the baby back...

He had to get hold of himself and think. Sam Ramsey was dead, but Lillian hadn't killed him. According to Trusty Joe, Sam had run from the road into the boathouse after Lillian was gone. No doubt Sam had been chasing the car, either to bring Lillian back or to make sure she didn't take the money—probably both. She'd knocked him out, but then was too scared to properly check his pulse.

Moments later, when gunfire hit the ammo in the boathouse, Sam Ramsey died in the explosion. His body was never recovered, but, in a gator-filled bayou, was to be expected. But why had Lillian stopped before telling the whole truth? Shane was sure she'd seen whoever shot his Uncle Silas, and sure she was telling the truth about blocking it out. Her slight hesitation told him she'd considered mentioning the money, which was definitely in the car. Now he decided to keep playing his own cards close to the vest. All hers weren't on the table, and he wanted to know why...

At least insofar as he could think about such things.

After all, he was still riveted on her last words. *I want to take Little Shane back to Ethel.*

"What do you think, Shane?"

He thought giving up the baby would break both their hearts. "If we take him back," he managed, "you know we'll never see him again. Big Apple Babies is an adoption agency, not a holding company."

"I know."

Apparently she'd been sitting here for hours, holding the baby, saying goodbye. All day, she'd been considering giving up Little Shane, to protect him against something bad that might not ever happen. Witnessing her bravery and sacrifice, Shane knew he'd never cared for her more. As his eyes lingered on his namesake, Shane's heart lurched, but his tone remained even. "It's after midnight now. We…can't talk to Ethel until tomorrow."

Her eyes registered the truth of that.

He leaned toward the rocker, stroking her cheek, smoothing another tangled strand of fallen hair. "What say, we sleep on it?" he asked, buying time to find a way out of this for all of them.

Her eyes narrowed as she considered. "Okay."

"C'mon," he murmured, rising. "He's sleeping. Let's put him down."

Together they laid the baby in the crib, then Shane clasped Lillian's hand, twining his fingers through hers. For a long time, they stood side by side, simply staring down at the child who, though no formal words had been spoken, was becoming theirs. The proof was in how Lillian knew Shane had to be involved in any decisions about his future.

"I guess I ought to change," she finally said.

"You'll feel better after a nice warm bath." Still holding her hand, he led her into the bathroom. Flicking on the light, he wordlessly turned on the faucets and started filling the deep whirlpool. "What say, I make it lukewarm?"

"Thanks, Shane. When I got home, I just…"

Her voice trailed off as he stopped in front of her. With his hand, he once again brushed back tendrils of her hair, gently tracing wisps that had curled in the humidity, framing her poreless rose cheeks and tangling near her temples and dark eyes. Cupping her chin, he grazed his thumb back and forth across her lower lip, then let it rest.

Funny, he thought. She was so beautiful, but her physical beauty meant absolutely nothing to him at this minute. He wanted so much more—her heart and soul. It was so much to ask that Shane had never intended to ask it of anybody. Until now. He became conscious of the rushing water in the bathtub, and the sound reminded him of their first kiss—of the pounding rain and the flood of their mutual need.

Leaning, he nuzzled her, rubbing his nose and cheeks and mouth over her delicate skin as he deeply inhaled her scent. Drawing back, his eyes searched hers, the gaze penetrating. He knew it was time for the words he'd never dreamed he'd say to anyone. "I've fallen in love with you. You know that, don't you?"

She sank against the counter. "I…I'd hoped so, Shane." Her breath caught. "I love you, too."

His heart was pounding hard. Right now, every word was so important. It was their future. He needed to say it again. "I love you. I want to stay together."

"Me, too."

His heart pulled, swelled. "I love that little boy in there, too, Lillian."

She blinked back tears. Her voice was a soft rasp. "I thought you might. I'd hoped."

Questions remained—at least a thousand. About where to take things from here. About the baby. About how to reconcile her dangerous past with an uncertain future.

But those questions were for tomorrow. Tonight, they needed to shore up their energies for what was to come. Not that they'd give up Little Shane, Shane assured himself as he pressed up against her, carefully unpinning what was left of the twist in her hair. He'd find a way out for all of them. Picking up a brush, he slowly ran it through the loosened strands.

Her eyes drifted shut and her head pulled with the strokes, exposing her slender creamy throat. The sheer intimacy of her yielding began to arouse him. Not with what Shane thought of as lust, but with a whole new kind of aching want—an outpouring, a straining need to share himself.

Heat was coming through her dress, making him warm, and her hip was hard against him, rhythmically pressuring his groin, stirring him as her body pulled with the brush strokes. His free hand soothed her side, his palm dampening on the lightweight summer fabric.

"There," he murmured, finally setting aside the brush. "Feel better? At least for now?"

She nodded.

He gently undressed her, lifting her limp white dress over her head and removing her bra, his arousal thickening as he freed her generous breasts. Dark tangled curls peeked from a white triangle of panty and he hooked both hands inside the silk scrap, pulling it slowly down her long legs, his nostrils flaring as he leaned, catching the intimate scent of her musk.

"Ah, sweetheart," he murmured, as she braced her hands on his shoulders for balance and stepped from the panties. Powerless to rise, he circled his arms around her thighs and drew her close, just holding her for a brief moment, pressing his cheek to the soft triangle of hair, pressing a chaste kiss to the moist, musky haven.

Then he rose, feeling heavy with emotion and gestured toward the tub where the water was still rising, now almost too deep. His voice was almost a whisper, "Go on, sweetheart."

"Coming?"

He hadn't even thought about it, he'd been so intent on simply wanting to bathe her, to make her feel better. "Yeah. After you."

He watched her head for the tub, get in, and turn off the faucets. Seating herself on the whirlpool steps, she let her legs dangle, the water lapping at the swells of her breasts. He started undressing in front of her—taking off his boots, his T-shirt, opening his belt and unsnapping his jeans, then his lean hand paused on the zipper, and he was suddenly conscious of where his hard sex was pressuring denim.

His head swam. She'd never seen him in the light; she'd never seen him naked. The realization left him so unsteady that his hand shook. Swallowing against the dryness of his throat, he brought down the zipper. Shedding his jeans and underwear, he stood up straight, feeling unaccountably vulnerable, but letting her dark eyes touch him with love.

Then he headed down the steps, stopping only to lay

a thick sumptuous towel at the very edge of the bathtub, so Lillian wouldn't slip on the tiles when she got
out. Bending his knees, Shane immersed himself to his
chest, found a wash cloth and, soaping it, floated in front
of her. Suddenly conscious of the mirrors surrounding
them, he caught a glimpse of himself and realized he
was a man transformed. His eyes were full of the same
naked emotion he saw reflected in Lillian's each time
he looked at her.

"Everything's going to be all right, Lillian," he
whispered.

"You promise?" she whispered back.

"I promise."

In the silence, he could hear her shallow breath, his
own heart pounding. A water droplet plunked from the
faucet into the still pool, sending a ripple. Right before
he pressed his lips to hers, offering a gentle, loving
kiss, he murmured, "We're all going to stay together.
You, me, and the baby. Everything's going to work out
fine."

"You never struck me as the type to believe in happy
endings, Shane."

"You've made me believe in them." He took her
mouth once more, then started bathing both her and
himself—running the cloth around his neck and over
his chest. Resoaping it, he lifted her feet and hands,
working the sudsy cloth between her toes and fingers.

He didn't know when he quit washing her and simply
started loving her. But the cloth, slick with suds, slid
between her legs with only the tenderest pretext of washing. Soon, his soaped finger followed, easing open her
cleft, exploring until a soft cry pressed into his shoulder,
and she murmured, "Shane, I think I'm about clean."

Leaning back a fraction, he saw the slightest of smiles lift her lips. Maybe that was why he loved her so much. Because no matter what trouble she'd been in, she'd stayed brave and kept going. She'd started a new life for herself—and she'd made that life work. No matter what a hundred tomorrows brought, she'd always be strong. And she'd always love him. His voice was too strained to be called husky. "Clean? I think I might have missed a spot."

"We wouldn't want that."

"No, we wouldn't."

"Here…" His hands—one covered with suds now, the other with the cloth—lathered her breasts until the constricted darkened tips were all that peeped from the white foam. His soap-slick hands slipping, he cupped her breasts from the sides, lifting and pressing them together. Rinsing the cloth, he wrung it, sluicing water over her, then he lathered again until her chest was covered.

"Oh, Shane," she whispered, her slender fingers suddenly kneading his shoulders, her long legs moving edgily in the water, floating around him, opening again. He felt simply reverent—moved from their confessions of love, and from the depth of what was passing between them. He couldn't articulate it, didn't think it in words, but he felt the emotions. He was loving her in the light now, soaping and bathing her. They were coming clean.

When the soap slipped from his grasp and slid over the bath tiles, she stretched but couldn't reach it.

His low-voiced drawl was whispered against her cheek. "I'll get it." Rising from the water brought his aroused sex close to her, and Shane suddenly gasped as her hands unexpectedly slid between his thighs, then boldly held him, urging him against her chest. Flooded with sensation, flooded with love, Shane felt his knees give out. Sinking, he braced himself as she thrust her breast against him, pressing his aroused length to where she was slick with suds.

He uttered something ragged when she nestled him into her cleavage. He'd become so thick now, painfully engorged. Water eddied around his knees as his hips moved, thrusting once between her breasts. "Yes—" His voice caught. "Ah, Lillian."

Far more than the physical sensation, he felt the stretching of his heart as he sank into the water again, found her hand, then urged her up with him, into his embrace. Their warm, wet bodies dripped and clung while their lips caught with gentle greed. The kiss was thirsty, a spring rain gulping at roots—as tongue met tongue, and as he slid his over her teeth and licked at the inside of her cheek.

"Love," he whispered thickly against her mouth. "Take me to bed."

Turning in his arms, she started ascending the steps, but their eyes caught in the mirror—and then they were both lost. His wet chest was pressed against her back, his heart beating against her, and seeing the full front of her in the mirror made him shudder. That sight—her breasts, stomach, the sweet bush below—completely swept him away, and he squeezed his arms around her, holding tight as his mouth sank onto her shoulder. Kissing her neck, he suckled, taking with his teeth and tongue. And when he managed to release her, their eyes linked in the mirror, stormy with love.

"Go," he said hoarsely, his hands on her shoulders.

Instead, she backed down a step, and simply leaned over the tub's edge, resting her belly on the white towel on the tiles. He didn't argue. Gliding between her legs that floated open, his hands roved as his eyes did, over her backside and arched spine. He pressed into her hot tight readiness, pushing in just a fraction, feeling the slick moisture that was no longer soap and water now, but that was all her.

And then, splaying both hands on her waist and holding her in place, he pulled her to him, even as he drove his whole body forward with a stroke so deep it made her shout out with the pleasured intensity of it. She stretched so completely open for him that he was utterly lost inside her, drowning in heat and darkness, gasping for breath. And then riding, until the reins were lost.

Unbalanced, he half opened his veiled eyes—and realized she was everywhere. In the mirrors, he watched her fists clench and unclench on the towel where she lay. Watched how he'd wound up crouching over her—how his hands reached around her and fondled her breasts, and how a finger found her mouth, letting her suckle. The visions took him to the edge. His words were thick, ragged. "Are you ready?"

"Yes! Yes!" Her gasps said she, too, was at the brink.

Crouching even lower, he strained and caught her mouth in a starving kiss. Somehow, he shut his eyes and kept them hovering for those few last precious seconds of love. He wanted to give her so much more, a lifetime of it—this woman he'd watched and wanted so long in the dark, whom he'd pursued for years. Whom he'd found. And who'd become, along with a baby, his destiny.

When his eyes opened again, he cast them around the room—and saw she was still everywhere. In every mirror. But now Shane felt her only one place—inside his heart.

"Lillian—" He gasped out. "Delilah. I don't know even know what to call you now."

"Wife," she said with a strangled whisper. "Shane, I'm your wife."

Wife. She rose to meet the last hard penetration that brought her climax, her body pulsing and shaking, and as he felt her plummet, Shane exploded, following her into oblivion, his consciousness almost fading from it, his head swimming, and the world becoming hazy and dark.

But her last words were still in his heart, claiming him. *I'm your wife.*

CHAPTER TWELVE

IT WAS DARK AND QUIET, maybe *too* quiet, Lillian thought when she woke with a start. And Shane was no longer in bed with her or near the crib. Had he taken the baby to the kitchen for a bottle? Had a nightmare from the past awakened her?

Instinct told her to get up, and her heart's sudden skip warned her not to turn on the lamp or call out for Shane. It was the faint prickle at her nape that really got her moving, stealthily going to the crib while she dressed in what her groping hands found first—panties, Shane's T-shirt and her robe.

Despite her uneasiness, seeing the baby sent a glimmer of a smile across her lips, and she gently rubbed his tummy. Hours ago, she'd meant to give him up, to make sure he'd always be safe from the past that haunted her, but right now she was just as sure she couldn't.

Touching the baby definitely calmed her. After what happened to Jake yesterday, it was no wonder she was having bad dreams again. Shane was probably just in the kitchen. She glanced at the clock. It was 5:00 a.m. "I just had a bad dream," she murmured. "That's all."

But something sounded behind her.

She froze. Listened. Her heart pounded too hard, her breath turning shallow. A shot of adrenaline begged her to run, but she crept to the bathroom. Flipping the switch, she blinked against the brightness and stared inside. Nothing dangerous here. Seeing the clothes and damp towels strewn across the floor, another fleeting smile touched her lips. Well, she guessed her and Shane's lovemaking was dangerous.

"Lone Star?"

The dog wasn't here. Nor was the bogey man or the Big Bad Wolf. Suddenly feeling silly, Lillian extinguished the light. She'd wake the baby if she called for Shane, so she padded toward the kitchen. In the living room, she stopped again. *Something's wrong.* Had they left the terrace doors uncovered? Open? She couldn't remember. Far off, orbs of light floated, undulating on the Hudson. Anchored boats. At the other end of the hallway, a bar of yellow light shone under the front door. She squinted. Was the door open a crack? It looked as if it was.

"Shane?"

He didn't answer.

"Lone Star?"

She glanced back toward the bedroom. Should she have brought the baby? It was definitely too quiet in here, and now the watchful silence seemed purposeful. *Shane's walking the dog!* The thought came in a flash. Lone Star must have awakened Shane, needing to go out, and Shane hadn't shut the door. It explained everything.

She sighed in relief but still moved with caution. When she swung open the kitchen door, nothing happened, so she hit the lights. And gasped. Her knees buckled, then she over-compensated, her legs becoming stiff as boards. She blinked hard against the shock.

Her husband—her other husband, her wrong husband, her *dead* husband—smiled back.

"Ah, sweet Delilah," he said. "So we meet again."

Only the kitchen table, its four chairs neatly tucked in for the night, lay between them. It wasn't nearly enough protection. "You're dead!"

"And damn good-looking for a ghost."

"If you don't say so yourself."

"Exactly."

Her first thought was for the baby. She wrenched around. "Who else is here?"

"I'm alone. I wanted to have a private chat."

"How did you get in here?"

"Slipped past downstairs security, then picked the locks on your front door."

Sam Ramsey's voice, though deep and melodious, sent a shiver down her spine. He was big and tanned, just as she remembered, and shooting her a deceptively glib smile. He hadn't changed much, though his sun-streaked hair was longer, in a ponytail. He was good-looking, and she well knew he could be dangerously charming. It was why she'd been so taken in by him. No doubt he'd been watching the apartment for a while. Maybe he'd seen Shane go out to walk the dog, then used the opportunity to creep inside.

"My poor Delilah—" He clucked his tongue. "Did you really think you'd killed me?"

She realized she was still gaping at him, completely stunned. *Yes.* She'd suffered the guilt for years. She could still remember the panic she felt as she drove down the dark private road at the plantation, fumbling at the Oldsmobile's dashboard, trying to find the headlights. Suddenly, Sam darted from the trees. Knowing she'd overheard him talking to the woman on the phone, he'd come after her. He'd gotten a head start while she'd been in the garage, and was rushing toward her on foot. She'd wrenched the steering wheel, but swerved too late. In the next second, Sam's body thudded against the hood. Leaping from the car, she'd rushed to his side. She was positive she'd killed him. "Yes, I was sure you were dead," she managed.

"I thought so. But I was only dazed." He leaned his body, which was sleekly encased in tight black jeans and a tighter black shirt, casually against the counter. The eyes perusing her possessed all the warmth of a snake's. "You'd like me dead, though, wouldn't you, Delilah?" he taunted. "So you and your latest husband can spend my money."

Her eyes widened.

"Oh, yes. I know all about Shane Holiday. And if you fork over my money, Delilah, then maybe I'll go away, nice and quiet, and let you have your other man."

She barely heard him. Her mind was racing. The money. Of course. Sam hadn't solely resurfaced to threaten her marriage to Shane. Now she noticed that some drawers and cabinets were open. Did Sam really think she still had the money? Had he come to search for it? Seven years of fearing a showdown must have paid off. Since she'd already lived a night such as this in her worst nightmares, she had practice, and she was very pleased to find her voice didn't even shake. "Where's Shane?"

"Where's my money?"

Terror suddenly welled within her. Did Sam know she had a son now? Did he know the baby was here?

And had he done something to Shane and Lone Star?
"Where's my husband?" she demanded sharply.

"*I'm* your husband."

The words made her queasy. But she guessed it was true. She was married to two men. "Technically."

"Whatever."

"You're not really my husband!" *Shane is.*

"Oh yes I am, Delilah. And if you don't start talking, I just might demand my marital rights." The lascivious glance that swept down her emphasized the threat. "It's been a long time since we've been together, now, hasn't it?"

Panic surged through her. Especially when she saw what was at the other end of Sam's big dangling hand. "Glock 9 millimeter," he explained. "Plastic. With a silencer."

She had no idea what such words meant—Glock. Millimeter. Plastic—only that the gun looked menacing. Silencers she'd heard of, of course. Which meant Sam obviously intended business.

Whatever you do next, stay calm. Her eyes sized up the situation: If she ran, the table would slow him down. But by the time she got Little Shane, he'd catch her. Sam was leaning against the knife drawer, but the sharpest knives were on the counter, wedged in a wood-block holder, almost within her reach. The bright yellow tea kettle on the top burner was heavy and had a rubber-coated handle. Last month, when she'd seen it at a furniture shop, the handle, which was marketed as a "firm-grip innovation," had sold her on the kettle. Now with any luck, maybe she could get a "firm grip" and innovatively brain Sam. Or maybe Shane—who she prayed was walking the dog—would come home.

She just hoped the baby didn't cry, alerting Sam to his presence.

"Don't even think about trying to fight me," Sam said, his dry chuckle grating on her raw nerves. "You'd think running me over with the car would have been enough."

"Apparently not," she tossed back.

Her feigned indifference only further infuriated him, and his brown eyes deepened to black. "I hid out from my daddy for years," he said, his voice low. "When everybody thought I'd died, I laid low. I wasn't taking any flak for not controlling my women—"

"Your women!" she exploded, noting he used the plural. "Just how many *women* did you have? I was your *wife!* I wasn't a possession! A trophy!" The man was sick.

Sam ignored her. "What you're going to be is sorry. Now where's that money? Tell me or you'll wind up getting shot like that man next to you on the sidewalk yesterday."

Jake? She gasped. "You shot Jake Lucas?"

Sam shrugged. "I don't know who he was. But next time, you'll be the target. I just wanted to let you know that you could wind up like that if you don't start talking. I saw you drive away with the money that night, so I know you had it. And if you spent it, I demand compensation. You can make this easy or hard. It's your choice. But you owe me."

She was reeling from Sam's confession that he'd shot Jake. She couldn't believe an innocent man could have died because of her. "I don't have it!"

They both knew she was lying. Sam's arm rose slowly with the Glock.

A low growl sounded. Then Lone Star lunged from behind a cabinet—a ball of bristling fur, flouncing hair bows and barred teeth—gaining remarkable height given that she was minus a leg. Sam swiped for and missed the bandanna gracing Lone Star's neck, then yelped as her fangs sank into his gun hand. Lillian raced for the stove, grabbing the kettle.

Poof. Poof. Poof.

She froze. Bullets sounded, muted by the silencer. But Lone Star didn't howl, and Lillian felt no pain. Belatedly, she registered splintering wood; the bullets had hit cabinets. Realizing she and Lone Star were safe, she swiveled from the stove, brandishing the kettle. "Shane!"

He didn't respond, simply kept barreling from his hiding place behind the door. He was barefoot, barechested, wearing only jeans—and going straight for Sam. Catching Sam's wrist, Shane wrenched it backward, making the gun drop, then he kicked it toward Lillian. She wasn't about to pick up the lethal-looking weapon, but when Sam ran at her, she swung the kettle like a razor-sharp scythe.

Not that Shane let Sam get anywhere close to her. Lifting a chair in midstride, Shane swung, narrowly missing Sam's head. Forgetting Lillian, Sam pivoted, grabbing Shane in a bear hug. Their bodies locking with slaps and thuds, the struggling men crashed onto the table, overturning it when they fell to the floor in a grunting tumble.

"Arf! Arf!" Lone Star dived low, attacking Sam's ankles, while Lillian feinted left and right, waving the kettle, looking for an opening into the melee. It came when Sam's thrashing foot caught Lone Star; the dog

whined, temporarily scuttling to the side, just as Sam got
Shane in a wrestling hold from behind. Shane elbowed
Sam's gut, but Sam was still coming for Lillian, kicking
aside chairs.

"Stop!" she shouted.

Sam was hurting Shane! Without another thought,
Lillian lunged, wildly thrusting the kettle. When Sam
spun to avoid the blows, she leaped onto his back, bouncing up and down.

Sam wrenched. "Get offa me!"

"I've wanted to do this for years," she announced,
right before hitting him. Dazed, Sam staggered. "Now let
my husband go," she warned, "or I'll hit you again!"

"Damn it, Delilah," Sam snarled. "You're my wife
and you've got my money!"

"She's *my* wife," Shane bit out.

"Prove it, you bastard," Sam spit back, panting hard
and suddenly heaving Lillian from his back like a lightweight coat. She sailed through the air, hit the floor hard,
then rolled, her hipbone cracking. Nerves inflamed by
the fight, she barely felt it. With superhuman strength,
Shane had whipped around.

"You want me to prove she's my wife, Ramsey?"

Sam clenched his fists. "Yeah."

Shane came like a prize-fighter, his well-honed body
taut, his fists pummeling every inch of Sam. It was
brutal, but Sam deserved it, and Lillian just wished she
had more time to admire the rolling, rippling muscles
of Shane's bare back. His every muscle flexed with a
fast sharp one-two jab that caught Sam's nose and sent
blood gushing. Lightning-quick gut-level punches followed, making Sam crumple.

JULIE McBRIDE   215

Lillian realized she'd better intervene. "Shane," she called nervously. "I guess we'd better not kill him!"

Her voice brought a maddened Shane to his senses. Grabbing Sam by the shirt collar, he dragged him toward the refrigerator. While Sam kicked and thrashed, Shane whipped handcuffs from his back pocket, looped them through the double doors of the refrigerator and secured Sam, then grabbed the phone. Lillian thought he was calling the police, but Shane kept pulling, ripping it right out of the wall. With the cord, he trussed Sam's legs.

"He looks like a turkey," she managed, completely stunned by the display.

Shane wasn't even winded. He glanced up. "Pig."

Lillian squinted. "Excuse me?"

Tightening the cord, Shane drew Sam's ankles and hands together, just close enough that Sam was kneeling uncomfortably next to the refrigerator. "I'm hog-tying him, sweetheart."

"I'm impressed," she managed. Shane was an ex-cop, of course, but she'd never considered what he might look like in action. "Always good to have a cowboy in the house."

"And a guard dog," added Shane.

Taking the cue, Lone Star came close, her beady eyes settled on Sam, and with a low growl in her throat she dared the man to move.

Not that Sam was through talking. "What are you two brain surgeons going to do now? Call the cops?"

Lillian frowned. He had a point. She was living under an assumed name, and she'd fled Louisiana with three million dollars that was earmarked as a payoff for dirty cops. Still, they couldn't let Sam go. From down the hallway, the baby wailed. She glanced anxiously over her shoulder.

"Go on," Shane said softly. "See to the baby. I'll take care of Sam."

Only the baby could have pulled her away. Right before she turned, Shane hauled a chair upright, spun it on one leg, then straddled it, sitting backward and resting his elbows on the high back. Jogging to the bedroom, she was unable to believe this was happening. Was Sam Ramsey really alive and in her apartment?

She was so shocked, she'd reached the bedroom before realizing she was still wielding the tea kettle. She was breathless, too, and anxious to know what was happening in the kitchen. But she managed a soothing coo as she checked the baby. He was fine, just damp. Leaving him, she flicked on the bathroom light and got a fresh diaper. Little Shane quieted, as if knowing relief was on the way.

"That's right," she somehow managed to say in a steady voice. "Mama'll fix you right up."

She was coming back out, diaper in one hand, kettle in the other when a dark gloved hand suddenly reached out from behind her and clamped down hard over her mouth. Something feeling suspiciously like a gun pressured her ribs. Her first panicked thought was that Sam had a partner. But then Sam said he'd come alone. Not that she trusted Sam.

A man said, "Don't scream."

How could she when his hand was clamped over her mouth? And who was he? What could she do? Swinging the kettle, she tried—and failed—to hit behind her.

"I said, don't scream."

She'd had it with all this manhandling. Who did these

macho jerks think she was? Some shrinking violet who took orders? Any semblance of the more demure Lillian Smith was long gone. Wrenching her head away, Delilah Fontenont screamed.

SHANE'S HEAD SHOT UP.

Sam chuckled nastily. "Guess I'm not your only intruder."

Shane rose from the chair, swiftly squeezing Sam's neck with just enough pressure to get the truth out of him. "Who's with you?"

"I swear!" Sam gasped. "I came alone."

"Watch him, Lone Star."

Lone Star bared her fangs as Shane hit the hallway at a run. Long ago the police academy taught him to respond quietly in such a situation, but Lillian and the baby's safety overrode everything he'd ever learned. He burst into the bedroom, slamming on the overhead light.

What he saw made no sense. His heart missed a beat; he paused uncertainly. Little Shane, sensing this was definitely not the best time to demand grown-up attention, remained thankfully silent—and Shane merely stared. An old man was backed against the wall near the bathroom door. He was holding Lillian hostage, and his gun was aimed at the wall, at least at the moment. Lillian's eyes, wide with fear, were riveted on a mirror opposite her. And in it, she was studying every nuance of her attacker's face.

"Trusty Joe?" Shane said.

"Yeah, Shane. It's me."

Of course it was. Shane knew every wrinkle of the old man's weathered features, since Trusty Joe and Uncle

Silas had been partners for years. Now he took in the
tough cop's familiar face and bald head, the body that
had remained strong and wiry, even after retirement. Joe
must have followed Sam Ramsey. Had he come to help?
Was he trying to solve Silas's murder? But no. Trusty
Joe was dressed in dark clothes and gloves. And one of
those gloved hands was covering Lillian's mouth.

"That's Lillian," Shane managed.

"Do I look stupid?" Trusty Joe snarled. "I know who
she is."

What was happening? Two days ago, when Shane
called, Trusty Joe said he was going on vacation, deep-
sea fishing. "If you know it's Lillian, then let her go."

"You just don't get it, do you, Shane?"

Shane was starting to. And he felt sick. Not to mention murderous; he was afraid of what he'd do next.
Before Shane made his move, Lillian wrenched around
again.

She gasped. "That's him!"

Trusty Joe grabbed her, pulling her to him.

"I saw him that night," she managed. "Shane, he
killed a man. I saw him! I tried to block it out. But I
saw him shoot someone."

Shane could guess who. He could almost see Lillian racing down the long driveway in the dark. She
looked back, maybe in the rearview mirror, and she'd
seen Trusty Joe in the shadows. Shane's Uncle Silas
was with him. But Trusty Joe had made a deal with the
Mob—and he wasn't about to let Silas get in the way.
Panicked, Trusty Joe turned and fired on Silas. Damn.
In the last moment of his life, with his last breath, Uncle
Silas had told Shane he loved him. It had been more

important for Silas to tell Shane he was loved, than to name his own killer. Shane's heart pulled.

Trusty Joe's grip tightened on Lillian. "Your little girlfriend destroyed my retirement package, Shane. Me and the Ramseys had it all set up. I was the one who was going to dole that three million dollars out to all the cops on the take. But when your girlfriend took off with the payoff and I couldn't stop her, Jack Ramsey wouldn't work with me anymore. The consortium started operating, but I never got my cut. Now, since you were nice enough to call with Delilah's whereabouts, and since you've got Sam Ramsey tied up, I'll just take that tidy little sum your girlfriend—"

"She's my wife," Shane said with deceptive calm that belied his building fury.

"I don't care who she is. I've been casing this place. I about fell over when I saw Sam Ramsey. I thought he was dead. Now I want the money he came for."

"Go ahead and shoot me," Lillian said calmly. "But you're not getting a red cent."

As much as he admired her spunk, Shane sure wished Lillian would quit taunting men with guns. It just wasn't healthy. He glanced toward the crib and swallowed hard. Raw fury made him want to throttle Joe. But Shane wasn't playing any risky games when Lillian's and the baby's safety were at stake. He kept his voice even. "Let her go, Joe. And then we can make a deal."

Lillian's eyes were bugging. "Don't make a deal, Shane! I saw him shoot somebody. I saw—"

The gloved hand clapped over her mouth again. "Got yourself a jabbery little thing, didn't ya, Shane? Well, you best start making her sing about my money. And, Shane, if you move, I will shoot you."

Shane tried to buy time. "You've known me all my life, Joe. Would you really shoot?"

Trusty Joe's eyes had turned cunning, crafty. "I shot your uncle, didn't I?" He chuckled harshly. "Or hadn't you guessed? You two were both fools. Upholding law and order, when every other cop on the block was making a killing. I tried to tell your uncle not to stake out the Ramseys that night…"

Lillian's eyes widened in shock. For the first time, the implication sank in. Shane had been there the night she'd fled Louisiana.

"I was on the case," Shane explained softly, his eyes never leaving Trusty Joe's. "And I came here to solve my uncle's murder. I—"

Trusty Joe cut him off with a defensive whine. "Damn right I shot Silas, before he hauled me into the precinct. He mighta been my partner, but no man was taking me down."

"So you really did it. You killed my uncle." It wasn't a question.

"What do you want it in, Shane? Blood?"

"That's exactly how I want it."

Suddenly, Lillian wrenched again, swinging the kettle. She missed Trusty Joe, but gained Shane the precious second he needed. He shot across the room, grabbing the gun. Lord, Shane wanted to kill the man. All these years, he'd continued trusting Joe—only to find out Joe had killed his Uncle Silas. The man had some nerve coming in here, threatening Shane's family. Clutching Trusty Joe's arm, he dragged him across the room and down the hallway. And he didn't stop until he reached the terrace.

"Shane!" Lillian's steps pounded behind him. "Please, don't throw him over!"

She would say *please* in an instance such as this. Delilah Fontenont, a.k.a. Lillian Smith, was a very strange mix of lady and hellcat. But she was right, too. This was a matter for the authorities. Scanning the Hudson, Shane saw the surveillance boat's searchlight bobbing in the water, and realized whoever was out there had probably noticed the action. No doubt Fin was on his way. Realizing he was still holding Trusty Joe dangerously close to the terrace rail, Shane blew out a murderous sigh.

"Take off your shirt, Joe."

The man did so, trembling in relief, seemingly realizing Shane wasn't going to do him any more bodily harm. Ripping the shirt to shreds with his bare hands, Shane tied Trusty to the terrace rail with the strips. A second later, Lillian's arms flew around Shane's neck.

"Are you all right?" she said.

"Are you?"

She nodded. "I…I didn't realize your uncle died at the Ramseys'." There were questions in her eyes, but there was trust, too, that Shane would tell her everything. Right now, he was just glad that she and the baby were safe. Maybe he hadn't protected his parents. Or Uncle Silas, who'd been like a father. But he'd defended his wife and baby.

"Your face," she whispered.

Only as Lillian's gentle fingers pressed his skin did Shane realize Sam had gotten in some licks. "It's nothing that won't heal," he assured in a low rumbling drawl. Besides, she'd already given him all the healing he needed when she'd accepted his love.

"You were like an animal." She tried to look disapproving.

He smiled, wincing against the pain in his battered body. Smoothing back her hair, he said, "You bring it out in me."

"Thanks."

"Anytime." Lowering his head, he delivered a quick kiss, then said, "I don't know what we're going to do now, but I do know I love you, Lillian."

What was almost a smile curved her lips. "Whoever said bad things come in threes?"

He narrowed his gaze. "Hmm?"

"Well, first there was Sam. Then Trusty Joe. And now the best-looking guy in the world is telling me he loves me. So, maybe bad things only come in twos."

Shane was about to agree when Fin strode came through Lillian's front door and headed straight for the living room.

Lillian turned in Shane's arms. "Who are you?"

"Fin Huff," said Fin, nodding a greeting at Shane. "And you're under arrest, Ms. Fontenont."

Lillian's eyes shot to Shane's. "What's this?"

"Unfortunately," muttered Shane, still holding her tight. "It's bad thing number three. And four," he added.

Because Ethel was on Fin's heels. And everything in the caseworker's expression said she'd come to take away Little Shane.

CHAPTER THIRTEEN

SHANE WOULD NEVER FORGET what followed. Not how Fin's agents stormed the apartment, hauling off Sam Ramsey and Trusty Joe Beaujolais. Or Lillian's betrayed expression when she realized Shane had been working with the agents—and for how long. He'd tried to go to her, but agents held him back.

"Sorry," Fin said coolly. "You crossed the line, Shane. We've got to arrest her now."

Her chin had quivered, her dark eyes blazing. "What was I—and the baby? Just a job to you?"

She knew better than that. Shane couldn't believe she'd even said it. Only hours ago, he was bathing her, loving her. Surely she knew the depths of what he'd shared had come from the heart. "It wasn't only that."

"Not *only* that!"

That wasn't what he meant. His eyes begged her to understand that torn loyalties had ripped him apart. "I came here to find out about my uncle, Lillian. You were a potential witness to his murder. Ever since I got here, I've been trying to find a way out of this for us."

Nothing he said mattered. And when Fin began questioning her, Lillian still coolly maintained she didn't have the Mob's money. When Ethel came from the bedroom, carrying Little Shane and the diaper bags, Lillian cried out, just once, and ice-cold fear slid through Shane.

He'd never believed this could really happen. Lillian lunged for the baby. Shane lunged. But people held them both back.

"Sorry, Lillian—" Ethel's eyes filled with tears. "I didn't want to do this, but Fin explained everything to me. I have to take the baby now."

"That's our son!" Shane exploded.

Ethel looked uncertain. "Shane, Fin told me this was nothing more than a sting operation. Are you saying you *want* this baby?"

Did he *want* his son? Shane had rushed forward, dragging along four agents who stopped him from getting to Ethel. His voice became a murderous command. "Put him back in his crib."

"If you're interested in the baby, maybe you can arrange to see him," Ethel said nervously.

Shane could only shake his head, his eyes riveted on where Ethel was backing away with the baby. Little Shane awakened and waved his arms. His sudden strangled cry of despair punctured Shane's heart like a knife.

You can't take our son! You can't come in here and snatch him from his crib! But Ethel had. And, after letting Lillian dress, Fin took her from the apartment with the same unbelievable ease.

Now Shane sat near the terrace, his hand resting on the spot between Lone Star's ears. "If I could just *think,*" he muttered.

Through the terrace doors, the predawn world wasn't encouraging. Gray haze settled on the shimmering Hudson, waiting for the sun's searing heat to shave it off like thick dark cream from butter. The surveillance boat's bobbing light had vanished. With Lillian gone, what was worth watching?

When Lone Star nuzzled Shane's thigh and whimpered, Shane glanced down. He took in the sheriff's badge pinned to the dog's red bandanna, her downturned ears, the sad dark droopy eyes and star-shaped barrettes. His heart pulled at the reminders of Lillian. How could his wife and son be gone?

Think of something, Shane!

Fin had taken Lillian for questioning, not even granting Shane a seat at the interview. Now that Shane had successfully bagged both Sam Ramsey and Trusty Joe, he was suddenly "too personally involved in the case." After years of dedication and putting in unpaid time, he'd been shut out. All Fin wanted was credit for making the collars.

Shane *really* had to think…

"To hell with thinking," he muttered. Ever since he'd moved in with Lillian, he'd been trying to think his way out of this. "What say we *do* something, Lone Star?"

"Arf!"

Shane headed down the hallway with Lone Star. Pulling on a T-shirt, Shane stepped into his boots as he picked up the bedroom phone and punched in a number. Listening to the phone ring, he glanced at the crib, and braced himself, feeling sick. Where was Little Shane right now? In a cab with Ethel? Crying in a crib at Big Apple Babies? Well, wherever he was, Shane thought, he wasn't where he should be—at home with his parents.

When Jefferson Lawrence finally answered the phone, Shane didn't waste any more time. He explained everything from start to finish, then said, "Meet me at your office."

"AND YOU HAD THE NERVE to bring your dog?" Jefferson fumed.

Lone Star thumped her tail uncertainly on the sidewalk.

Shane resettled his hat more firmly on his held, then held up a hand. "Please, Jefferson. I feel riled enough without enduring more of your caustic tone."

"A *dog*," repeated Jefferson.

Lillian's boss had forced Shane to get a warrant before coming to the building, which meant Shane had go through Fin—who was now in charge of what had become a full-scale official case against the Ramseys. Despite being ticked off by the politicking, Shane had acted professionally, in order to obtain the warrant. Still, swallowing his pride left a bad taste in his mouth. Besides which, they were wasting precious time. Shane wanted Lillian and Little Shane back. Now.

"You insisted on bringing *your* dog," Shane wound up saying.

"You'd better believe I called the honorable Judge Tilford Winslow," Jefferson returned, his usually melodious baritone now rough around the edges because of his mood. Caught on his morning run, Jefferson was wearing bright red runner's shorts and a ventilated shirt. As he headed through the lobby door toward the judge, who waited at the security desk, the gadgets hanging around Jefferson's neck—a stopwatch and pulse-monitoring device—thumped against his chest.

"Tilford," Jefferson continued, his voice rising, no doubt to embarrass Shane. "I told Mr. Holiday I'm not proceeding one step further without my attorney present! Oh, no, I'm not! Not after what Mr. Holiday's done to poor Lillian!"

Mr. Holiday. Poor Lillian. Shane blew out a testy sigh. *Go ahead,* he thought. *Perceive me as the enemy. See if I care.* He followed Jefferson toward a bank of brass elevators.

Judge Winslow followed, looking grouchier than Jefferson. By nature, the judge was formidable—well into his eighties, corpulent and bald. But Shane had met him twice, and he suspected the judge, like Jefferson, had a softer side. Both wealthy men helped fund the Big Apple Babies adoption agency and recently their previously anonymous contributions had come to light.

"Sorry if I got you out of bed, Judge Winslow—" Shane struggled for diplomacy, grabbing Lone Star's bandanna and coaxing her inside the elevator. "I appreciate your coming. I—"

"I do assure you I was wide-awake, young man," Judge Winslow said coolly.

Glancing over the elderly judge's wrinkled gray suit and tie, Shane decided not to mention that the white shirt stretching over his considerable paunch was crookedly buttoned. Shane sighed. "Right."

Judge Winslow cleared his rheumy throat while Jefferson angrily stabbed the button for the executive floor. "Truly," the judge continued in an acerbic tone. "I'd only started my morning coffee, Mr. Holiday. In fact, I was sitting down to a nice quiet breakfast, but of course I jumped right up to rush over here. Nevertheless, seeing as it's scarcely 7:00 a.m., I do have a very long day left ahead of me, during which I'm sure I can find an uninterrupted moment to read the *New York Times.* Since my semi-retirement, I like to start my mornings with a nice, long leisurely break—"

Shane gritted his teeth. "Like I said, I'm—"

"Oh, shut up," growled Jefferson. "Tilford and I don't care how sorry you are." Jefferson leaned and repeatedly stabbed the elevator button to make his point. Not that it helped. The elevator was padded, pressurized and ponderously slow. The executive suite was on the sixty-seventh floor.

Shane and Lone Star stared up at the bar of extinguishing lights above the door, while Jefferson continued ruminating, half talking to himself. "Lillian's very fragile. And I knew she was in trouble. I just knew it! Well, I certainly hope you're satisfied with yourself *now,* Mr. Holiday…."

Floor twenty-seven. Floor twenty-eight…

"…you've ruined her life. And the baby. My God! What are we going to do about the *baby?*"

Floor twenty-nine. Thirty.

"…to see her used! Seduced! What were you thinking when you married her? Don't you know that wedding vows are sacred? Or do you care?"

Thirty-one. Thirty-two. Shane exhaled a long-suffering sigh. "I could really do without all the flak right now, Jefferson. Okay?"

"Arf!" agreed Lone Star.

"You ruined her life," Jefferson continued as if he hadn't heard a word. "And she waited so long to get a baby! She can't have any, and that might have been her only chance!"

Shane had about had it. That his and Lillian's son was in a crib at Big Apple Babies, instead of at home, wasn't helping his own mood in the least. "Lillian," he reminded flatly, "fled Louisiana with three million dollars in her possession that not only belonged to a crime consortium, but that was going to be used as payoff money to the police."

Jefferson's eyes narrowed. "Exactly. It was the Mob's money. Not Lillian's. She was running for her life, poor girl. Not that she'll get in trouble—" His voice rose. "I want you to know I've been making phone calls. I've got a lot of pull in this town, and I've already hired lawyers—"

Shane raised his eyebrows. "You've hired lawyers to argue Lillian's case?"

Jefferson shot Shane a smug, self-satisfied smile. "I'm sure you've heard of Joyce Moon, Orsen Daily and Bert Taylor?"

The three high-profile defense attorneys were the highest-paid and most sought-after in the country. Relief flooded Shane, not that he could get a word in edgewise, to thank Jefferson.

"They'll rip you to shreds," Jefferson continued. "Everything concerning your illegal surveillance of Lillian and will come out. You won't have a prayer."

Shane told himself not to rise to the bait. It would definitely be easier if Jefferson would calm down and realize they were on the same side. "Jefferson," he finally said. "Whether you choose to recognize it or not, I'm trying to help her."

"Oh, now you're running scared!" Jefferson fumed. "Now that I've mentioned the lawyers, you're backing off! Well, just so you know, I'll take you all the way to the Supreme Court for violating Lillian's civil rights!"

Shane was getting genuinely aggravated. "She's my wife."

"I believe she's technically still married to Sam Ramsey," interjected the judge coolly.

Which meant Shane could be forced to testify if he found evidence against her. "I love her," Shane said, defending himself.

"With love like yours," Jefferson snapped, "who needs enemies?"

Judge Winslow sighed. "Gentlemen, may I suggest we continue this incredibly long elevator ride in silence?"

Shane was about to snap. "She broke the law. She's been living under an assumed name."

"And now you show up with a warrant to open my personal office safe!" Jefferson burst out. "Clearly, you're amassing more evidence against her. How could you pretended to love her? Even marry her? And all for your measly ambition, your fool case."

Shane's voice was low, deceptively controlled. "Jefferson, I've about had it. The case you're talking about involved my uncle's death."

That brought a tense silence that lasted until the doors opened. Shane looked out—at Lillian's work area overlooking the cubicles and Jefferson's glassed-in space, which included a spectacular view of the Manhattan skyline.

"C'mon, Jefferson—" Judge Winslow's palsied, liver-spotted hand patted his friend's back as they exited the elevator. "Let's just open that safe for Mr. Holiday."

Jefferson stopped at Lillian's desk. "I forget where Lillian keeps the combination."

Shane yanked open her desk drawer, taking the paper from beneath her work books. "Here."

Jefferson gasped. "He's obviously searched her desk before. Isn't that illegal? Can't we get him on that, Tilford?"

Judge Winslow nodded. "Hmm. Illegal search and seizure."

"I'm about to have a seizure," muttered Shane, heading into Jefferson's office with Lone Star close behind. "Now, where's the safe?"

"He has a warrant," Judge Winslow reminded. "We may not want to help him prosecute your assistant, Jefferson, but we have no choice. It's the law."

"But I don't want him in my safe."

Shane wanted to throttle the man. "What's in there?"

"I don't know," Jefferson admitted. "Lillian has exclusive access. And I, unlike some people, trust her implicitly." Suddenly looking wounded, Jefferson strode across his office, took a book from a bookcase and pressed a button behind it. Shane watched the bookcase pop from the wall like a door, exposing a wall safe behind. So that was it. If the office wasn't surrounded by glass and open to prying eyes, Shane would have quickly found it. Heading for it, Shane quickly began spinning the dial.

Jefferson sighed loudly.

"You know," Shane couldn't help but say, "I think it's you who doesn't trust her, Jefferson. Otherwise, you wouldn't be so worried about what we're going to find."

With a final click, the door of the safe swung open.

And Shane's heart sank. Had he really been hoping to see three million dollars in cash? Okay, so maybe he'd imagined getting the money, turning it in to Fin and cutting a deal for Lillian.

But the safe was empty, except for a manila envelope, which he withdrew. He pulled out the papers inside, the top one of which was an envelope addressed to him in

Lillian's handwriting. He opened it while Judge Winslow and Jefferson clawed through the remaining contents. "Shane," the note began, "if you're reading this, something bad's happened to me."

His eyes skimmed the explanation that followed— it detailed her parents' deaths, her marriage to Sam Ramsey, how she'd fled and adopted an assumed name. Everything was much the same as she'd related last night.

Last night? It seemed as if a lifetime had passed between then and now. Shane kept reading. "I'm asking you to be Little Shane's guardian. When you held him the first time, I knew everything would be all right. You need each other." Shane's heart thudded. Damn right he needed his son. Lillian, too. But where was the money? That was the key to getting them back, and she hadn't said a word about it.

He glanced into the safe again. It was empty now. And, for a second, despair engulfed him. Remembering the dark rushing river that took his parents' lives, he realized he could no more control his fate now than he could that night. Dammit, when would that dark river leave him alone? When would darkness quit rushing through his life, taking his family?

Judge Winslow sighed wearily. "Ah," he said, rustling through some papers. "Won't criminals ever learn? Why, this is the same code Mackie the Money used in 1937." The judge began reminiscing. "Yes. I was just a young whippersnapper then…"

"Mackie the Money?" Shane interrupted.

"A numbers runner," Judge Winslow explained. "It was one of my very first cases…."

Shane stared down at the senseless pages of numbers in Judge Winslow's wrinkled hand.

"I'm sure it tracks intended payoffs to the police," continued the judge. "All you need is the…" He shuffled through the papers. "The key. Yes, here. Poor girl. She's in terrible trouble. Good thing *Jack* Ramsey didn't find her. She'd probably be dead by now. Well, I believe you can pick up the whole crime consortium on the basis of this, Mr. Holiday." The judge thrust the papers at Shane. "Now may I please return to my home and to my breakfast, which is no doubt cold?"

Not yet. Evidence against the Ramseys wasn't going to help Shane get Lillian and the baby back. "Was there anything in the envelope about the money?"

"It's in Zurich," Jefferson announced, perusing another stack of papers.

Relief flooded Shane. "Zurich?"

"She's been trading in international currencies," Jefferson continued, shaking his head with worry. "I always tell her stocks. Even bonds. Overseas currencies are so volatile right now." Grudging respect and pride crept into his tone. "It was terribly risky. But my, my, my. Lillian has made a killing."

"She's been investing the money?" Shane said.

Jefferson nodded. "Between her night school education and whatever advice she's picked up around this office, she's become one very wealthy woman."

Shane could merely stare. Her personal bank accounts showed she pinched pennies better than most. But… "Wealthy?"

"Yes. And the dear girl never squandered her principal." Jefferson sighed with sudden contentment. "The three million dollars is untouched. And I'm sure she'll be happy to turn it over to the government." Jefferson suddenly chuckled. "Of course, she did quadruple the principal…"

Shane raised his eyebrows. "Where's that?"

"She gave it all to charity," Jefferson said.

Somehow, Shane wasn't all that surprised. He'd discovered a giving heart in the woman he loved. "Which charity?"

"Big Apple Babies."

Judge Winslow clamped a hand to his forehead as if to say he should have known. "Jefferson!" he exclaimed. "All this time, the woman on the phone—"

Jefferson nodded. "The one who'll never meet us face to face—"

"It was Lillian?"

Shane listened as the two older men pieced it together. Apparently, as soon as Lillian came to work for Jefferson, she found out about Jefferson's secret backing of Big Apple Babies. Meantime, she was in possession of a huge sum of money and afraid to go to the police. In good conscience, she could never touch the money because it was blood money, belonging to a crime consortium. So, using Jefferson's financial advice, she'd slowly begun to invest it. Later, she introduced herself to Big Apple Babies anonymously—first through a letter, then through a phone call. She offered the group the considerable interest she was earning. Becoming a secret philanthropist was the perfect solution to her predicament.

"And to think—" Jefferson shook his head. "Every time the Big Apple Baby backers met on the phone, Lillian and I were on the same conference call. I was in my office—" His gaze strayed to the glass wall separating their desks. "And she was in plain sight."

"My," the old judge said in shock. "She's certainly a very clever girl."

"For some time, she's been Big Apple Babies' most secretive and generous contributor." Jefferson sighed. "Remember her donation for the new security system…"

Lillian had paid for the new, state-of-the-art security system that Shane had installed at Big Apple Babies? It was mind-blowing. Countless emotions rushed in on him—among them love and pride. Lillian was so damn smart. And gorgeous. And high-spirited. But Shane didn't have time to think about it. He was already on the run with Lone Star.

Judge Winslow said, "Where do you think you're going now, young man?"

Shane and Lone Star turned at the door. "Look, Jefferson, could you please call Ethel? Explain everything. And Judge Winslow, you're with the family courts. Pull any strings you can. I'm headed over to Big Apple Babies. I want my son back."

Now that things were looking brighter for Lillian, Jefferson's mood had improved considerably. "And then?"

"And then I'm going to get Lillian."

EVERYWHERE SHE LOOKED, Lillian saw Shane. Right now, she was crossing the threshold over which he'd carried her on their wedding night. Then she headed for the room where they'd made love. Wherever he'd gone this morning, he'd worn his Stetson, but Lillian could still imagine it, resting behind her on the marble-topped entry table, as if he'd left it there just to torture her.

"Are you ready to start?" Joyce Moon said.

Lillian turned in the hallway and stared at the three defense attorneys Jefferson had sent. Joyce Moon was about thirty, with straight dark hair. Orsen Daily was older, about forty, with a spindly body and wire-rimmed glasses. The youngest—Lillian thought he'd said his name was Bert Taylor—looked too slick for his own good. It was lucky, he'd said as he paid her bail for the fraud charges, that all three lawyers happened to be in Manhattan at the moment. Lillian guessed they were all highly sought-after, but then Jefferson would only hire the best.

"Are you ready?" Joyce repeated.

"Please take a seat in the living room," Lillian managed. "I think I need a minute alone."

"Sure." Joyce Moon nodded, blazing a trail on down the hallway.

Lillian went inside the bedroom, her high heels clicking on the hardwood floor. She was underslept and her head hurt, and as she opened the curtains and blinds, summer sunlight flooded the room, piercing her eyes. Catching a glimpse of herself in a mirror as she headed for the crib, she was amazed she'd managed to look so good. Somehow, she'd pulled her hair into a decent French twist, and when the agents gave her a minute to change, she'd put on her best navy suit. If she was going anywhere near a jail, she'd decided, she'd be damned if she'd look cheap. Or ruffled.

She'd only called out for the baby once.

And she wouldn't again. Not even now as she stared into the crib. She hadn't cracked when the agents who questioned her threw her relationship with Shane into her face, either. Oh, they went into details. Apparently, he'd been obsessed with solving his uncle's murder, and so he'd tailed her for seven years. He'd watched her from a boat in the Hudson, too. *And married me. Helped me adopt Little Shane.* She fought down the pain that came with the deeper thoughts.

And the anger. Because she should have known. She should have pieced it together when agents burst into the apartment while she was baby-sitting. That day, something about one of the men niggled at her mind. Now she realized it was because he'd been in her apartment before, dressed as a mover.

"Dressed," she muttered, still staring blindly into the empty crib. That was the key word. Because it had all been a game. A charade. And Shane Holiday had been wearing a mask.

Oh, he'd come to love her. The baby, too. Jefferson had called the lawyers to say Shane found the papers she kept locked in the office safe. Right now, he was fighting to get the charges against her dropped. Not that she cared. Her eyes trailed over the room—seeing his clothes on a chair. The white dress he'd taken off her last night, which was still on the bathroom floor.

She leaned over the crib, torturing herself by touching Little Shane's things one by one—a baby-blue pacifier. A rattle. A pull toy he wouldn't have been old enough to play with for months...

Later, she knew, she'd been glad that the saga of the past seven years was over and that the dark shadows of her nightmares had been swept away. It had felt good to confront Sam after all these years. But now, all she could think about was Ethel taking away the baby. And Shane….

"Lillian?"

The word came from behind her in that low rumbling drawl that always reminded her of home. *Shane.* He had a lot of nerve, coming here right now. Not that she wouldn't face him. No, she didn't mind in the least. In fact, she was looking forward to it. Jefferson would do everything in his considerable power to help her get Little Shane back. And even before she did, Lillian was leaving Shane Holiday in the dust.

Choke on this, cowboy, she thought. Coolly, she turned toward him, knowing he'd never see how badly he hurt her. He didn't deserve any part of her, and she'd been betrayed one too many times. Her dark eyes settled on him, and her tone stayed calm. "What do you think you're doing here?"

His voice was as damnably cool as the gaze that was calculated to remind her she'd met her match in him. "I live here, Lillian."

She'd almost forgotten. He had nowhere to go. All his belongings were here. Her heart suddenly lurched, and she tried to pretend she wasn't hoping he'd come back to apologize. "Get your stuff and get out."

He shook his head. "You know I'm not going anywhere."

The hell he wasn't. She gaped at him. "You helped me adopt a baby. A *baby,* Shane. He's my son—"

"He's my son, too."

Her heart pounded dangerously hard, as she fought against the truth of that. "Not that it matters now," she said, keeping a tight rein on her emotions. "Shane, you knew I was being watched, you knew he'd be taken away. And you still helped me get him. I hate you for that. You know that, don't you?"

Holding up a finger, Shane said, "Hold that thought, Lillian."

Then he vanished from the bedroom doorway. Her eyes narrowed. A second later, he reappeared—with Little Shane squirming in his arms. Her heart ached so badly, Lillian could do nothing more than grip the crib's rail. How could Shane do this to her? He was seriously threatening her control, making tears press against her eyelids.

Not that he cared in the least. He was walking toward her, carrying the baby, and as he approached, he lifted his Stetson by the brim and sent it spinning onto the bed. "Judge Winslow, Jefferson and Jake Lucas had a powwow, and the upshot is that Little Shane stays with us while things are cleared up. If everything goes smoothly, which it will, then we keep him for good."

"Us!" she exploded, stamping a high heel. "There is no us anymore!"

"Of course there is." Shane stepped closer, bouncing Little Shane on his hip. "Look, I know the agents told you I staked you out for years. But you know what else?"

She wished he'd leave, but for some foolish reason, she felt compelled to indulge him. She shook her head. "What?"

"I fell in love with you the first time I ever saw you—" Shane glanced at her, his tantalizing drawl lowering, to soothe her. "I was tailing you on Bayou Laforche, where you stopped for a soda at a dusty old bait shack. You were wearing a white dress that day, and when you got out of your car, my whole world stopped."

She tried not to react, but her eyes widened.

"And, Lillian," he continued smoothly, "if I've loved and chased after you for seven years, I'm not going to stop now."

With that, he leaned and pressed Little Shane in her arms, and Lillian simply couldn't help herself. She nuzzled and kissed the baby and then, realizing she was shaking too much to keep holding him, she laid him in the crib. "What, Shane?" she managed, feeling desperate to fight the tears that suddenly shimmered in her eyes. "Is it really necessary to torment me some more?"

"Torment you? C'mon, you know me better than that."

But it was torment. She didn't want the baby here, if he could be taken away again. It hurt too much. "They could take him…"

"But they won't." Shane edged closer, and the eyes she could never resist settled on hers again. "Trouble is, it's a package deal, Lil. You have to take me, too."

"I don't have to do anything."

Swiftly, he turned and pressed up against her, his hands settling on either side of her, closing around the crib rail, pinning her. "Oh, yes, you do."

He was too close. She could feel the heat and strength coming from the body that had loved her so well. Her voice was traitorous, coming out with a hint of raspiness. "And why's that?"

"Because you love me."

Hadn't he heard her? "I hate you now, Shane Holiday!"

He grabbed her quickly. As his warm, muscular arms wrapped around her, hauling her against his chest, a lock of his hair fell and teased her forehead. Her sharp swift breath of protest only drew in his masculine scent, and feeling his body against hers seemed to sweep everything from the room—the rising summer heat, the slow turning of the ceiling fan.

"Well, you know what they say about love and hate," he returned. "There's a real fine line."

"It's always better not to cross the line, Shane."

The instant before his mouth descended, catching hers in a way meant to remind her of the passion they shared, he said, "But I already warned you, I always do."

Maybe she should have heeded all those warnings, but beneath Lillian Smith Holiday lay the decidedly wilder Delilah Fontenont, who liked to run barefoot near the bayous, dabble in high-risk financial markets, and fall in love with men like her husband, Shane. And so her arms suddenly wrapped around his neck and her tongue dueled with his, and she gave in to a slow sweet kiss that melted whatever was left of her resolve not to love him.

After a long moment, he drew away, ever so slightly. "I thought we might go home," he murmured against her lips.

Her mind clouded, as she wondered about what was going to happen with the baby, wishing for reassurance that the charges against her would be dropped and that they could keep him. "I guess we are home, Shane."

"I mean down South."

"Down South." Whatever breath she had left after Shane's kiss caught in her throat, making her heart hammer so that it almost hurt. If the Ramseys were imprisoned, was there a chance she could go home to

Louisiana? Her gaze trailed past Shane to where Little Shane was gazing up from the crib at his parents, his eyes sleepy. He yawned, as to say this family needn't have a care in the world. Somehow, she found her voice. "You know…I guess I'm still legally married to Sam."

Shane's lips twisted in a quick wry smile. "Somehow, I'm sure there are grounds for divorcing him." Shane's eyes caught hers, the pale irises darkening, turning smoky with his feelings. "I want you to marry me, Lillian."

"I want that, too. But you know I'm in trouble now."

"I'm here to stick by you."

She was running out of arguments. Especially when his steady eyes came a hairbreadth closer, peering right into hers. "Lillian," he said softly, "when this is over, you're going to have that white brick house with the picket fence."

"I am?" she whispered.

"You are." And it was as simple as that. Without another word, Shane's lips closed over hers again, and her adventures were done. Or just beginning. Because she and her two Shanes were on their way home.

EPILOGUE

SHANE WATCHED LILLIAN breeze through the gate in the white picket fence with Little Shane, big at almost a year, slung around her hip. She was wearing a short pale yellow sundress, and her hair was dark now. What hadn't grown out she'd dyed back to its natural color, and now it was hanging loose and wild to her shoulders. Not that Shane had ever gotten used to calling her Delilah. Somewhere along the way, she'd turned into a Lillian. Or a Lily. Or a Lil. All the names of which reminded Shane of sweet young women with hearts as wide open as lily pads and nothing to hide from anyone, particularly not their husbands.

"Shane, honey," she called out now, in a soft drawl that got thicker the longer they stayed in Louisiana, "your Aunt Dixie Lynn wants you to finish shelling those crawfish."

"I'm working on it." Or he had been. But the minute his wife and son started up the walk toward the front porch, the whole world had stopped for Shane. He paused, as he always did, to admire her, forgetting everything else—the crawfish and the sounds of the bayou and the soft classical music playing on the radio.

Smiling, Lillian headed up the porch steps, then unceremoniously settled herself and the baby onto Shane's lap. "C'mon," she said, "everybody up at the big house is starved."

He smiled back at her. "And your sitting in my lap is supposed to make me hurry?" Running a palm easily over her back, he felt the light fabric, then the silk of her bare shoulders, tease his fingertips. He winked at Little Shane, who giggled and tried to grab his daddy's nose.

"No, but maybe this will." Lillian leaned, making the baby coo with delight at being squinched between his parents.

"What will?"

"This." She leaned a final inch and delivered a hot, sweet, salty wet kiss. Even though it was meant to be an I've-been-missing-you-all-day kind of kiss, it quickly turned risky, and when Lillian leaned away, she looked terribly pleased with herself. And then she groaned, shifting the baby on her hip. "He's sure getting big," she said with a smile. "I guess this means I should start a college fund."

"I doubt you'll have much trouble doing that," Shane said dryly, even as his heart swelled with pride over her business acumen.

She laughed again, and he glanced across the neatly landscaped grounds of the old restored Fontenont plantation—the stately mansion, the white-columned porch and the rose garden once tended by her father. It was such a great place that Shane didn't even miss the log cabin he'd sold back in East Texas. Here, the nights were quiet and warm, just the way he liked them. Fireflies winked in the berry bushes and birds cawed, diving into the bayou while gators slid under the mossy trees.

No, there'd never been a finer day, Shane thought,

than when he'd packed up Little Shane, Lillian and the
U-haul and headed through the Holland Tunnel, with
a map on his lap and Manhattan's skyscrapers in the
rearview mirror. New York was a town with a lot of
heart. But it wasn't for him. Or Lillian. Or the family
they wanted to raise.

Long before they left, everything fell into place.

Judge Tilford Winslow helped facilitate Lillian's
quick divorce from Sam Ramsey, and she'd married
Shane at Trinity Church again, this time inviting Shane's
aunts and his brother, Doc.

In exchange for her testimony, Lillian was given complete immunity, a deal cinched by the high-powered
attorneys Jefferson had hired. And also by the fact that
Lillian hadn't understood the significance of all the
papers in her possession, which had now been used to
shut down the Ramsey crime consortium for good. With
Trusty Joe and Sam Ramsey in jail, there was nothing
more to fear. Oh, Shane figured there might still be a
few angry dirty cops in Southern Louisiana, but it was
nothing he couldn't handle. He'd proven he could protect
his family.

With the consortium gone, the Fontenont plantation
had gone to auction—and Lillian had gotten it back.
Since then, right on the property where she'd grown up,
Shane had built them a small white brick house with a
picket fence.

Otherwise, the plantation was now a functioning
small hotel—with an airstrip, guest bungalows and
stables. Shane spent his days managing it—fixing everything broken, making sure the grounds and buildings
were maintained, and sometimes giving boat tours of
the bayou to his and Lillian's guests. He didn't regret

hanging up his holster. He liked staying safe. And as far as action went…well, he got plenty of that with Lillian. At least when she had time.

She was busy, scouring the *Wall Street Journal* and investing all the hotel's profits. Not to mention filling out paperwork, so she and Shane could adopt another baby. If the Louisiana caseworker who was coming next week didn't work out, there was always Big Apple Babies.

The adoption agency's staff was in close touch. After all, Ethel, ever the soft touch, had wanted to see Lillian, Shane and Little Shane together again. In fact, the plantation was becoming a haven for countless Big Apple Baby staffers who were seeking a getaway from the city. Shane's brother, Doc, had just visited with Frankie and the baby, and Jake and Dani Lucas planned to vacation here with their kids.

Shane suddenly realized Lillian was staring down at him, and he reached up, finger-combing the dark strands of her hair. "Too bad I've got to shell the crawfish," he murmured throatily, thinking he'd like to make love to her, right here and now. "But if I don't, Aunt Dixie Lynn'll have my hide."

Lillian giggled. "And Jefferson will have mine."

Shane chuckled, gazing across the grounds toward the front porch of the big plantation house, where a hungry Aunt Dixie Lynn and Jefferson Lawrence were swinging in the porch swing, holding hands, and waiting for their supper.

"Who would have thought," Shane mused, shaking his head. Even now, Aunt Dixie Lynn couldn't quite believe her husband had been killed by the partner he'd trusted, and the events had brought back so many memories of Silas that she'd taken to driving down from Bayou

Teche to Bayou Laforche for long weekends. Aunt Dixie
Lynn said the only thing that helped was spending time
with family.

Meantime, Jefferson had started flying in mysteriously on those same weekends. Ostensibly, he came to
make sure Lillian and Shane were managing the hotel
in a way he found fiscally sound, but he really came to
see Aunt Dixie Lynn.

Glancing over the porch, Shane's lips tugged into a
wider smile. Just weeks after they'd arrived in Louisiana, Ms. Lone Star had taken the final plunge into
womanhood, taking up with a shaggy black shepherd
named Rebel. And now, their six puppies were clumsily
crawling over the porch.

"They do make a lovely couple," murmured Lillian.

Shane chuckled. "Who? Dixie Lynn and Jefferson
or the dogs?"

Lillian elbowed him. "Dixie Lynn and Jefferson."
Her eyes suddenly softened. "And so do we."

He nodded, his gaze following hers as it swept the
landscape again. After a moment, she said, "We belong
here, Shane."

He smiled, raking his hand under her nape. "Deep
down, when I first saw you, I think I knew…" he found
himself saying, his fingers tightening in the strands of
her hair, pulling her head down towards his for another
kiss.

"Knew what?" she said huskily.

He shrugged. *That one day I'd be sitting in a rocking chair down South, on a hot lazy afternoon with our
warm skins touching, and you and a baby in my lap.*
But somehow, with Lillian's lips so close, it seemed like

too much to say, so right before Shane's mouth settled
on hers for a slow deep kiss, he sighed and said, "That
we'd fall in love."

Fall in Love with...

MEN
in UNIFORM

YES! Please send me the exciting *Men in Uniform* collection. This collection will begin with 3 FREE BOOKS and 2 FREE GIFTS in my very first shipment—and more valuable free gifts will follow! My books will arrive in 8 monthly shipments until I have the entire 51-book *Men in Uniform* collection. I will receive 2 free books in each shipment and I will pay just $4.49 U.S./$5.39 CDN for each of the other 4 books in each shipment, plus $2.99 for shipping and handling.* If I decide to keep the entire collection, I'll only have paid for 32 books because 19 books are free. I understand that accepting the 3 free books and gifts places me under no obligation to buy anything. I can always return a shipment and cancel at any time. My free books and gifts are mine to keep no matter what I decide.

263 HDK 2653   463 HDK 2653

Name _____ (PLEASE PRINT)

Address _____ Apt. #

City _____ State/Prov. _____ Zip/Postal Code

Signature (if under 18, a parent or guardian must sign)

Mail to the **Harlequin Reader Service:**

IN U.S.A.: P.O. Box 1867, Buffalo, NY 14240-1867
IN CANADA: P.O. Box 609, Fort Erie, Ontario L2A 5X3

* Terms and prices subject to change without notice. Prices do not include applicable taxes. Sales tax applicable in N.Y. Canadian residents will be charged applicable taxes. This offer is limited to one order per household. All orders subject to approval. Credit or debit balances in a customer's account(s) may be offset by any other outstanding balance owed by or to the customer. Please allow 4–6 weeks for delivery. Offer available while quantities last. Offer not available to Quebec residents.

Your privacy: Harlequin is committed to protecting your privacy. Our Privacy Policy is available online at www.eHarlequin.com or upon request from the Reader Service. From time to time we may make our lists of customers available to reputable third parties who have a product or service of interest to you. If you would prefer we not share your name and address, please check here. ☐

MUBPA10

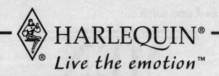

HARLEQUIN®
Live the emotion™

Love, Home & Happiness

HARLEQUIN® *Blaze*™

Red-hot reads.

HARLEQUIN® HISTORICAL:
Where love is timeless

HARLEQUIN® *Romance*®

From the Heart, For the Heart

HARLEQUIN®
INTRIGUE®
Breathtaking Romantic Suspense

HARLEQUIN®
Medical Romance™...
love is just a heartbeat away

HARLEQUIN®
Presents~
Seduction and Passion Guaranteed!

HARLEQUIN® *Super Romance*®

Exciting, Emotional, Unexpected

HARLEQUIN®
nocturne™
**Dramatic and sensual tales
of paranormal romance.**

Want to try 2 FREE books?
Visit: **www.ReaderService.com**

HDIR10

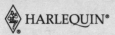
HARLEQUIN®

**Invites *you* to experience
lively, heartwarming
all-American romances**

Every month, we bring you four strong,
sexy men, and four women who know what
they want—and go all out to get it.

From small towns to big cities, experience
a sense of adventure, romance and family
spirit—the all-American way!

Love, Home & Happiness

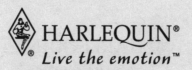

www.eHarlequin.com   HARDIR09

HARLEQUIN®
INTRIGUE®

BREATHTAKING ROMANTIC SUSPENSE

Shared dangers and passions lead to electrifying
romance and heart-stopping suspense!

Every month, you'll meet six new heroes
who are guaranteed to make your spine tingle
and your pulse pound. With them you'll enter
into the exciting world of Harlequin Intrigue—
where your life is on the line
and so is your heart!

THAT'S INTRIGUE—
ROMANTIC SUSPENSE
AT ITS BEST!

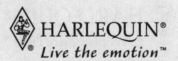

HARLEQUIN®
Live the emotion™

www.eHarlequin.com   INTDIR06

HARLEQUIN®
Presents®

The world's bestselling romance series...
The series that brings you your favorite authors,
month after month:

Helen Bianchin...Emma Darcy
Lynne Graham...Penny Jordan
Miranda Lee...Sandra Marton
Anne Mather...Carole Mortimer
Melanie Milburne...Michelle Reid

and many more talented authors!

Wealthy, powerful, gorgeous men...
Women who have feelings just like your own...
The stories you love, set in exotic, glamorous locations...

HARLEQUIN®
Presents®

Seduction and Passion Guaranteed!

HPDIR08

www.eHarlequin.com

...there's more to the story!

Superromance.
A *big* satisfying read about unforgettable
characters. Each month we offer *six* very different
stories that range from family drama to adventure
and mystery, from highly emotional stories to
romantic comedies—and much more! Stories
about people you'll believe in and care about.
Stories too compelling to put down....

Our authors are among today's *best* romance
writers. You'll find familiar names and talented
newcomers. Many of them are award winners—
and you'll see why!

If you want the biggest and best
in romance fiction, you'll get it
from Superromance!

Exciting, Emotional, Unexpected...

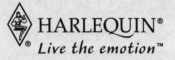

www.eHarlequin.com   HSDIR06

Harlequin® Historical
Historical Romantic Adventure!

*Imagine a time of chivalrous
knights and unconventional ladies,
roguish rakes and impetuous
heiresses, rugged cowboys
and spirited frontierswomen—
these rich and vivid tales will
capture your imagination!*

*Harlequin Historical . . .
they're too good to miss!*

HARLEQUIN® Romance®

The rush of falling in love

Cosmopolitan
international settings

Believable, feel-good stories
about today's women

The compelling thrill
of romantic excitement

It could happen to you!

EXPERIENCE
HARLEQUIN ROMANCE!

Available wherever Harlequin books are sold.

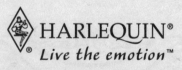

HARLEQUIN®
Live the emotion™

www.eHarlequin.com

HROMDIR09